中西文化文学十论

张平功 著

Chinese and Western Cultural and Literary Studies

By Zhang Pinggong

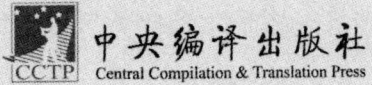

中央编译出版社
Central Compilation & Translation Press

图书在版编目（CIP）数据

中西文化文学十论／张平功著. — 北京：中央编译出版社，2013.12
ISBN 978 - 7 - 5117 - 2000 - 9

Ⅰ.①中…　Ⅱ.①张…　Ⅲ.①比较文化 - 中国、西方国家 - 文集②比较文学 - 文学研究 - 中国、西方国家 - 文集　Ⅳ.①G04 - 53②I0 - 03

中国版本图书馆 CIP 数据核字（2013）第 309181 号

中西文化文学十论

出 版 人：	刘明清
出版统筹：	董　巍
责任编辑：	霍星辰　曲建文
责任印制：	尹　珺
出版发行：	中央编译出版社
地　　址：	北京市西城区车公庄大街乙 5 号鸿儒大厦 B 座（100044）
电　　话：	（010）52612345（总编室）　　（010）52612363（编辑室）
	（010）52612316（发行部）　　（010）52612315（网络销售）
	（010）52612346（馆配部）　　（010）66509618（读者服务部）
传　　真：	（010）66515838
经　　销：	全国新华书店
印　　刷：	三河市天润建兴印务有限公司
开　　本：	710 毫米×1000 毫米　1/16
字　　数：	350 千字
印　　张：	17.75
版　　次：	2013 年 12 月第 1 版第 1 次印刷
定　　价：	50.00 元

网　　址：	www.cctphome.com　　邮　箱：cctp@cctphome.com
新浪微博：	@中央编译出版社　　微　信：中央编译出版社（ID:cctphome）

本书为广东外语外贸大学 2013 年度出版资助项目的研究成果

Contents

Part One

Part Two

Acknowledgements

Any extended process of research and writing incurs many personal debts. This project has been far more extended than anticipated so the debts are considerable.

I am very grateful for the following academics and scholars who have given me advice, helped shape some arguments, provided intellectual support and autonomous research spaces at Staffordshire University in England: Barry Taylor, David Bell, Tim Edensor, Maggie O'Neill, Tony Spybey, David Alderson, Shaun Richards, Helen Chapman, Mark Featherstone, Malcohm Henson and Nick Bentley.

I have received valuable support from Wang Ning at Tsinghua University. Two pieces of writing in this book are the revised proceedings I submitted while attending the international conferences organized or chaired by him. He is always generous in relaying academic information and providing constructive academic assistance. Thanks to Luan Dong and Sheng Anfeng for their valuable help.

Z. P.

Part One

Tracing the Signifier:
Barthes and Althusser

Introduction

Drawing on the Swiss linguist Ferdinand de Saussure's basic concepts (e. g. the signifier/signified and langue/parole distinctions, the idea of underlying codes and structures, and the arbitrary nature of the sign) (Hall, 1997:46), the French literary critic and semiologist Roland Barthes developed his theory of mythology. In "Myth Today" in *Mythologies*, the collection of demystifying essays (originally published in 1957), his theory of myth is demonstrated through illustration of concrete examples of French popular culture. According to Barthes, myth is a "second-order" signification based on the "first-order" of the language system—Saussure's linguistic model. What Barthes is interested in is cultural and ideological meanings of myth as well its applications in modern society, and how it is assumed and sustains significance. Barthes's purpose is to see through the process of mythical construction in order to reveal the significances which are manipulated and distorted by myth, and how manipulation and distortion usually take place in specific historical circumstances and concern particular class interests, shifting "from semiology to ideology" (Barthes, 1968: 139). Essentially, Barthes's conception of ideology seems to be more consistent with structural Marxism, and with Althusser in particular, than with traditional Marxism, in that the myths in popular culture are viewed as serving the interests of a bourgeois class. The former argues that ideology is a force in societies in its own right, while retaining Marx's emphasis on economic determinism. As to Marx's base-superstructure model, Althusser interprets that the superstructure is not only determined by the base but by numerous secondary factors of a local and external kind. Thus, ideology has a "relative autonomy" from the material base. The relationship between the theoretical model of Barthes' mythology and the ideological thinking of Althusser's Marxism can be seen in the way that Althusser's ideology, as a "representation of the imaginary relationship of individuals to their real conditions of existence" (Althusser, 1971:153) parallels Barthes's theory of mythical representation in that what people represent to themselves in ideology and representation is misleading. The relationship between themselves and the real world is far from factual, but "underlies all the imaginary distortion that we can observe ⋯ in all ideology: what is represented in ideology is therefore not the system of the real relations which govern the existence of individuals, but the imaginary relation of those individuals to the real relations in which they live" (Althusser, 1971: 153-154).

This essay expands the discussion of their relationship by referring in detail to Barthes' model of representation and Marxist theory of ideology, with special attention to Althusser's work in this regard.

Barthes's Theoretical Model of Mythology

Barthes's theory of mythology has its roots in the thinking of the Swiss linguist Ferdinand de Saussure (1857—1913) (Barry, 1995:41). In the linguistic argument of Saussure, the relation between the "signifier" (which is a sound image) and the "signified" (which is the concept to which it refers) is arbitrary, which is to say that words achieve their meaning from association in the mind, not from any natural or necessary reference to entities in the real world. These associations work through the principle of exclusion, which is to say any sign achieves meaning diacritically, or through a system of differentiation from other signs. Thus, language is not a way of naming things which already exist, but a system of signs, whose meaning is relational. Therefore, only a social group can produce signs, because only a specific social usage gives a sign any meaning. Barthes makes a step forward from this argument. According to him, myth is "second-order" association based on the "first-order" of the language system—Saussure's schema. It is understood that in order to engage in the process of signification the "second-order" system relies upon the "first-order" system, the language system. A sign in the "first-order" system, a word or a thing, becomes a signifier in the "second-order" system of myth. By using the symbolic or concrete language of other systems, myth comes into being and thus becomes a metalanguage because it can refer to other languages (Strinati, 1995:113). It may also be understood that through providing this additional signifying system, social meaning can be associated with signs in a similar way to that by which connotations are embodied in words. The loaded sign "becomes the signifier for the next sign in a chain of signification of ascending complexity and cultural specificity" (Turner,

1996: 18).

Myth as a process of representation has a great effect on people's life in modern times. As Hawkes explains, "nothing in the human world can be merely utilitarian: even the most ordinary buildings organize space in various ways, and in so doing they signify, issue some kind of message about the society's priorities, its presuppositions concerning human nature, politics, economics, over and above their overt concern with the provision of shelter, entertainment, medical care, or whatever." (1997: 134) More demonstrative examples can be found in the well expounded *Mythologies* by Barthes, such as, the difference between boxing and wrestling; the significance of eating steak and chips; the styling of the Citroen car; the cinema image of Greta Garbo's face; a magazine photograph of an Algerian soldier saluting the French flag, and so forth (1973). Barthes's theory of representation based on symbolic language, like other theories of structuralism, carries much weight in analysis of contemporary cultural and social identity, as Sarup suggests: Structuralists would want to stress the importance of language in the organizing construction of identity. It is through the acquisition of language that we become human and social beings: the words we speak situate us in our gender and our class. Through language, we come to "know" who we are. (Sarup, 1996)

Myth as "one particular type of signifying practice" or "one particular form of cognition" is a concept of ideology, for it is constituted by imagination and has become "part of the repertoire of every society, in some culturally organised way" like forms of "dreams, songs, fantasies, myth and stories" (Appadurai, 1996: 53).

One of the characteristics of bourgeois ideology is to deny the existence of the bourgeois class. The bourgeoisie seems a nameless class because myth functions as ideology to ensure that it is not named. Myth and ideology function together so that "individuals are reconciled to their given social positions by falsely representing to them those positions and relationships between them as if they formed a part of some inherently significant, intrinsically coherent plan or process" (Bennett, 1979:116). To make it more obvious, the example of "democracy" is a case in point. People believe that democracy is the ideal political system in keeping with the nature and needs of people in society; history has been an evolution and revolution of political forms towards democracy; once states have all reached democracy, all they have to do is avoid reverting. There is no need for more progress in term of political improvement. People also assume that democracy is the political system best suited to the nature and aspirations of humans.

In the final analysis, Barthes believes that myth as ideology is functional in shaping people's outlook. Bourgeois ideology, through a long history of forming and transforming, is firmly cultivated in people's minds in capitalist society.

Althusser's Work on Ideology

Most modern Marxists, in a variety of Marxisms, have drawn upon, developed or expanded the school of thought jointly founded by Karl Marx (1818—1883) and Friedrich Engels (1820—1895). In *The Communist Manifesto* of 1848, Marx and Engels established the theory of economics called "Communism", in which they proclaim that the aim of Marxism is to create an ideal world, a world without classes, poverty, etc. Their philosophical viewpoint is materialism, treating the world in a concrete, scientific and logical way, as opposed to idealist philosophy. The latter has a belief in a spiritual or supernatural world. In Marxist theory, there are two well known propositions which are worth emphasizing: although numerous philosophers have so far put forward theories of various kinds to interpret the world, what is important is to change the world; secondly, in Marx's words,

"The mode of production of material life conditions the social, political, and intellectual life in general. It is not the consciousness of men that determines their beings, but on the contrary, their social being that determines their consciousness" (Marx, 1859).

The traditional Marxist theory of society and culture begins by understanding another crucial "but seemingly contradictory" (Williams, 1980: 31) proposition of a determining base and a determined superstructure. The base refers to the material means of production, distribution, and exchange and the superstructure is the "elevated" world of ideas, art, religion, law and so on. What is important for Marxism is that the superstructure is not independent, but is controlled or "determined" by the reality of the economic base. This theoretical model, known as economic determinism, is the kernel of traditional Marxism.

Nevertheless, traditional Marxism had attached little importance to the idea of culture, regarding it as part of the superstructure of society and therefore, a mere product of the economic base. However, as Saussure's concept of the social function of language suggests, this does not recognize the way in which language exercises a determining influence over solid social realities—including the foundation of capitalist society—the material base (Turner, 1996: 23). Therefore, in the history of Marxism, modern Marxists have made a great contribution, especially in reframing the place and function of culture. In the creative work done by the leading modern Marxists, Louis Althusser's (1918-1990) theory on ideology is central and draws most attention. For Althusser,

"Ideology is a system (possessing its logic and proper rigour) of representations (images, myths, ideas or concepts according to the case) endowed with an existence and an historical role at the heart of a given society. " (Barry, 1995:163; quoting Goldstein, 1990)

It can be understood that ideology should be examined not only in language and representations but also in its material forms—the institutions and social practices through which peopleorganize and live their lives. This argument is different from traditional Marxist understanding of ideology in that the latter treats ideology as "false consciousness", "the system of ideas and representations which dominate the mind of man or a social group" (Althusser, 1997: 149), as contrasted with underlying reality of economic and class relations. Althusser's ideology "represents the imaginary relationship of individuals to their real conditions of existence" (Althusser, 1977: 151-153). Althusser further emphasizes that ideology creates us as persons, that is, it "hails" us, calls us into being.

In his significant essay entitled"Ideology and Ideological State Apparatuses" (1969), Althusser describes "Repressive State Apparatuses" such as the army, the courts, the police, which can be deployed to "force" the implementation of hegemony. "Ideological State Apparatuses" such as school, the church, the family, the media and political system assist in the reproduction of the dominant system by creating subjects who are ideologically conditioned to accept with "consent" the values of the system. Through this system of "natural" recognition, ideology is addressed to individuals and their identities are recognized.

Althusser's theory of structural Marxism is influenced by the psychoanalysis of Freud and Lacan. Althusser is interested in how subjects and their deepest selves are "interpellated" (originally the term of Freud), positioned (from

Lacan) and patterned by what lies outside them. For Althusser, psychoanalysis was very effective in suggesting that the human being has no essential "centre", except in the imaginary misrecognization of the "ego", i. e. in the ideological formation in which it "recognizes" itself. This "structure of misrecognition" of Althusser is important to an understanding of his theory of ideology (1971: 218-219). According to Butler,

"The Althusserian use of Lacan centers on the function of the imaginary as the permanent possibility of misrecognition, the incommensurability between symbolic demand (the name that is interpellated) and the instability and unpredictability of its appropriation" (Rajchman, 1995: 239).

A Comparison between Barthes and Althusser

Althusser defines ideology as "a system (with its own logic and rigor) of representations" (images, myths, ideas or concepts), which coincides with Barthes's semiotics, regarding contemporary mythology as ideology, "a realm which has purged itself of ambiguity and alternative possibility" (Eagleton, 1996: 117). In "Myth Today", Barthes gives a convincing analysis of the way in which the mythologies of advertising, fashion, popular culture and the mass media attempt to "transform what he calls the 'bourgeois norm' (Storey, 1997 : 81) into a universal 'nature'". He perceives these cultural phenomena as mythologies as well as ideologies, because the purpose of these ideas is to naturalise modern bourgeois society, making it appear "normal" and "obvious". In the meantime, all the contradictions and differences in the society are covered up. By means of the structural approach, both Althusser and Barthes deal with ideology and mythology in a similar way. For Althusser, ideology is a system of representations. But these representations are only imaginary, a "structure of misrecognition" (1971: 218-219).

Therefore, since ideology is "a representation of the imaginary relation of individuals to the real condition of existence", it is always mystifying. "Ideology became the backbone of a mass discourse whose function was to make the poor dream the same dream as the rich" (Martin-Barbero, 1993:165).

To see through ideology, one has to tell the real from the imaginary by employing discourse analysis. In addition,

"···attention must be turned away from that mythical popular subject immediate to observation and focused instead on the relation between two different kinds of practice: a 'first-order' practice of everyday culture, and the 'second-order' practice of analysis of it conducted by a reader endowed with significant cultural capital" (Frow, 1995:87).

With his focus on the powerful use of language and the insights of Saussure, Barthes proposes that the mythic process of signification is equally ideological. Myth as a "second-order semiological system" is the subtle form of communication conveyed by a discourse. As opposed to the arbitrariness of the signifier/signified, mythical signification is always certain and purposeful. One is able to realize this by adopting a social and historical analysis of "the seemingly obvious" (Storey, 1997:120).

In the theory of Althusserian Marxism, ideological structures appear to be natural, carrying out their tasks "according to the order of things", which is a process of naturalisation by the state ideological apparatuses—by the churches, the schools, the family, and through cultural forms, such as literature, music, advertising, etc. Similarly, Barthes, before moving to a post-structural way of thinking, shared this viewpoint on ideology, with its close relation to mythical representation through the mass media and other forms of popular culture. For Terry Eagleton, Ideology seeks to convert culture into Nature, and the "natural" sign is one of its weapons. Saluting a flag, or agreeing that Western democracy represents the true meaning of the word "freedom", become the most obvious, spontaneous responses in the world. Ideology, in this sense, is a kind of contemporary mythology (1996:117).

Althusser believes that ideological structures purport a reasonable interpretation of the history of mankind. It can be seen that ideology in its concrete and material forms appears to be in agreement with the logic of historical development. The assumption is that the present state of historical development is natural, with regression being out of the question. Barthes points out in his theoretical model of mythology that myth can only be approached in terms of the way it functions to recreate concrete social phenomena that come to be naturalized, but which are in reality a "specific structure of imperial power" in the historical context (Strinati, 1995:115).

For Althusser, ideology is not only realized in language and representation but also in concrete social and political organizations and formations. The comprehensive application of ideology has a direct effect on social norms. Barthes, on the other hand, while focusing on the theory of myth, emphasizes more the process of signification, the creation of meaning and its popularization in society, even though the process of signification carries a no less political overtone. Referring to the war in Algeria (1954-1962) Barthes remarks, "myth has…a double function: it points out and it notifies, it makes us understand something and it imposes it on us" (Storey, 1997:84).

All in all, with the Marxist tradition and Saussure's modern linguistic theory as background, Althusser and Barthes have a lot in common in treating ideology and symbolic representation, though they differ in methodology. Both Althusser and Barthes point out that political and social institutions carry out their "tasks" through the reproduction of values, ideas of the world, system of images and conceptions of the society. Both of them suggest that the function of social institutions is to legitimize the current situation of the society and make it acceptable to all. They indicate that in order to achieve this goal, the use of force and adoption of oppression is an inferior strategy compared to "social cooperation" or teaching on a general scale. For Althusser, the state ideological apparatuses (the churches, the schools, the family, the media) are functional and for Barthes, the cultural media (such as literary works, music, advertising, fashion, photography, etc.) are effective in this case. The theories of Althusser and Barthes exercise great influence on the way of thinking by social beings.

REFERENCES

Althusser, Louis. *Ideology* (1994). ed. Terry Eagleton. Harlow: Longman.

Appadurai, Arjun. *Modernity at Large: Cultural Dimensions of Globalization* (1996). Minneapolis: The University of Minneapolis Press.

Bennett, Tony. *Formalism and Marxism* (1979). London: Methuen & Co Ltd.

Bennett, Andrew and Royle, Nicholas. *An Introduction to Literature, Criticism and Theory* (1995). Hertfordshire: Prentice Hall & Harvester Wheatsheaf.

Barry, Peter. *Beginning Theory: An Introduction to Literary and Cultural Theory* (1995). Manchester: Manchester University Press.

Butler, Judith. "Subjection, Resistance, Resignification: Between Freud and Foucault" in *The Identity in Question* (1995). Ed. John Rajchman. London: Routledge.

Chiders, Joseph and Hentzi, Gary. *The Columbia Dictionary of Modern Literary and Cultural Criticism* (1995). New York: Columbia University Press.

Eagleton, Terry. *Literary Theory: An Introduction* (1996). Oxford: Blackwell Publishers Ltd.

Frow, John. *Culture Study & Culture Value* (1995). Oxford: Oxford University Press.

Hall, Stuart. *Representation: Cultural Representation and Signifying Practices* (1997). Ed. London: SAGE Publications Ltd.

Hawkes, Terence. *Structuralism and Semiotics* (1997). London: Routledge.

Jenkins, Richard. *Social Identity* (1996). London: Routledge.

Loomba, Ania. *Colonialism / Postcolonialism* (1998). London: Routledge.

Larrian, Jorge. *The Concept of Ideology* (1979). London: Hutchinson.

Marx, Karl. "Preface to A Critique of Political Economy", from *Karl Marx: A Reader* (1986). Cambridge University Press.

Strinati, Dominic. *An Introduction to Theories of Popular Culture* (1995). London: Routledge.

Sarup, Madan. *Identity, Culture and the Postmodern World* (1996). Edinburgh: Edinburgh University Press.

Storey, John. *An Introduction to Cultural Theory and Popular Culture* (1997). Hertfordshire: Prentice Hall / Harvester Wheatsheaf.

Turner, Graeme. *British Cultural Studies* (1996). London: Routledge.

Williams, Raymond. *Keywords: A Vocabulary of Culture and Society* (1983). London: Fontana Press.

Williams, Raymond. *Base and Superstructure in Marxist Culture Theory* (1985). London: Verso.

Studying Raymond Williams
in a Chinese Perspective

Introducing the Cultural Theorist

"Culture is ordinary." That is the place to start from. The man behind this provocative idea is Raymond Williams, the Britain's great post-war intellectual. The journey Williams took from the country to the city, from one nation to another, from one class to another changed the way we think about culture and society. Williams once remarked,

> "We use culture in two senses, to mean the whole way of life, the common meaning, or to mean the art and learning, the special processes of discovery and creative effort. Some writers reserve one or another of the senses. I insist on both". (*Culture is ordinary*)

Williams is from a working-class family. He challenged the idea that culture only means high culture and that only elites can call themselves cultured. The idea of Raymond Williams was influential in the social and cultural scene as something special in Britain in the 1950s. All the ideologies about class, about social change, and above all, about culture became open to challenge. Society's hierarchy of values so firmly established began to break up because of such writers as Williams. His first major book *Culture and Society* is a radical re-reading of literature and history, which shows just how much traditional definitions of culture had the taste of one class built into them. Reading this influential book, readers thought the ideas advanced by Raymond Williams were incredibly exciting. For instance, students at the English Faculty of Cambridge were very interested in his theory and wanted to be taught by the writer, also a lecturer at the institution. Raymond Williams' understanding of culture and society appealed considerably to many literary and cultural critics at that time, because they wanted to know as well as to find the way of thinking and re-conciliating literature and history together. There is something in Raymond Williams' works that show the possibility of the reconciliation and intellectual energy being released from there. Raymond Williams' contemporaries thought that Williams was a formative influence on the life of numerous young persons on the left, many thinking figures in the labor movement, in fact, anybody who cared about culture and books and testimony of history. There was not another one who had the reputation of shaping and influencing the minds of the people who claimed to be a thinker on the left. Terry Eagleton, a student of his at Cambridge, now the well-known English professor and cultural theorist, said about his teacher thus:

"Raymond was the man who almost single-handedly launched the idea of culture. He had things to say that nobody else could say, that nobody else was saying".

Williams' re-definition of what we mean by culture owns much to the fact that he came from a very particular background, from a particular place, from a particular time. He was born in 1921 in Pandy, the border country in south Wales. But through his own family ties, he was strongly connected to industrial working class. His father was a railway signal man. Therefore, in the context of the 1920s and 1930s, through the working post on the railway, the family was connected to all of the modern world. Alternatively, this is the life connected up from the very beginning when one thinks about Williams' background as provincial and limited because it was local. Williams once recalled that his father was one of the three signal men in the big, old west railway box. The telephone and telegraphy were especially important for the signal men. Through telecommunication with other signal men over a wide social network, talking to the men whom they may never meet but knew a lot through voice and opinions and stories, they became modern industrial working class. For Williams, this is special environment of familiar, domestic and communal community. Pandy is an English-speaking region, where like elsewhere in the UK, the schools put an emphasis on artistic and cultural achievement for the pupils. Young Williams proved to be a talent in his school days. In his novel *Border Country*, Raymond Williams recorded his study life and occasions very vividly. One of the strengths about Williams was the fact that he came from what must have been an extraordinarily supportive environment of working-class solidarity. That is the environment of mutual-support, strength and harmony of the working-class community where he grew up. The boy has observed many of the hardships the railway men and coal-miners had experienced in the 1920s and 1930s, especially his father who was sacked after joining in the strike against wage-cuts and poor working and living conditions of the miners. From his childhood, Williams has made himself a strong-minded, self-sufficient person, and prepared himself for the rest of life. In his primary school years, he has distinguished himself with highest marks. Then he entered grammar school through examinations as a top student. The school is the well-known Abagavanny Grammar School. It is natural to realize that a boy from an ordinary village school to a prestigious grammar school clearly shows some sight of promise on scholarship. That is the first step leading to his consequent attendance of Cambridge.

In 1939, the year when Britain was at war with Nazi Germany, Williams won the scholarship to Cambridge, then a remarkable achievement for someone of his background. Also, there was vivid description in his novel of *Border Country* of his depart from Pandy with his father sending him off. That is not an ordinary journey out from Wales. It's border-crossing, physically and spiritually for Williams.

The outbreak of war had hardly touched the normal life situation of Cambridge with most public school intake. Cambridge in those days was still an aristocratic school, and Williams was quite unprepared for it. He was curious about the university culture and social composition of the student organizations. For example, for joining the students union, you needed a proposer. Of course, Williams did not know anybody. He realized the curiosity of his position when he was asked a question "Haven't you got friends from school?" However, Williams discovered the Socialist Club and joined the organization and became a member of comradeship. During this period of time Williams read Marx's *On Capital* and Engels' *Anti-Duhring* and other works. He was then deeply interested in the theories of Marxism. Soon after joining the Socialist Club he joined the Communist Party and did many sorts of work as a Party member. Basically, the Socialist Club at Cambridge became a home from home for Williams. Too much time spent in writing public propaganda materials left little time for him to seriously research in literature. Cambridge was in the 1930s the centre of intellectual communism and Williams found it naturally adaptable in the socialist society on campus. But according Eric Hobsbawm, a postgraduate at Cambridge and his senior, Williams was not a communist in the strict sense, he was somewhat more of a communist militant, an anti-fascist militant. In the more general environment Williams was influenced by the British Left. Within the English faculty he was influenced more by F. R. Leavis. At that time Raymond Williams was a left-wing Leavist, a communist and a young man from Welsh working-class background combined and fitted altogether. Then political activities and propaganda took up much of his time, and academic study went on like separate existence. Williams later dropped out from the Communist Party because he could not tolerate the organizational disciplines of the Party, and because he married a lady who was so-called "politically unconscious". In literature studies, he was critical of Bernard Shaw and George Wells, and of the social novels in general. In the very early 1940s, the attitude toward the Second World War in Britain was changing when Nazi invaded Soviet Union in 1941. Soon after his marriage, Raymond Williams was called up as a soldier and then an officer to fight in the front. He was commissioned as a captain into the Royal Tank Army and went into the battles in the West Front and Normandy after D-Day. In one of his works, Williams gives a frank and frightening account of his experience in Normandy fighting of 1944. Such "chaos and dreadful things" of the battlefield in wooded countryside are carefully depicted: the high level of deaths and casualties, the bombs dropped on you from your own planes, not knowing whether you were firing on the enemy or on your own troops, the sight of tanks with people you know in them burning, exploding, the constant fear you lived with, confined with that little mental interior of the tank surrounded with hundreds of rounds of high explosive ammunition and a considerable amount of diesel fuel, and so forth. The consciousness of guilt at the moment, especially guilt of cowardice that comes when you realize terrible things are being done, is also recorded. In 1945, Williams came back from the war to a "different or another Cambridge". The pre-war atmosphere had gone and English intellectual life seemed to have shifted rightwards. The British government appeared to be rapidly accommodating to capitalism. He resumed his academic work fanatically, even setting up such lifelong priorities as analysis and criticism of cultural politics at an early stage. At that time, military ex-serviceman would submit a 15,000-word thesis for the degree. Williams took Ibsen as his topic. The 19th century Norwegian playwright spoke most closely to his own condition which appealed to Raymond Williams a great deal. Basically, the war experiences have influenced Williams in two ways. He became more mature and hardened as a man. And he became more rigid and ruthless in his argument. There was a famous incident about the argumentative exchanges between L. C. Knights and Williams on the themes of horror of mechanical civilization, loss of organic world, meaning of neighbors and so on. By then Williams began to ponder on the relationship between culture, literature and society. On one occasion, he talked about the academic lifestyle by remarking,

"It seems very strange that every academic man of all human possibilities should be selected above all others as an example of intelligence …It is mostly clerical work, in a most strict sense, shifting words from manuscript to print, from print to manuscript then back to print again, regardless of their value" (*Second Generation*).

Upon his graduation Raymond Williams found a job not in academia but in adult education. He taught English literature and other subjects. It proved a correct and proper decision. Because almost all arguments, all ideas that he later put into his *The Long Revolution* and *Culture and Society* are coming out of the adult education movement, such as how culture and literature merge into society, how society structures itself, how mass media influences politics, what an advertisement means and so forth. Raymond Williams delightedly involved himself in adult education for more than 15 years. Besides teaching at local communities, he was following a hectic writing schedule and working in nearly complete isolation. His student Terry Eagleton said about him launching the notion and project of cultural studies and criticisms single-handedly, as he had no collaborator. The key theme of *Culture and Society* is the concept of cultural democracy, an idea to let everybody speak, to be heard, especially to listen to the voices of the working class. To Williams, "There are, in fact, no masses. There are only ways of seeing people as the masses". He believes that "Cultural criticism is concerned with evaluation, with comparison, and with standards."

(*Culture is Ordinary*)

Williams suggests that the notion of culture emerges in response to the social changes that come with industrialization and modernization. As time went on, it came into conflict, for some thinkers at least, with the idea of democracy, which was seen as a threat to culture. The notion of culture also became more and more isolated and specialized, and confined to the keeping of a smaller and smaller, and somehow partly ideal or imaging minority—from Coleridge's elitists, through Arnold's remnant people, to Leavis' "educated public". Williams tries to acknowledge what he felt are valuable elements in the idea of culture—its stress on wholeness, nurture, growth—while rejecting its mystifying patterns, its social and political conflict, its confinement to a minority, and its elite construction. In a more practical way, Williams' ideas can be seen as cultural democracy as well as sociology of literary studies.

When Raymond Williams was invited back to Cambridge in 1961, heading Jesus College, he was regarded as a novelist and a major literary and cultural critic. Not only because he wrote widely-read novels, but because his cultural ideas have provided crucial information for many other cultural thinkers at the time, drawing primarily from his own background and experience. For many, Raymond Williams' cultural theory serves as revelation of reality and actuality of both social and cultural situation in his times. Regarding literature studies, Williams criticized some kinds of literary grading and judging as a game, and a snobbish game. He was simply not interested in it. What interested Williams or informed him most was the way literature fed into society and expressed important ideas of society.

Those influenced by Raymond Williams began to see the case against capitalism was not an economic case but a case of capitalism destroying private as well as public communal collective culture. As he considered, society creates elites, elites take over culture, writers gang together and they try to impose sorts of literary canons from above. As a matter of fact, for him, literary impulses are much more complex. They come from many more sources, from many different voices. Literary writings can obviously be a whole variety of popular forms, including sports and entertainment, even cultural tourism and theme parks. All are of realist taste without much emphasis on social distinction.

Williams' exploration in *Culture and Society* develops in a range of important ways. To change the distinction between "art" and "ordinary experience", he takes up the idea, based partly on contemporary work in biology, that our "seeing"—our interpretation of sensory input according to a set of rules—is a set of learnt rather than natural activities. Reality, as we experience it, is after all a human creation and this creation has two sources, i. e. the human brain as it has evolved, and interpretation carried by our cultures. Though the brain gives a common basis for our interpretative activity, our ways of seeing are not fixed and constant. Different cultures see the world in different ways, and ways of seeing within a culture change over time. Precisely, human beings change them in response to the interactions between learnt, culturally inherited patterns and the contemporary environment. The artist also responds to these interactions and communicates his experience, and thus participates in the process of change. "Art" and "ordinary experience" are not separate. In other words, art is an aspect of the general process of human creativity and communication. Art, like culture, is ordinary.

The cultural standing and ideas of Raymond Williams were not popular at Cambridge. He was criticized in the press and ostracized by some of his fellows for what wrote in *Culture and Society*, *Long Revolution* and other works. In spite of the fact that he was sitting in the parlor of his faculty, he could not speak his left principles loudly. The atmosphere for Williams in Cambridge then was suffocating. Williams introduced film analysis in some of his lectures and even ran film episodes for illustration at class, almost unheard at that time. Some students said their generation went to the college in order to be taught by him, but he refused to teach them and turned them out to be taught by other people. His mind was on more important things, as some students recalled. But in the eyes of students and colleagues, Raymond Williams was a benign man, personally, not in his writings. In the 1960s Raymond Williams was active in social and political movements and activities. He was a hero in activities against American involvement in Cambodia and the Vietnam War. For an academic of literature to be intensely involved in social protests was very unusual at that time.

By 1970 Williams has became a nationally known figure, and he was invited to take part in a BBC program entitled "One Pair of Eyes". In this program, he said that university is not only the place of learning.

> "What I found when I first went there was another reality. Many of the colleges were beautiful and people came to look over them···I could still see them as country houses I've seen from outside: railways, walls, gates, lodges, parks built into the shape of class, an old property class, into its way of life. Learning is not regarded as discovery, but as something young gentlemen need to know. It is of interest to make comparison and contrast of different Cambridges as boarder-crossing." (*One Pair of Eyes*)

Raymond Williams wrote a few books on television, some being very critical. He was the first intellectual who gave TV a thorough scrutiny. Referring to the rapid development of mass media and TV, Raymond Williams said,

> "It is clear that the extension of communications has been part of the extension of democracy. Yet, in this century, while the public has extended, ownership and control of the means of communication have narrowed".

He also remarked,

"The ownership of the means of communication, old and new, has passed or is passing, in large part, to a kind of financial organization unknown in earlier period, and with important resemblance to the major forms of ownership in general industrial production. The methods and attitudes of capitalist business have established themselves near the centre of communications. There is the widespread dependence on advertising money, which leads to a policy of getting a large audience as many as possible, to attract and hold advertisers. From this it becomes one of the major purposes of communication to sell a particular product and program. All the basic purposes of communication—the sharing of human experience, can become subordinate to the drive to sell. " (*Communications*)

It therefore can be seen that what annoyed him is this sort of power and control over the media: who is controlling them, for whom, in whose purposes, against what? Much attention needs to be paid to the scheduling and the flow in television programming, as he advises.

In 1973, he published a book named *The Country and the City*. The city and the country, according to Williams, are inter-connected from the beginning. They are combined in an interesting way. One theme of the book is concerned with the country or the city as a distinctive way of life, with the city being modern, civilized, illuminated, sophisticated while the country backward, simple, out-of-date. On the other hand, this contrast can be turned the other way with the city being full of senselessness, over-crowding, noise, crime, power, and the country simple, innocent, old-value. All and again one will find a way to trace back to the valuable past and regret of something that is just disappearing, because of industrialization and urbanization. (*The Country and the City*)

In the early 1980s, Raymond Williams began to retreat because of his personal crisis, getting further and further away from English politics. Williams' relationship to his wife and his growing sense of Welshness have supported him through the crisis. He was becoming more aware of his Welsh identity. The last book he wrote, *The People of the Black Mountains*, is very significant to understand the life journey of Raymond Williams. What makes this work very moving is the connection between the personal and the public. He was very clear about his own identity, his own movement from Welsh working class through all different stages and places to Cambridge. Further, what makes the best writing of his is the connection of his personal journey and whole cultural history where he spent his life trying to participate, to analyze and to understand. And he never let one replace the other.

A brief representation of life journey of Raymond Williams and some of his theoretical ideas will not suffice for doing justice to the great cultural theorist. In the light of the current worldwide research and debates on his ideas and expressions, introducing and reviewing some of his theories and lessons may help us with the task of studying and criticizing Chinese cultural realities in the present time.

Studying Williams in a Chinese Perspective

With the introduction and growing study of his cultural and critical work in China from the 1980s, Raymond Williams' central contribution to Cultural Studies is not only regarded as increasingly influential and significant in the English-speaking world but also in contemporary China. This part of article explores some key concepts and ideas advanced in Williams' seminal works such as *Marxism and Literature*, *Culture and Society*, *Communications* and *The Long Revolution*. By a shift of context in which his theories or more general Cultural Studies are approached, regulated and critically applied in China, the author will consider the functions, opportunities as well as constrains which shape the situation in which the changing Chinese cultural realities and landscape are studied and assessed in contemporary times. A range of cases will be used to indicate how and why Raymond Williams is applied. I will also offer an argument for the continued relevance of Williams' thought to Chinese cultural debates to date.

Culture is ordinary (Williams, 1963). That may serve as a start of this essay as well. With the introduction and growing studies of his cultural and literary theory in China from the 1980s, Raymond Williams' central contribution to Cultural Studies is not only regarded as increasingly influential and significant in the English-speaking world but also in contemporary China. In this essay, a number of cultural and critical issues and ideas advanced by Williams will be analyzed and considered in both Western and Chinese context. The purpose of the analysis and study of Williams is to look at his major cultural concepts from a different angle, to try to apply some of his ideas in the current situation of cultural and literary studies in China, to find a way of thinking and reconciling culture (high, middle and low cultural ideas and practices) and history together, and finally to see if Williams' cultural thought can exert further impact on the Chinese cultural politics.

Higher Education and Politics

In his first major book *Culture and Society* (1958) Raymond Williams employs traditional Marxist theory in articulating and redefining culture and literature. It presents a radical re-reading of literature and history, which shows just how much traditional definition of culture had the taste of one class built into them. This, among others, was an exciting idea in the 1950s, and is also interesting at the present time. It seems that in this important book Williams wanted to establish a kind of Marxist cultural theory of his own. He remarked,

"Marx himself outlined, but never fully developed, a cultural theory. His casual comments on literature, for example, are those of a learned, intelligent man of his period, rather than what we now know as Marxist literary criticism." (1961:258)

However, Williams could never afford to overlook or neglect the significance and value of Marx's social and economic theory, particularly the work of *Critique of Political Economy* (1859). Naturally, Williams applied in his work many crucial concepts from Marx and Engels, such as, structure and superstructure, levels of control, interaction (Engels), as well as economic conditions of production.

Williams has formulated the theory of culture as the study of relationships in a whole way of life, which can be found in *Culture and Society* and in almost all major theoretical works of his. In effect, he was producing the sociology of culture that was initially derived from the English tradition of criticism. On the basis of "a hundred of schools of thought" in Europe, Williams began to make connections across various theoretical directions and frame important cultural issues by means of theoretical abstraction. This he named cultural materialism, which promotes "the analysis of all forms of signification within the actual means of conditions of their production" (1958).

A look at the theoretical development of Marxism in China in the period of time roughly within the comparatively short life time of Williams' (1921-1988)

generates disparate phenomena. The divide can be located around the Great
Cultural Revolution. Before the radical nationwide movement, especially in the
1920s and 1930s, some or very little introduction and translation of global
Marxism (more accurately Western Marxism or New Marxism) was conducted in
China. As a result, the spread of philosophical and cultural ideas and works of
Western Marxists was very limited. After the Cultural Revolution, especially in
the early reform era of late 1970s and 1980s, a systematic and larger scale study
of Western New Marxism began in earnest. A large number of works by Western
cultural theorists and literary critics are carefully studied, introduced and
translated, such as Weber, Freud, the classical Frankfurt School critics,
Harbamas, Lukacs, Althusser, Gramci, Luxemburge, Eagleton, Jameson and
the "New Left" critics. Admittedly, as David Aldson remarks,

"Marxism is a tradition of thought which includes numerous
interpretations, developments and modifications of the insights of Marx
himself, some of which constitute necessary amendments to the inherent
limitations of those insights whilst others result from attempts to be consistent
to then in historically changed circumstances" (2004:9).

It was noticeable that the research and scholarship in philosophical, cultural
and literary study and application kept balanced with the result that there was a
general prosperity in Marxist studies in the Chinese context, a very open and
democratic context in the 1980s. However, reflecting on the Chinese endeavors
in this respect, it is clear that most Chinese Marxists were scholars, learners,
translators and disseminators. Very few of them can be credited as Marxist critics
or theorists, unlike Raymond Williams or Terry Eagleton. The former, such as
Xu Chongwen and Wu Yuanmai at The Chinese Academy of Social Sciences,
Wang Ning and Yu Wujin at Tsinghua and Fudan University respectively, did
invest considerable energy and efforts in rendering and explaining crude theory
and teaching of old and new Western Marxist interpreters and critics in China

while the latter not only authenticated Marx' and Marxist theory but also went deeper in order to propose and advance new ideas and criticism. Therefore, it is understandable that in China, original Marxist cultural and literary critics are surely in great demand. Some even commented that what is urgently needed in today's China is the Marxist scholars and critics of the Frankfurt School type.

The reason for theoretical advancement and contribution behind such creative Marxist critics as Raymond Williams is that he came from a working-class background in rural Britain, and later went to Cambridge as a "scholarship boy". At Cambridge, from 1939, Williams devoted more time to political activity than academic work. He discovered the Socialist Club and joined the organization and became a member of Communist comradeship. Instead of concentrating more on English literature, Williams has read Marx' *Capital* and Eagles' *Socialism* and *Anti-Duhring*. In his college years, he was well introduced to Marxism, not unusual for his generation. Williams was able to concentrate on his academic work only after the Second World War, in which he took part as a soldier and officer. In the peaceful years and environment of Cambridge, Williams resumed his academic work fanatically, establishing his lifelong priority: theory and practice in cultural politics.

Williams did many things and accomplished a lot, including finding his young and smart lady of political consciousness to marry. He shared many important ideas with his wife, Joy, who eventually became his good assistant in both domestic and academic sense. On one occasion he commented on their exchange that at a certain time she could be considered as "joint author" in certain chapters of his books (McIlroy, 1993). Williams' involvement in all of these events and issues and topics can be viewed with a steady gaze in the Chinese context. The first issue at stake is obviously the "scholarship boy", regardless of different educational system and selection tradition. It can be seen that there is some degree of overlapping if we try to compare the selection of "scholarship boys" in both British and Chinese context, though it is only a recent phenomenon for some of key middle schools to send their best students to the national prestigious universities in China. But the key middle schools in China are in some way similar to the grammar schools in Britain in terms of hardware (construction of campus) and software (teachers and means of teaching) rather than school tradition and history. In view of unequal distribution of educational resources in China, it is questionable if students of excellent school records in the remote countryside can be selected as the "scholarship boy" type and are able to enter quality institutions of higher education in China. The second issue is the college culture and academic requirements for the college students. Technically, this can be seen as the standard practice of credit system and social involvement. Williams entered Cambridge to study literature, but he was heavily involved in politics. For some time during his college life, he was called upon to join the army. And eventually he graduated from Cambridge and became a thinker, educator and writer. We need to be reflective in considering our annual college entrance exams and in re-evaluating the current school curriculum. The third issue is related to the school culture. It is clearly indicated that during Williams' career as a cultural theorist and literary critic, he went through a lot of personal and academic crisis. But through his great attachment to his wife and growing sense of identity, he was never bitten or defeated. Evidently, there are more activities and organizations for socialization and friendship undertakings in Anglo-British colleges and universities (including religious activities and organizations) than in Chinese schools. The administration and management of such activities and organizations also vary accordingly. There seems to be necessary for our educators to create more space and provide more freedom for our national asset. The students' rights and the management's obligations must be ensured so as to promote progressive and healthy college culture.

Adult Education

Soon after his graduation from Cambridge, for 15 years (from 1946 to 1961), Williams served as a staff tutor for the Oxford Delegacy for Extra Mural Studies, organizing and teaching adult classes in collaboration with the Workers' Educational Association. This is a very important period for him as some of his major cultural and literary works were produced and published during this time, such as *Culture and Society 1780-1950* (1958), *Reading and Criticism* (1950), *Drama from Ibsen to Eliot* (1952), *The Long Revolution* (1961). The period also witnessed the making of an intellectual, and reveals Williams' searching analysis of the conditions for a genuine learning society in Britain.

That Williams chose to work for Oxford University's adult education delegacy for his personal and academic reasons can be understood equally well in China. The personal reason is mainly the financial. A newly graduated college student with a family to support is always in need of reasonable income. That is why William gave up the senior scholarship from the University and took up the adult education job which was better paid. The academic reasons are more interesting and thought-provoking, and are certainly more crucial for Williams. As far as Williams was concerned, the Tripos or a thesis is of secondary consideration in his circumstances. For some, they are mostly obsessive if not unreasonable and not worth years of commitment. Williams had a clear idea of how much emotion and energy he should devote to academic work. The beneficial lesson we can draw from his choice and determination can be that Williams has set an example in terms of becoming an intellectual and a man. He denied the commonplace earthly demands and requirements of higher education institution and followed his own path: taking adult education classes, writing novels, collaborating with friends in running a journal and a magazine, building up a press, even making films. Moreover, for academic reasons, and I believe that they are also of Chinese interests, Williams made comparison between becoming a full-time academic at the University and adult education tutor, and wisely took advantages of the latter. Being involved in teaching WEA classes, he was first of all in the position of benefiting from the freedom to choose one's own syllabus and gear this to whatever one happens to be researching or writing on. Secondly, he had the opportunity to study literary texts and topics at much greater depth than the pressures of time and crowded survey syllabuses in English departments allowed for. Thirdly, he could take the opportunity to teach beyond the usual frontiers of English, not only into cultural studies but into, for example, European and American drama. (Mcllroy, 1993). Williams showed us that a thinker is not the one who forever thinks. It is naturally important for a thinker who has constant dialogues with the masses, should be confronted with adult learners from all walks of life in his case, and above all place much importance on experience. Consequently, he offered us this dictum, "There are in fact no masses, only ways of seeing people as masses".

The above discussion does not indicate that Williams was totally confined within adult education. Instead, he made abundant use of his teaching time and conditions. He was becoming more and more productive and creative during this time equally owing to his utilization of a range of intellectual resources and his unusual determination as a true scholar. We in China have become accustomed to such idioms as "long sitting in the solitary chair" (zuo lun ban deng), "ten years of academic diligence can turn out a quality work" (shi nian mo yi jian) and so forth. It is more realistic, in Terry Eagleton's words, for Williams to work with his personal resources without significant collaboration or institutional support, i. e. almost single-handedly. Again in the Chinese context, what Williams performed and contributed to Cultural Studies can be seen as a practical model. For social science workers and academics in the institutions of higher education in China, serious researchers and academics (including not so serious researchers and academics) are able to obtain research funding of different quantities fairly easily. Research-active people can successfully apply grants from departmental to ministerial to state functionaries. However, the financially assisted research projects are sometimes administered and managed in an ineffective or irresponsible manner. The end results or the publications are often considered as poor in academic standard. Reports of academic cheating and some "unconventional" means by some applicants of winning the favor of the appraisal and evaluation organizations for private and personal interests are not uncommon. In view of the route Williams has followed as a cultural and literary thinker, we feel a need to exam and scrutinize our academic appraisal system and conventions for flaws. Radical measures are obviously needed to amend professional policies and regulations and to cultivate a healthy learned environment.

Media Culture, Film Studies and Audience

In an empiricist cultural environment, it is special to see that Williams was not only erudite but also courageous and experimental. At Cambridge he was the first don to run film classes, which was unheard of in that ancient institution. Williams has recalled that he used to view a large range of films at the Cambridge University Socialist Club. These films were mostly the representation of the situation and realities of domestic and European societies and histories and they "were particularly important". As above discussed, Williams had wanted upon graduation to make his own films, a very innovative project. Before and after he became the University lecturer, he had always been a unique type, exerting a formative influence on the young generation at the time. Moreover, what he did in the teaching of new subjects in media and film proved significant in the subsequent development of the then embryo discipline of film studies and further in the later time in Cultural Studies. In a way, Williams intended to establish the new study area and to move further towards the institutionalization of the subject. This was eventually realized as one of subject areas of research within The Center for Contemporary Cultural Studies (CCCS).

Theoretically, in his cultural and literary works in later periods, Williams tried to incorporate theory and practice of film-making and media study into his general theoretical framework of "structure of feeling". The ideas of visual cultural production together with other cultural conceptions seem to make his critical work more comprehensive. In other words, drawing from his analysis of films, Williams succeeded in uniting his analysis of totality and experience, and in characterizing the function of art.

Williams' pioneering work in film studies and media analysis is still hugely influential today. In *Communications* he defines society as "a form of communication through which experience is described, shared, modified, and preserved" and says that

> "The emphasis on communication asserts, as a matter of experience, that men and societies are not confined to relationships of power, property, and production" (Prendergast 341).

One way of interpreting those words by him is related to his notions of culture being ordinary and of culture as "a whole way of life". Another way of understanding him can be in disagreement with the conceptions of Marxism that emphasize on the mode of production and productive relationships, because Williams was seen as too subjectivist and empiricist in insisting on a role for "experience". As issues of media in China are quite similar in the reform era, Williams' analysis of media production and reception is obviously supportive in explicating and analyzing these issues.

Since entering the era of globalization, the renewal of knowledge has accelerated in China. Modern sciences and IT technologies have introduced foreign culture to Chinese society. The large flow of foreign business people, capital, technology, products and languages has actually blurred the distinctions between Chinese and foreign cultures. The computer popularization and commodity internationalization impel Chinese people to learn from foreign cultures. This fusion of Chinese and foreign cultures has contributed to mutual cultural exchange and formation of new cultural identities.

With ubiquity of the global media, especially television and the Internet, media development has undergone yet another transformation. Chinese people now have a seemingly limitless access to activities, attitudes, and aesthetic ideals that do not necessarily relate to the assumptions about taste and sensibility that are promulgated by the standards of a dominant culture. The result has been the increased confusion of what had once been rather clear distinctions between highbrow, middlebrow, and lowbrow culture. Because of this overlap, critics today often use the terms "popular culture" or "the culture of the masses". As suggested by Williams, the meanings of popular culture can also be the culture "well liked by many people", "inferior kinds of work", "work deliberately setting out to win favor with the people", and "culture actually made by the people for themselves". In Chinese context, media culture is characterized by its commercial features since its development is linked with both the global norms and the country's economic reform. In view of cultural realities in China, the rise of popular media has led to the prosperity of cultural market. It has also served as catalyst in the development of economy. At the same time, the situation has deconstructed the existing symbolic hierarchies and caused the "paradigm shift" to appear in Chinese cultural landscape.

Media technology and its development in China, like the development of politics, economy and cultural progress, are neither even nor well-balanced, bearing the features of Chinese socialism. Continuous social development has created a situation where at one end one has the information super highway via computers, modern management and high technology, while at the other end, cultivation is still carried out manually in some areas. This has created at present a mixture of farming, industrial and information cultures in "pre-modern", "modern" and "post-modern" stages. Thus, the current Chinese media culture is obviously marked with characteristics of being at once fragmentary and unifying, heterogeneous and homogenizing. Geographically, there has been the diversity of media formation and distribution in various parts of the country. Chinese people in the reform era are also entitled to the variety of media production and selection under "direct State control" and with "planned flow", in Williams' terms (*Communications*).

The meaning of the word "audience" suggests a relationship between offering and receiving parties, which can be described as "a client relationship". According to Williams, this is significantly true in the case of advertising, where the audience is targeted by the advertisement. In the study of audience in media production and Cultural Studies, the concept of audience is often defined against social background. As the audience consuming media products or reading cultural texts are heterogeneous, the cohesiveness and integrity of the audience does not actually exist, since the consumption of a text differs due to status and identity of audience, time and place. Alternatively, the strategies and responses of audiences to a media product or a text are never identical or unified. Different kinds of people interpreting different media types can produce feedback in different ways. In this sense, the general concept of mass audience is actually hard to find.

In a review of theoretical contributions to research in media audience, the work of Williams, who examines the relationships between audience, texts and cultural perspectives, is seminal. In his early works, Williams (1962, 1976) argued that print capitalism and the commercialization of the media lessened the importance attributed to any one text, and emphasized instead the continuous supply of cultural material over the quality of cultural work. His theoretical debate on the key concept of "flow technology" represented by television production, as well as his cultural analysis of media production, is still significant. Williams' cultural approach to media differs from the previous textual research on media and therefore brings great changes in cultural interpretation of media products.

Influenced by Raymond Williams, his fellow-socialist Stuart Hall advanced a theoretical model of "encoding and decoding of meaning" (1992), which involves a critical analysis of the media producer and consumer. Basically, Hall argues that the relationship between producer and audience is a fractured one, which indicates that the correspondence between encoding and decoding is questionable. In other words, what the audience derives from the text may not be the same as what the media producer thought they had inscribed in the text. Essentially, Hall proposes three strategies of dominant, negotiated and oppositional readings, with particular emphasis on the social differences and power structures of the audience. These reading positions are effective at "differentiated moments within the totality formed by the social relations of the communicative process as a whole." (1992)

Fiske and Hartley (2003) study "audience's responses" in the media context. For them, the variety of reading strategies and responses to media products has generally been influenced by the changing economic and social system of capitalism over history. Based on but also surpassing the previous positions of "encoding and decoding" and "meaning systems", Fiske and Hartley focus on the overwhelming effects of ideology on the audience, because powerful groups have long perceived mass media as sites for the dissemination of dominant ideology. This view and Fiske's other crucial ideas of "active audiences" and "interpretive pleasure" have also been widely debated, though there is partial recognition of their theoretical persuasiveness but no consensus on the issues (Croteau & Hoynes, 2003).

In the era of globalization, the hegemony of national politics has greatly been challenged by the globalizing force of mass media. Benefiting from new information technologies, people in developed countries are able to participate in the process of creating new cultural expressions and of contributing to the formation of global culture. It is imperative that the West is dominant in terms of controlling most advanced media production and manipulating the consumption of media products worldwide. However, discussions of the "global information balance", "communication rights" and "diasporic audiences" (Ibid) have practical significance in contemporary China.

Culture and Society

The book with such a title by Williams is regarded as his best-known and most influential work. It can then be regarded as one of the great contributions to cultural and literary studies. Many of his fertile ideas and concepts are eloquently theorized and discussed in detail in this monumental work. His understanding and interpretation of culture and society appealed very much to many literary and cultural critics in that historical period, and to Chinese cultural and literary writers in modern time as well. A number of issues and problems Williams addressed in that long historical time remain of interest for Cultural Studies practitioners today as those issues and problems cry to be reconsidered with new references. For Williams, "The development of *culture* is perhaps the most striking among all the words named," and he further remarked that

"The question now concentrated in the meanings of the word *culture* are questions directly raised by the great historical changes which the changes in *industry*, *democracy*, and *class*, in their own way, represent, and to which the changes in *art* are a closely related response. The development of the word *culture* is a record of a number of important and continuing reactions to these changes in our social, economic, and political life, and may be seen, in itself, as a special kind of map by means of which the nature of the changes can be explored" (*Culture and Society*).

In this important book, Williams drew our attention to a number of words which had acquired new meanings in that specific period and after, such as *ideology*, *intellectual*, *rationalism*, *humanitarian*, *utilitarian*, *romanticism*, *bureaucracy*, *capitalism*, *socialism*, *liberalism*, *collectivism*, *commercialism*, *masses*, *highbrow*, *isms*, *operative* (*noun*) and so forth. This unfinished list of terms and concepts are still attracting, puzzling and sometimes enlightening us. Williams later dealt with these complex ideas in his *Keywords* (1976). Contemporary writers further discussed these concepts and more related terms in *New Keywords* (2004), in the newly-published keyword references in China, which forms a link of the cultural study genealogy from the earlier master.

In actual fact, it is in the context of the British Industrialization that Williams conducted his critical analysis of culture and literature. He discussed the nations of culture with reference to the idea of democracy and learning communities. He analyzes how the notion of culture gets increasingly isolated and specialized, and confined to the keeping of partly ideal or imaginary minority— from Coleridge's clerisy, through Arnold's remnant, to Leave's "educated public" in the 20th century. According to him, culture tends to become restricted to a rarefied "aesthetic sphere" towards the end of the 19th century. Williams emphasizes the valuable elements in the open-minded ideas of culture such as its stress on "wholeness, tending, nurturing, and growth" and on the culture of majority, the masses.

It may not totally be inappropriate to consider the notion of culture that developed in the era of modernization in China with that in the time of the Industrialization in England. Some cultural elites such as Yu Qiuyu, propagate about the "ontological implications of culture" (wen hua ben wei) and "absoluteness of cultural values" (wen hua de zhong ji jia zhi) and about the divorce of cultural ideas and practices from society and politics. By way of romanticizing or criticizing Chinese traditional culture, Yu has taken up the job of making culture seem to be a floating signifier. There is a general lack of context in which cultural skills and cultural values can be estimated in Yu's theoretical argument. On the other hand, in almost all Williams' cultural works cultural analysis is always rooted in society, history and political events. Socialist culture, common culture or working-class culture, for Williams, is organically related to the then social change, to literary movement and figures, to Marxism, to trade union, to the masses, to classes and alike.

However, Williams' cultural discussions provoke some questions in current Chinese cultural context. First, we might ask, what is the benchmark theory for talking about and classifying "masses" and "classes" in China's transit period from a traditional state to a (post) modern state? Take the key notion of "cultural fever" (wen hua re) in the earlier decade for example. This seems to be associated with the China State policy of reform and opening to the outside world. The "cultural fever" is part of reflection on the transformation of current Chinese cultural situation, and is further seen as the inevitable consequences of Western cultural influences. The value of Chinese traditional culture and its "dominant mode" (Williams) was being wakened. Even Williams' defined "democracy" had yet taken another layer of implication in the open and liberal China, for the fact that communication means and technology have been revolutionized and the media users have played the role of a communicative agent rather than being placed on the receiving end.

Williams' attempt to identify an idea of the impact of the nineteen-century tradition is particularly enlightening in China. One thing was prominent during the 1990s and that is the revival of national learning (guo xue). This cultural move is thought to be a continuum of the cultural fever of the earlier decade. As opposed to the influence of the Western culture, national learning aims to articulate new subject positions for the intellectual elites by consecrating pure, autonomous scholarship or learning on the one hand, and to promote cultural nationalism or an "anti-Western movement" by advocating a nativist value system and exploring Western mistreatment of China in modern and the contemporary era on the other. The advocates of the culture fever in the 1990s argued that due to the unbalanced flow of information, there comes the domination of Western culture which was threatening the cultures of developing countries such as China. Global media play a key role in the process, when Western countries' military colonization gave way to "electronic colonization". The postcolonial strategy of the world capitalism is arguably seen as "cultural hegemony" in China. At the same time, Chinese intellectuals have rediscovered the value of the Chinese cultural legacy. For them, the time has come to identify their academic lineage and ethical traditions with Chinese culture. A lot of work had been done in systematic research projects, re-editing and printing of the classics, and issuing learned journals. Likewise, Williams devoted half of volume to critical appreciation of a number of nineteenth-century thinkers and literary writers in order to show that tradition and heritage should duly be cherished because they are the basis of extending meanings and values of a particular culture.

Science and Theory

An example of combination of scientific knowledge and theoretical analysis by Williams can be found in *The Long Revolution* (1961). It seems reasonable to say that his scientific discussion of art and literature is authoritative or integrated in terms of authenticity and scientific accuracy. Through his efforts in exploring the relationship between science and theory, we have a better understanding of Williams as unique. To discuss similarities between "art" and "ordinary experience", Williams takes up the idea, based partly on modern research in biology, that our "seeing"—our interpretation of sensory input according to a set of rules—is a largely learnt rather than "natural" activity: "reality as we experience it is a human creation". This creation has two main sources: "the human brain as it has evolved, and the interpretations carried by our cultures" (p34). Though the brain gives a common basis for our interpretative activity, our ways of seeing are not fixed or constant. Different cultures see the world in different ways, and ways of seeing within a culture change over time—or, more precisely, human beings change them, in response to the interactions between learnt and culturally inherited patterns and the contemporary environment. The artist also responds to these interactions and communicates his experience, and thus participates in the process of change. "Art" and "ordinary experience" are not separate: art is an aspect of the general process of human creativity and communication. Art, like culture, is ordinary.

With this interesting discussion only, it is not easy to reflect upon or fully appreciate his work as a body of theory. The instance of Williams' experimental discussion can now simply be taken for granted in both the West and China. Two examples will suffice. In the prosperity of translating global culture within China, it is commonplace to see the fact that a number of translators take advantages of the achievement of contemporary work in modern sciences, and apply scientific concepts and formula in their study of cultural and literary subjects. Xu Yuanchong, a Chinese scholar in translation study, re-shapes ideas from some of the latest developments in science, such as "super conduction" in modern physics, "chemical reaction aesthetics", "cloning" and mathematic $1 + 1 > 2$ (acquisition of meaning through reading between lines), in his translation theory and practice. He concludes that translation is not only a problem-solving discipline but also creative art. Xu believes that through translation of literature, it is possible to transform the beauty of one culture into the beauty of global culture. He has formulated the theory of introduction of "quality gene" in literary translation in an attempt that the translated language will be as good as the original, and even better, i. e. the "target text" to be equally good as the "source text" and even better. In practice, Xu sincerely applies his creative thoughts in the translation of a number of English and French canonical works such as Shakespeare, Scott, Byron, Shelley, Hugo, Balsac, Moppassant, and Roman Roland. In his translated publications of Chinese classics, such theories and methods are also experimented with considerable success.

In a similar way but towards a different direction, Yang Zhenning, an American-Chinese scientist and Nobel Prize laureate, is interested in solving the mystery that China has fallen behind the West in modern times when the country "between the first and thirteenth century A. D. reached a level of scientific knowledge unapproached in the West." (Needham, 1995) Yang shares the view of most European observers that superstition and ancient mysticism prevented the rise of true scientific thinking in China. *The Book of Changes* is arguably chosen for such criticism by Yang. And his choice of such a book provokes obvious disputes and argument in Chinese cultural and academic circle. Critical opinions concentrate on that Yang, as a serious scientist, has failed to find some positive elements in *The Book of Changes*. There is possibility of finding the ancient thought system in *The Book of Changes* that can be thought as a "viable alternative, a kind of mental approach, associative thinking, and co-ordinative thinking" (Pp162-163). In a word, it is a special system of scientific thinking in ancient China. In this case, it is not difficult to reflect upon Williams' borrowing of modern biological work in his argument on cultural perception and art.

Structures of Feelings

There seem to be some differences between plural and singular form of this crucial concept by Williams, which may be seen as common knowledge. Repeated consultation of his works of *Preface to Film*, *The Long Revolution* and *Politics and Letters* show the two forms were used interchangeably without substantial difference. To be brief, "Structures of feelings" refer to the sensibility of a generation, its socially reflective experience articulated in cultural forms. As a heuristic approach to study cultural representations and to investigate organizations of life, Williams develops the concept of "structure of feeling":

"It is as firm and definite as 'structure' suggests, yet it operates in the most delicate and least tangible parts of our activity" (*Long Revolution*, p64).

Williams' definition of this concept in *The Long Revolution* is complicated, but we should attempt a summary, given its importance throughout his work. In one sense, the "structure of feeling" is the culture of a period. It is not learned in any formal way, but each new generation creates it—using, in part, elements from the past—as it shapes its response to the unique world it inherits. A "structure of feeling" corresponds, in some ways, to the dominant "social character" (Erich Fromm) , which Williams uses to denote "a valued system of behavior and attitudes" (*Long Revolution*, 63)—but, more importantly, it expresses the interaction between the dominant "social character", alternative "social characters", and lived, experiential reality. In all actual communities, it is a very deep and wide possession, since communication depends on it. But it is not uniform throughout a society, and is primarily evident in the dominant productive group. At this level, however, it is different from any distinguishable "social character" as it has to cope, not only with the public ideals, but also with their lived omissions and consequences.

The fusion of "structure" and "feeling" epitomizes Williams' approach in all his work—a search for system combined with the desire to acknowledge "the most delicate and least tangible parts of our activity". We may ask with "structure of feeling", as with the "wholeness" of "a whole way of life", what constitutes it as a structure—why "structure" rather than, say a field of attitudes and affects? How far "structure" is more than a metaphor for "organization" and "interconnectedness",—the metaphor the later 20th century prefers to that of organic formation and circle? The temporal dimensions of the concept are also a problem. "Structure of feeling" has synchronic implications, but Williams' stress on the concept, throughout his work, is diachronic, concerned with historical experiences and realities. But how do "structures of feelings" change with time and reality, and in what sense, when they change, do they remain "structures"? *The Long Revolution* seems to suggest that they change with "the new generation···feeling its whole life in certain ways differently, and shaping its creative response into a new structure of feeling" (*Long Revolution*, 65). But if a "structure of feeling" changes with each new generation, the difficulties remain of delimiting a "generation" and of accounting for the possible persistence and co-existence of "structures of feelings" across and within different generations. In his later work, Williams tries to define the concept in a more reflective way, but it remains a shifting signifier. That scholars and theorists conduct systematic research on the complicated implications of the concept in his works and on its varying meanings in others who have employed it would be valuably necessary.

It seems that the notion of "structure" has been much used to challenge the idea of the free, autonomous individual: structures make men, not vice versa. Williams stresses in *The Long Revolution*, however, the role of human agency, indeed human creativity, in shaping "structures of feeling" and the "creativity" is not confined to the artist, who partakes, rather, of a general human process of creativity and communication. A confinement can be made within the Chinese context for the application of structures of feelings in the reform era in China.

Marxism and Literature

It is laudably interesting that Williams has put considerable stress on process, on specificity, and on activity. Today, such terms are hardly likely to meet with disapproval from anywhere, as can be testified in some Keyword-style analysis. But the central problem with *Marxism and Literature* is suggested by Williams' remark, in the Introduction, that his contact with international Marxist thought in the 1970s gave him the sense of belonging to a sphere and dimension of work in which he felt comfortable with (*Marxism and Literature*). This confession reveals a recognizable poignancy of protracted isolation. Williams' insistence throughout the book on "the full social and historical material process" is helpful for our understanding of the writer. Despite his reiterated stress on creativity, the "full social process" is totalizing, and transcendent, which is in general agreement with the ethos of historical materialism.

Historical materialism, according to Williams, is of human creativity, and he provocatively claims, "At the very centre of Marxism is an extraordinary emphasis on human creativity and self-creation" (*Marxism and Literature*, 206).

The question of why actually existing socialism has so often stifled creativity, and not only in the arts can therefore be raised. Williams strives to retain a sense of the specificity of the practices that have, in his view, been isolated as "art" and "literature". As a matter of fact, "structure of feeling" sometimes seems like an attempt to preserve such specificity politically and culturally. As the concepts of art and literature irreplaceable for him, Williams tries to displace the experiences for which those concepts stand into a socio-political awareness that especially manifests itself in certain artistic practices.

Williams' affirmation and creative thoughts in *Marxism and Literature* are somewhat sensitive in the Chinese theoretical and literary field. That innovation and diversion of traditional Marxist discourse and interpretation is allowed within a limited circle does not mean lack of new perspective or silence of criticism. Williams' cultural materialism is being paid attention to and focused not only in institutions but also among students who want to draw more inspiration from Marxism. His unique emphasis on human agency and cultural creativity is meaningful in terms of distancing his ideas from the traditional crude Marxism and setting up new criteria for understanding and judging the use and value of literary and artistic works in China, without sticking dogmatically to the existing standard or scheme.

Conclusion: Williams Will Not Go Away

It is pitiful that Williams was not able complete his last work due to his acute blindness. The unfinished nature of Williams' work is stressed by his premature death. But his unfinished Welsh trilogy project forms, nonetheless, a totalizing course, a sustained attempt to integrate personal experience, cultural, social and political analysis, literary criticism and theory, fiction and drama, and socialist commitment into a continuing practice that sought both to interpret and change the world. It was this combination of his personal efforts, social impact and his Marxist theorizing of cultural realities that Williams came to call "cultural materialism".

Raymond Williams is inspiring resources for many in many respects both in his times and in our times. His very virtues, his critical decency and his incisive ideas represented in his works and speeches are always enlightening. It is only natural that he is regarded as not only a kind, modest and erudite man, but an important thinker. Williams' theoretical and practical contributions such as generation of heuristic concepts and approaches, opening of new investigation fields, concern for specificity, difficulty and complexity, continued and disinterested commitment are both morally and intellectually exemplary. His work is a serious call to thought and responsibility. By the 1990s, Williams was being unreasonably dismissed as passé. His ideas had been superseded by various schools of thought, especially post-learning of various sorts, and so forth. This hasty judgment is largely explicable in terms of the decline of belief in socialism and the feasibility of a "common culture". The fact is, however, that the problems he addressed remain of critical significance and, no doubt, Williams' pioneering work will continue to be an available source of inspiration for the future development of cultural analysis in the whole world, including the West and China.

REFERENCES

Books by R. Williams

Williams, R. (1954), *Preface to Film*, Chatto & Windus.

— (1963) *Cultural and Society 1780-1950*, Penguin.

— (1963) *Border Country*, Chatto & Windus.

— (1965) *The Long Revolution*, Chatto & Windus.

— (1962) *Communications*, Penguin.

— (1964) *Second Generation*, Chatto & Windus.

— (1968) *May Day Manifesto*, Penguin.

— (1975) *The Country and the City*, Chatto & Windus.

— (1974) *Television: Technology and Cultural Form*, Fontana.

— (1976) *Keywords: A Vocabulary of Culture and Society*, Fontana / Croom Helm.

— (1977) *Marxism and Literature*, OUP.

— (1979) *Politics and Letters: Interviews with New Left Review*, New Left Books.

— (1980) *Problems in Materialism and Culture*, Verso.

— (1983) *Writing in Society*, Verso.

— (1989) *Raymond Williams on Television: Selected Writings*, Routledge.

— (1983) *Writing in Society*, Verso.

— (1966) *Communications*, Penguin.

— (1954) *Drama in Performance*, Muller.

— (1970) *The English Novel from Dickens to Lawrence*, Chatto & Windus.

Others

Aldson, D. *Transition: Terry Eagleton* (2004), New York: Palgrave.

Croteau, D. & W. Hoynes. *Media Society* (2003), London: Sage.

Eagleton, T. *Literary Theory* (1996), Oxford: Blackwell.

Mcllroy, J. & S. Westwood. Ed. *Raymond Williams in Adult Education* (1993), Leicester: NIACE.

Prendergast, C. *Cultural Materialism: on Raymond Williams* (1995), Minneapolis: University of Minnesota Press.

Needham, J. *The Shorter Science and Civilization in China* (1993), CUP.

Critiquing Irigaray's
Post-modern Feminist Theory

In *Ce sexe qui n'en est pas un* (This sex which is not one) and elsewhere, Irigaray focuses on the absence of women from the social order and explores analogies between sexuality and language. Irigaray finds out that, throughout the entire Western cultural tradition, women have been assigned no place in history. Alternatively, women have been put in the schizoid position of being simultaneously in history and not in history—"written out" of history by male power. They appear as exterior representations of various kinds or as objects of men's desire. Therefore, Western tradition is shaped by masculinity. Women's desires are not represented and the feminine is suppressed. For Irigaray, however, there are connections between women's bodies and women's meaning-making in language. She argues that *difference* is shaped by the female body and rests in women's capacity for decentred, multiple sexuality and women's language. She concludes that women's identity can be autonomous and explorable only within a radically separatist women's movement. This interpretation of some thematic concepts of feminist theory advanced by Lucy Irigaray will shed light on the understanding and criticism of Irigaray's feminist theory and, more generally, of the French school of thought on gender politics.

Essentially, French feminists, such as Kristeva, Irigaray and Cixous are concerned with language and psychology. They take as their start-point the insights of major post-structuralists, especially Lacan, Foucault and Derrida in their treatment of subjectivity and femininity. For these feminist theorists, the claim of sexual difference is the site of a different kind of feminine voice. This special voice is variously described by Lucy Irigaray as *parler femme* ("woman speaking"), by Helene Cixous as *ecriture feminine* ("feminist writing"), and by Julia Kristeva as the semiotic. None of these women philosophers fully accepts the distinction between "man" and "woman"; further, they question the binary logic which supports the male/female duality. However, for the reason that this binary logic is most clearly related to language, it can only be subverted by a different type of language. This different, revolutionary language is for each of these thinkers a female or woman-identified language: a language celebrating women's identity.

Focusing on Irigaray's ideas on sexuality and language, the author of this paper attempts to analyze the essential themes of this "French side of the divide", indicating that although their theories are characteristically radical in their own right, they are far from functional in political and social applications.

There are two major sources of influence on French feminist criticism, namely, Derrida's deconstruction and Lacan's deconstructive approach to the theory of psychoanalysis by Freud.

The term deconstruction is virtually synonymous with the work of Jacques Derrida, who has used it to characterize the kind of critical effort that he advocates. Derrida's most immediate point of reference was the notion of structure. It involves the dismantling into their constituent features of all types of unities, systems, theories, etc. Thus, if structuralism aims to "construct" the system of logical relations governing the disposition of individual elements in a text, deconstruction is, among other things, a critique of structuralism, which is seen as simply one more stage in the history of metaphysics. Derrida argues that metaphysical systems are "centered" structures that depend on a paradoxical logic according to which the centre is understood as both present in, and independent of, the structure. In this form, the relationship between centre and structure appears as a hierarchical opposition in which one term is understood to embody truth and the other is seen as merely a negative copy: norm/deviation, sane/mad, mine/yours, authority/obedience (Eagleton, 1996:164), or as an especially important case for Derrida—speech/writing. This last opposition displays the curious logic of the supplement, which, when teased out by a deconstructive reading, can be seen to subvert the process by which a piece of writing is said to produce meaning. Instead of appearing as a mere representation of the truth that is present in speech, writing is thus shown as, according to Derrida, a field of limitless play, which is characterized by the movement of difference, a word invented by Derrida combining "differance" and deferral (Storey, 1997:94-95).

Deconstructionists argue that linguistic meaning is "constructed" through contrasts between binary opposites such as black/white, and that the choice of one of these terms as positive (usually white) depends on the negation or oppression of the opposite term (usually black). Deconstruction pulls apart (deconstructs) the process which creates and naturalizes these oppositions, deconstructing, for example, the ways in which women are associated with nature (inferior) and men with culture (superior).

French feminists are determined to replace this ideology with alternative women's language, *parle femme* or *ecriture feminine*. The writings of Lucy Irigaray, in particular, contain new forms of expression, using attributes of female sexuality (of *jouissance* and multiple pleasure) to replace phallocentric (male) pleasure which is singular (the Phallus). Irigaray's account emphasizes the multiple or plural styles of female sexuality and expression, which can also be interpreted ambiguously in terms of her claim of female sex being not one

(Irigaray, 1985:28-30). Her persuasive description of the features of the sexual lips that are constantly "in touch" with special sensuality of the female body is both symbolic and tactical. It aims at producing difference that can be attributed to women the right to voicing themselves differently. Irigaray is not mystifying the nature of language. What she debates about is the creation of women's language. In Irigaray's words, what women want is a language of their own, a currency of exchange or a non-market of economy. For her, this language can only emerge from women's sexual difference. As she remarks,

> "Female sexuality has always been conceptualized on the basis of masculine parameters. Thus the opposition between 'masculine' clitoral activity and 'feminine' vaginal passivity, an opposition alternative which Freud—and many others-saw as stages, or alternatives, in the development of a sexually 'normal' woman, seems rather too clearly required by the practice of male sexuality" (1981:99).

Jacques Lacan's theory of psychoanalysis also influences French feminism immensely. Lacan creatively updated and reworked the principles by Freud, with the understanding that it is through an attendance to language and linguistic structures (as theorized via Saussure and Jakobson) that the structures of the unconscious are to be understood. His most famous pronouncement is "The unconscious is structured as a language" (Barry, 1995:111). According to Lacan, the patriarchal system comes in at the Symbolic stage and it silences women. They are excluded and outcast as "the others". They are deprived of language because they cannot escape from the Imaginary into the Symbolic order, as males can, or, strictly, they can enter the Symbolic but only by being what they are not, which is a way of masquerade.

Paradoxically, Lacan's marginalization of women has given a boost to post-modern feminist theory. Interpretation of structuralism informs that the meaning is not an independent representation of the real world understood by an already constituted subject, but part of a system that produces meaning, the world and the possibility of a subject. If identity is a construction and not an absolute fixed reality, then this opens up immense scope for feminist thinking. In light of this, Lacan's idea of the self as fictitious can be seen as weapons for French feminism.

> "Debates in the area of feminism, sexuality and textuality have been explored and ‘dramatized’ in the work of the French feminist deconstructivists—Irigaray, Kristeva and Cixous—in their dialogue with the work of Derrida and Lacan" (Brooks, 1997:69).

Different from Freud's or Lacan's theories of sexuality particularly, which define women as negatively imaginary, incomplete, an empty signifier (the vacant womb), French feminists, Irigaray in particular, view feminine sexuality as either subordinate to the needs and desires of men (imagined sexuality by men) or autonomous and explorable only within a radically separatist women's movement (a schizoid duality). The reason for this choice, according to Irigaray, is that women have been put in the schizoid position of being simultaneously *in* history and *not* in history—"written out" of history by male theory.

Irigaray's style of writing is experimentally feminine, "sexism in language" (Humm, 1995:258). She articulates,

> "Not to mention her language in which ‘she’ sets off in all directions leaving ‘him’ unable to discern the coherence of any meaning. Hers are contradictory words, somewhat mad from the standpoint of reason, inaudible for whoever listens to them with ready-made grids, with a fully elaborated code in hand. For in what she says, too, at least when she dares, woman is constantly touching herself. She steps ever so slightly aside from herself with

a murmur, an exclamation, a whisper, a sentence left unfinished ⋯ When she returns, it is to set off again from elsewhere. From another point of pleasure, or of pain. One would have to listen with another ear, as if hearing an 'other meaning' always in the process of weaving itself, of embracing itself with words, but also of getting rid of words in order not to become fixed, congealed in them. " (1981:103)

This peculiar style can be defined as women's body language or feminist vocabulary which can further be defined as different semantic usage.

"The relatively secure meanings of 'ordinary' language are harassed and disrupted by this flow of signification, which presses the linguistic sign to its extreme limit, values its tonal, rhythmic and material properties, and sets up a play of unconscious drives in the text which threatens to split apart received social meanings" (Eagleton, 1996:163).

Like *ecriture feminine*, the language of Irigaray's *parle femme* can be regarded as the explanation of "female physiology", something worth celebrating for women.

Technically, Irigaray tries to dismantle phallocentric language by adapting the strategy of mimetism, grammatical alteration and a method of "excess". Burke says,

"Like Derrida, Irigaray underscores the functions of spaces, pauses, and the white of the page in the act of reading by stressing their roles as 'figures' in signifying practice" (1994:255).

The commonality of their styles is double fold. One is in the graphic, ranging from rhythm to syntax. The other is in what "they come together" on the question of style—the manner of "deconstructive encounter of texts" (Weed, 1994:83), as can be demonstrated in most Irigaray's works.

The user of such language is seen as a kind of freedom-fighter in the linguistic environment. Because this style of writing is "transgressive, rule-transcending and intoxicated" (Barry, 1995:128), it is hard to be theorized in a conventional way. This stylistic weirdness is sometimes compared to e. e. cummings or James Joyce, namely, avant-garde or experimental style characteristic of distortion and free manipulation of linguistic devices (Hu, 1997: 25-26). However, in view of Irigaray, this language derives from women's sexual difference. This language difference, according to modern linguistics, is classified as one of "semantic usage in women's genderlects" (Humm, 1995: 144).

Irigaray's "erudite background" suggests that although she is working primarily in philosophy, she is also a psychoanalyst and linguist at the same time (Whitford, 1990: 106). The reason that she was expelled from Lacanian "school" is because of her outspoken critiques. Like Cixous, Irigaray advocates the possibility of feminist writing which has always been radical and controversial. Feminist writing is probably the first theory to rewrite most forcefully the basic concepts and reality from the standpoint of women. Thus it has revolutionary significance. Writing and language of the body seemly enable women to enter history (Zhang, 1998:105). As a "counter attack" to patriarchy, they believe that exploration of women language generates social change. Through this writing of women, by women and for women, the creation of concepts of woman culture and the establishment of new social institutions are possible.

Nevertheless, feminist writing theorized by Irigaray as a source of political inspiration is only Utopian imagination. Consequently, it has some limitations. According to Toril Moi, writing can only be used as medium for liberation, but not as instrument. As a signifying practice, the function of language is limited in changing social reality. Thus feminist writing lacks acting power (Zhang, 1998: 125). Writing of the body is not the same as social discourse because the former is a "textual strategy of essentialism" (Braidotti, 1994:124), a strategy based on the belief that essential differences between females and males are crucial for women's subjectivity, while the latter is a place where power and politics meet. Isolating sexuality from social reality results only in inefficiency in practical reform. Writing the body does not bring forth liberation of women for the reason that this writing is but psychological experimentation, "thought work", to be exact. The poetic and radical style of feminist theory is therefore powerless in dealing with political and social issues for women. Focusing on biological gender difference, Irigaray's theory is thought to be conservative in nature. Her over-emphasis on the specificity of woman's body boarders on separatism and physiological fatalism, thus causing more problems than solutions.

Irigaray gives language predominance over social and political issues. As a matter of fact, differences of sexes are "the rhetoric of difference" (Humm, 1995:39) that women come to realize from their bodies. Therefore, differences of body are dwarfed when compared with differences of races, classes, geographies and nationalities. Based on the theory of sexuality, Irigaray's attempt to generalize women of different situations regardless of these differences is characteristic of undesirable universalism.

Influenced by previous thinkers, Irigaray creates a fantastical philosophical genealogy or "feminist counter genealogies" (Braidotti, 1994: 121). With obviously Nietzschean style,

> "Her texts create a symbolic position for women in culture and elaborate sexual difference as the major philosophical issue of our age" (Martin, 1999:247).

She advocates that by establishing the subjectivity of women through representation and experience, they can find their place in human civilization and history.

Looking back in history, the record of the achievement of men and the civilizations they have built indicates that much of the world has been patriarchal. In historical accounts, very little is recorded about the thoughts, feelings and achievements of women. Indeed, women have been regarded hardly better than childbearers. "The problem", according to Irigaray, "gravitates around the fact that man has defined himself with reference to his own genre, and in so doing believed his divine to be representative of the whole of the genre human" (Martin, 1995:135).

"For woman is traditionally a use-value for man, an exchange value among men; in other words, a commodity. As such, she remains the guardian of material substance, whose price will be established, in terms of the standard of their work and of their need/desire, by 'subjects': workers, merchants, consumers. Women are marked phallically by their fathers, husbands, procurers. And this branding determines their value in sexual commerce. Woman is never anything but the locus of a more or less competitive exchange between two men, including the competition for the possession of mother earth" (1981: 104).

A statement by a lexicographer makes it clear:

"Properly speaking, a man is not married to a woman, or married with her; nor are a man and woman married with each other. The woman is married to the man…we do not speak of tying a ship to a boat, but a boat to a ship. And as long as woman generally lives in her husband's house and bears his name—still more should she not bear his name—it is the woman who is married to the man" (White, 1891:140) (Qin, 1996:20)[1].

Etymologically, this Latin word "maritare" meaning "to marry" or "married" is neutral with no preference in either males or females. For the reason that this viewpoint of Richard White is also mistakenly shared by other lexicographers, such as Noah Webster (1828), Walter W. Skeat (1918) and Ernest Weekley (1921), the prejudiced concept of matrimony remains to date (Ibid).

Against historical background of patriarchy, Irigaray believes that the mother-daughter relationship is vitally important. She regards this relationship as one of divinity. The significance of the relationship lies in its potential of establishing female as subject (Martin, 1999:248). In the process, the earlier traditional analysis of "mother" and natural function of "mother" is challenged and the double bind of the maternal issue is stressed. Therefore, motherhood becomes a weapon powerful both in patriarchal domination of women and for the strongholds of female identity. Luisa Muraro thus comments,

> "According to Irigaray, the genealogical link serves to symbolize what takes place between mother and daughter, allowing us to overcome the patriarchal regime of lack of differentiation and rivalry between women" (Muraro, 1994:324).

The theme of divinity is a crucial aspect of Irigaray's mimetic strategy for the possibilities of "women-becoming-subjects". For the male, the subjectivity is ensured by the Father-God. For the female, she "has no God, no divine, no goal. Without a God, what becomes of her will? To the extent that it can be said to be hers at all, it is a kind of amorphous meandering at best a passive nihilism ···" (Martin, 1995:135).

Therefore, a different concept of the divine is necessary for female subjectivity, that is, the divine relationship of the mother-daughter which is believed to realize female subjectivity. This notion of the divine for women prevents the dissembling of the mother-daughter relationship and keeps their self-reliance.

By revealing a concealed masculine bias in tradition and history, French feminist writing criticizes the gender structure of society. Irigaray's framework of genealogy of women is particularly useful in this aspect. In this framework, the relationship among women is subject to subject, rather than a negative copy shadowed by men. Feminist writing, as an anti-rational measure, brings plenty of pleasure and strength for women, with which they can create the future at their will.

In "The 'Mechanics' of Fluids", Irigaray elaborates the rhetorical feature of "fluidity". Irigaray suggests that female fluidity is what "leaks out" or "flows" out of the discourse of masculinity. The nature of woman's speech is fluid and hysterical as opposed to the straight-forward and rigid characteristics of the phallocentric. She interrogates,

> "Must this multiplicity of female desire and female language be understood as shards, scattered remnants of a violated sexuality? A Sexuality denied? The question has no simple answer. The rejection, the exclusion of a female imaginary certainly puts woman in the position of experiencing herself only fragmentarily, in the little-structured margins of a dominant ideology, as waste, or excess, what is left of a mirror invested by the (masculine) subject to reflect himself, to copy himself." (1981:103)

Among numerous ways of approaching Irigaray, according to Margaret

Whitford, two are outstanding. One is that she is seen as a biological essentialist, which suggests that there is an essential feminine difference deriving from biological differences. The performing of the difference is repressed by patriarchy. By "proclaiming a biological-given femininity", biology can somehow establish femininity. The other is the reading of Irigaray as a "psychic essentialist" within the theoretic framework of Lacan. This reading proposes that due to Irigaray's misunderstanding and misrepresenting of the major concepts of Lacan's theories, the issue of the feminine is misplaced in the stage of "a pre-given libido, prior to language". Thus specific female drives are found that posit "two distinct libidos—a masculine and a feminine" (Whitford 1990:107). The highlight by Whitford on the two approaches is of great importance. It suggests that Irigaray's theory of feminism is not a rationalist project. Rather, it is a historical break-through in terms of theory and practice in the postmodern times. It is believed that development of feminism today has entered a transitional period. The mode of postmodern feminism, in sociological terms, is still "up for grabs". For Irigaray, deconstruction is only a central theme in her analytic theory. Her commitment to feminist politics is the propaganda of theory of difference, i. e. motivations enabling women to develop "a separatist space" (Brooks, 1997:80).

As a feminist philosopher, Irigaray firmly rejects feminist ambition of equality "as an intelligible goal for women, on the grounds that the conditions for its intelligibility have not yet been met" (Whitford, 1994:380). The reason, for Irigaray, is that the desire to be equal to men does not mean a shift of binary structure of dominating and dominated, nor to engage desire attached to women. The achievement of equality may bring some necessary, temporary gains, but they will only mean that women are participating in the reproduction process of patriarchy. As a strategy, Irigaray agrees to women struggling for equal rights (Ibid). In a long run, effort for equality by women only "contributes to the erasure (effacement) of natural and spiritual reality in an abstract universal which is in service of a single master: death" (Ibid). The problem is that the poor and underdevelopment arising from women's submission by and to a culture that oppresses them makes of them a medium of exchange, with heavy exploitation. Women are only living in the possibility of the "quasi monopolies of masochistic pleasure, the domestic labor force, and reproduction" (104).

The idea of Irigaray is that women should be encouraged to be strategic about their undertakings. They need to be tactical in keep themselves separated from men for the benefit of defending their own desires. In terms of language acquisition, they should try to formulate their own language, and to

> "discover the love of other women while sheltered from men's imperious choices that put them in the position of rival commodities, to forge for themselves a social status that compels recognition, to earn their living in order to escape from the commodities of prostitute" (105).

For Irigaray, in order for them to obtain a favorable position on the "exchange market" and to avoid their proletarianization, women are in the need of breaking through these indispensable stages. The dilemma will appear: it is by no means desirable that the order of things should be reversed, because in so doing, "history would repeat itself in the long run, would revert to sameness: to phallocratism. It would leave roots neither for women's sexuality, nor for women's imaginary, nor for women's language to take their place" (105). In view of this, it can be concluded that Irigaray shares a deconstructionist notion with other French feminists in understanding that there is no subject beyond the fixed categories of gender and that woman is in the process of becoming.

NOTE

[1] In an article entitled "A Historical Study on the Gender Differences in the English Language—A Review of Grammar and Gender", published in

Journal of Modern Language, in 1996, in China, Qin Xiubei, a well-known Chinese linguist and educator, discusses etymologies of some English words, such as "woman", "wife", "marry" by drawing authoritative references form well-known lexicographers: Nathan Bailey, Charles Richardson and Joseph Emerson Worcester, to name but a few.

REFERENCES

Bennett, Andrew and Nicholas Royle. *An Introduction to Literature, Criticism and Theory: Key Critical Concepts* (1995). Hertfordshire: Prentice Hall / Harvester Wheatsheaf.

Brooks, Ann. *Postfeminism: Feminism, Cultural Theory and Cultural Forms* (1997). London: Routledge.

Barry, Peter. *Beginning Theory—An Introduction to Literary and Cultural Theory* (1995). Manchester: Manchester University Press.

Braidotti, Rosi. "Of Bugs and Women: Irigaray and Deleuze on the Becoming-Woman", *Engaging with Irigaray* (1994), ed. Carolyn Burke et al. New York: Columbia University Press.

Burke, Carolyn. "Translation Modified: Irigaray in English", *Engaging with Irigaray* (1994). ed. Carolyn Burke et al. New York: Columbia University Press.

Eagleton, Terry. *Literary Theory —An Introduction* (1997). 2nd Edition. Oxford: Blackwell Publishers.

Humm, Maggie. *The Dictionary of Feminist Theory* (1995). 2nd Edition. Hertfordshire: Prentice Hall / Harvester Wheatsheaf.

Hu, Quansheng. "A Comparative Study on American and French Feminist Criticism", *Journal of Foreign Literature* (1997, No. 1).

Irigaray, Luce. *This Sex Which Is Not One*, Translated by Claudia Reeder, in *New Feminisms*, ed. Elaine Marks and Isabelle de Courtivron (1981). New York: Cornell University Press.

Martin, Alison. "Luce Irigaray and Divine Matter", *Women and*

Representation (1995). ed. Diana Knight and Judith Still. Nottingham: WIF Publishers.

Martin, Bestsan. "Luce Irigaray", *Dictionary of Cultural Theorists* (1999). ed. Ellis Cashmore & Chris Rojek, London: Edward Arnold (Publishers) Ltd.

Muraro, Luisa. "Female Genealogies", *Engaging with Irigaray* (1994). ed. Carolyn Burke et al. New York: Columbia University Press.

Qin, Xiubei. "A Historical Study on the Gender Differences in the English Language", *Journal of Modern Foreign Languages* (1996, No. 2).

Storey, John. *An Introduction to Cultural Theory and Popular Culture* (1997), 2nd Edition. Hertfordshire: Prentice Hall / Harvester Wheatsheaf.

Whitfofd, Margaret. "Rereading Irigaray", *Between Feminism and Psychoanalysis* (1990). ed. Teresa Brennan. London: Routledge.

Whitford, Margaret. "Irigaray, Utopia, and the Death Drive", *Engaged with Irigaray* (1994). ed. Carolyn Burke et al. New York: Columbia University Press.

Zhang, Yanbing. "Criticism on the Theory of Language in French Feminism". *Journal of Fudan University* (Social Sciences Edition) (1998, No. 2).

China's "Cultural Fever"
in the Global Context

It is argued that the culture fever in the 1980s and 1990s is the reflection of traditional culture vis-a-vis social and cultural crisis and realization of the need to learn from Western cultures. What many Chinese intellectuals have yet to cultivate is a new sense of nationalism that would combine traditional values with the cultural essence of the modern world, particularly of the Western countries. Only through cross-cultural dialogue, can the Chinese communicate with the Westerners better and understand each other better. As a local identity, Chinese culture can be and should be part of global culture. And those who hold that Chinese culture may serve a critique of the discourse of globalization are ignorant of Chinese history and the tradition of cultural exchange between Chinese people and the peoples of the world.

A brief account of scientific and cultural interchange between China and the world is necessary to illustrate the point. In his monumental work *Science and Civilization in China*, Joseph Needham breaks new ground by presenting to the Western reader a detailed and coherent account of the development of science, technology and culture in China from the earliest times until the advent of the Jesuits and the beginnings of the modern science in the late seventeenth century. Dr. Needham also devoted much discussion on how scientific knowledge traveled between China and Europe, between China and the rest of the world, under such titles as "The Continuity of Chinese with Western Civilization", "Trade-routes between China and the West", "The Old Silk Road", "Chinese-Western Cultural and Scientific Contacts", "Chinese-Indian Cultural and Scientific Contacts", "Chinese-Arab Cultural and Scientific Contacts", etc. (Ronan and Needham, 1978). Equally important is the conviction of Joseph Needham and his writing collaborators that the contribution of Chinese science and culture to the humankind is a great one. The same can be said for Western science and culture. The "coarse racial classification of world peoples" (Diamond, 1998: 323) and its negative cultural implications should be abolished.

"No single people or group of peoples has had a monopoly in contributing the development and progress of humankind. All achievements should be recognized, and celebrated, if we are to move on our way to a universal brotherhood of Man" (Ronan, 1978:4).

Current debate on the Chinese cultural realities presents a picture which is quite thought-provoking. The focus of the discussion is placed on the relationship between traditional culture and its modernization in the era of globalization. One of the most popular culturalist approaches in China and abroad preaches that Chinese culture, dominated by the heritage of Confucianism, should exercise more influence on the cultures of the world, if not Confucianizing the world. However, in a long historical period of time, Confucianism itself has been rewritten and reconstituted by the intellectual elite and the cultural power blocs. Modern Confucian discourse is regarded as an integral part of the ideology of capitalist globalization.

"The best example of this is Japanese and East Asian manufacturing success and the contribution to this of particular cultural influences, principally consisting of Confucian (or post-Confucian) socialization process and institutionalized forms of social group. These have been significant in the development of organizational innovations" (Spybey, 1996:154-5).

Tu Wei-ming, a modern Confucian scholar of Harvard, confirms,

"There is strong evidence to show that the dynamic cultural forms enhancing economic productivity that industrial East Asia assumed have benefited from Confucian ethics" (Tu, 1991, quoting from Axtmann, 1997: 40).

Numerous other theorists of the West (Herman Kahn, 179; Roderick Macfarquhar, 1980; Peter Berger, 1983) emphasize greatly on the practical values of traditional Chinese culture. They attribute the economical miracles of East Asian countries to the influences of the legacy of Confucianism. They propose a "post-Confucian hypothesis", claiming that if Western individualism is a driving force for industrial development at the early stage, the Confucian collectivism and social mores are more suitable for the contemporary mass production. While recognizing the values of the "small traditions", they believe that there exist "two different kinds of modernization": the Western style modernization originated from Christianity and the East Asian modernization rooted in Confucian thought. In January 1988, seventy-five Nobel Prize laureates made a joint statement in Paris, calling for drawing wisdom from Confucianism, the founder of which lived more than 2000 years ago.

The overbearing attention to Confucianism is causing some puzzling problems in its home country. The revival of new Confucianism started in Hong Kong, Taiwan and Thailand after the liberation of China in 1949. For a long time after the liberation, Confucianism was seen as a "reactionary cultural force" and "feudalist junk". It was criticized heavily by both the State ideology and the masses. Then in the 1970s and 1980s, New Confucianism became popular as a global discourse owing to the promotion of some North American academics who were former students of Hong Kong and Taiwan Neo-Confucian masters, as well as to the official endorsements from the governments and authorities of Taiwan, Singapore, and South Korea.

In October 1994, an international conference on Confucianism was convened for the first time in Beijing. The participating countries and regions were Singapore, Taiwan, South Korea, Japan, Germany, United States, etc. The conference also drew the attention of the CPC and the State leadership. The head of the State met the delegates of the conference at the reception dinner and one State official was named President of the newly-established Confucian Association (Liu, 1998: 172; Spybey, 1996:69). The Beijing conference on Confucianism is by no means co-incidental, for it provides a great chance to promote "traditional culture" and mass education of patriotism, which is a composite part of "cultural nationalism" and "national learning". The State at the same time took the opportunity to launch a nationwide education of patriotism, which was more significant for the younger generation. The ideological nature of the event is obvious because in Chinese political discourse "patriotism and socialism are identical" (*Jiang's Speech on Education in Patriotism*, October 1996) in China's reform era. Further, besides theory of building "socialism with Chinese characteristics", the important contents of patriotism actually include efforts to "raise the national self-esteem and sense of pride among people nationwide", and "to carry forward the fine practice of viewing the love of the motherland and contributing all energy to building the motherland as the highest glory" as well as to follow "the tendency of viewing the impairment to the motherland's interests and dignity as the worst disgrace" (Ibid).

Therefore, in the Chinese cultural situation, Confucianism, traditional culture, national learning are generally progressing in the same direction. The fact that these cultural trends stay in harmony is because they are "politically correct" and development of them is one consequence of global capitalism. The rise of Confucianism and over-attachment to the traditional culture can be problematic in China, since they can be used to boost false romanticization of the historical past. In terms of the practical values of traditional culture, there can be a lot of debate on their feasibility and practical application for modern initiatives. Although glorious in history, traditional Chinese culture, which is historically defined before the time of the Opium War, is arguably not practicable in modern times due to its internal closure and lack of transformational generative capabilities. More doubtful is the claim that the Oriental or Chinese culture can be used to "save" the world.

A series of discussion taken place in the People's University of China in 1998 have clarified many ideas. [2] The most prominent aspect of the discussion is serious reflection of modern Chinese history and scientific treatment of traditional Chinese culture. Some concluded that modern history of China is essentially a history of adopting modern science and culture of foreign countries because classical Chinese culture or Confucianism has little connection with the history of modern science (Fang, 1998: 46). The humiliating defeat of the "middle kingdom" in the Opium War and Sino-Japanese War is clear testimony of the historical fact. From mid-19th century onwards, the elder generation of Chinese learned a lesson from backwardness and abandoned the imperial view of "the empire of all under heaven" (Ronan, 1978), and thus began searching for a viable dream of a strong China. The slogan then was "learn from foreigners and make oneself strong" ("shiyi zhangji"). Kang Youwei wished to copy the Japanese model and establish the "constitutional monarchy" in China; Dr. Sun Yat-sen dreamed of a republic similar to that of the United States of America. He drafted "Outlined Plans for China's Reconstruction" and even succeeded in the initial stage; Mao Zedong and his comrades cherished communist revolution and he succeeded in the founding of the People's Republic of China in 1949, which is in actual fact an evolutionary institution of the prototype of the Soviet socialism in Russia.

Chinese cultural theorists further investigated the features of current relationship between Chinese culture and foreign cultures to show Western influence. At the level of material culture, mass production and high technology are the important components of industrial formation of modern China. This can be treated as the continuum of the movement of learning modern science and technology of the Western countries in the mid-19th century rather than carrying on "artistic and agricultural" traditions (*Journal of Cultural Research*, No. 10, 1998, p. 43). To a great extent, Chinese institutional culture and mental culture are also imported from abroad. Its socialist system and the People's Congress are essentially the reformed polity on the basis of the models from the former Soviet Union instead of evolution from the country's feudal system. Deng Xiaoping, as successor to Mao Zedong, has made dramatic changes to the existing system and established his "theory of socialism with Chinese characteristics".

It is known to all that Marxism, the State's ideology of China, is brought home from the West by the earliest Chinese revolutionaries such as Chen Duxiu, Li Dazhao, Deng Xiaoping and Zhou Enlai. Moreover, in academic development, most subjects in natural sciences and social sciences in terms of their academic principles or structures, are introduced to China from foreign countries. The "four great inventions" in the history of China is a great pride for every Chinese but not many understand that they are mainly technological inventions rather than scientific. Similar is the discovery of ratio of the circumference of a circle to its diameter by Zu Chongzhi, the ancient Chinese mathematician whose accurate calculation of the ratio is said to be hundreds of years earlier than the Europeans (Li, 1998:151). However, it is a fact that "the Chinese suffered from a lack of deductive geometry——the very essence of precision in Greek science" (Ronan, 1978:2). Some Chinese researchers have pointed out that mathematics or scientific calculation has never been in full development in ancient China compared to the study of humanities and classical writings, because their importance never reached the height of human studies, the "millennial interest on human society" (Ibid). For this reason, they were forever marginalized in the ancient Chinese history of science and civilization. Textbooks of modern subjects are composed by "Mr. Science" and "Mr. Democracy" and they came to China only in the modern times.

In the transitional period of time, Chinese cultural discourse is becoming more and more diverse and complex. Different voices are heard concerning current directions of traditional culture and its modern application, the nationalistic writing, neo-Confucianism, post-colonialism and theory of cultural studies. In the past few years, "theory of globalization" came into fashion in China. Some introductory works as well as in-depth articles have appeared in the mass media and learned journals. Books have also been published for the demand, which can be seen as a resistance force to the spread of cultural nationalism. Discussion on the theory of globalization, globalization and post-modernism, post-colonialism and cultural studies (Wang, 1998:103-110) has drawn the participation of sociologists and cultural theorists nationwide and abroad.

It is generally agreed that we are living in an age of globalization. Useful conceptions such as "standardization", "dependency", "cosmopolitanism" are becoming the new global consciousness (Kumar, 1995:193). In an article published in a Chinese magazine *Pacific Journal*, Li Shenzhi, a cultural specialist in Beijing, offered his interpretation of the negative manipulation of nationalism emerging in some places in China. To make his point clear, Li gave a narrative account of a countryside woman who talked to her son studying in the United States on her newly installed home telephone at the Spring Festival of 1994. This woman felt sorry for her son who did part-time work in restaurants in order to pay school tuition. She encouraged her son with this word of comfort, saying "we will let them (the Westerners) come to serve out dishes for us after you have learned more knowledge and made our country stronger". Li then commented that "this is extremely vulgar nationalism which goes against both the trend of globalism and Chinese tradition" (Zhao, *The China Quarterly* , December 1997, p747).

We share Li's viewpoint that with all the countries being interdependent, the modern world has indeed become a "global village". "No man is an island". If China would like to play a bigger role in the future, it should follow the dominant trend of globalization and become a part of the whole, for an attempt to "reinvent the wheel" is impossible (Ibid). China should become more aware of what is happening outside its territory, make efforts to persist in opening-up, conscientiously learn the strong points of other nations around the world, and actively introduce advanced science and technology, managerial expertise, to enhance capability of the country and accelerate its development in all walks of life. Similarly, as far as cultures of globalization are concerned, Chinese culture should also follow the course of reform, opening-up and drive to modernization. It can shine with new splendor only through learning from cultures of the world and revitalize itself by benefiting from cultural communication.

NOTE

[1] The following titles are relevant: Luo Chuanfang, "Looking at Oriental Culture from a New Angle", *Chinese Cultural Newspaper*, 9 September, 1998; Fang Keli, "Western and Eastern Cultures in the Twentieth Century", *Chinese Cultural Research*, Winter Vol. 1997; Feng Tianyu, "Reflections on Cultural Transformation at the Thrshold of the New Century", *Chinese Cultural Research*, Summer Vol. 1997; Han Minqing, "Global Cultural Development and the Rise of Chinese Culture", *Chinese Cultural Research*, Summer Vol. 1997; Wang Desheng, "Cultural Transformation, Popular Culture and Postmodernism" *Shanghai Artist*, No. 5, 1998; Lai Xinxia, "Creating New Culture in the New

Century", *Oriental Culture*, No. 1, 1998; Ning Zongyi, "The 21st Century: Can Oriental Culture Be Dominant?", *Oriental Culture*, No. 1, 1998; Li Shenzhi, "My View of Oriental and Occidental Cultures", *Tianjin Social Sciences*, No. 1, 1998; Zhong Rui, "Is the 21st Century the Times of Oriental Culture? — Comments on Ji Xianlin's 'Theory of Cultural Replacement'", *Oriental Culture*, No. 3 1998; Wang Ning, "Cultural Studies: The West and China", *Foreign Literature Research*, No. 9, 1998; Wang Ning, "Postmodernity and the Challenge of Chinese Popular Culture", *Chinese Cultural Research*, Autumn Vol. 1997; J. Hillis Miller, "Globalization and Its Influences on Literary Research", *Contemporary Foreign Literature*, No. 1, 1998, etc.

[2] The pen talks on "Modern Transformation of Chinese Traditional Culture" by Cheng Fuwang, Yuan Jixi, Jin Yuanpu, Zhang Fa (The People's University of China, Beijing), Fang Delin (Beijing University), and Dou Zongyi (Atlantic University of America, USA), *Humanities Magazine*, No. 4, 1998, Xian; and Goa Bingzhong, "Meeting and Mixing of Chinese and World Culture", *Chinese Cultural Research*, No. 14, Winter Vol., 1996, Beijing.

REFERENCES

Axtmann, Poland. "Collective Identity and the Democratic Nation-State in the Age of Globalization" *Articulating the Global and the Local* (1997). Colorado: Westview Press.

Diamond, Jared. *Guns, Germs and Steel* (1997). London: Jonathan Cape.

Kumar, Krishan. *From Post-industrial to Post-modern Society* (1995). Oxford: Blackwell Publishers Ltd.

Liu, Kang. "Is There an Alternative to (Capitalist) Globalization? The Debate about Modernity in China" *The Cultures of Globalization* (1998). Ed. Fredric Jameson and Masao Miyoshi. Durham: Duke University Press.

Li, Zonggui. *A Survey of Chinese Culture* (1998). Guangzhou: Sun Yat-sen University Press.

Ronan, Colin A. and Joseph Needham. *The Shorter Science and Civilization in China: An Abridgment by Colin A. Ronan of Joseph Needham's Original Text* (1978). Cambridge: Cambridge University Press.

Spybey, Tony. *Globalization and World Society* (1996). Cambridge: Polity Press.

Wang, Ning. *Globalization and Postcolonial Criticism* (1999). Beijing: Chinese Social Science Press.

Globality and Cultural Trends
in Contemporary China

Introduction

Globalisation is becoming a fashionable term in China after the country joined WTO. Though widely used, its concept is from time to time misunderstood, for we often think of it in terms of economic connections and financial activities. The process of globalisation is, in actual fact, driven by a mixture of cultural, economic and political influences and covers a much wider complex area. With discourse of globalisation comes the question of identity. The problem arises once we perceived identity as fixed, natural and timeless. Such a conception makes it unlikely for contested and pluralized identities to emerge. In spite of the fact that global forces can be oppressive and erode traditions and identities, they can also provide new framework for people to rework or create identities. Discussion on globalisation and cultural identity is of great significance in contemporary Chinese context, as the country is getting more and more involved in the process of globalization.

Globalization is a term widely used nowadays, from political speech to business manual. Everyone talks about it, though it is not yet clear what we are talking about. The word has sometimes become vague and meaningless because it is often misused even abused. Globalization, as a general concept for describing the ever-intensifying networks of cross-border human interaction, covers a great variety of social, economic and cultural change. It is therefore not surprising that different disciplines have assigned different meanings to it and that this has led to often heated debates on various interpretations of its broad theme. However, globalization as an influential area of academic inquiry is essentially discussed in humanities and social sciences. The problem is that the scientific discussion of globalization is hampered by the multidimensional and multidisciplinary characteristics of its content as well as by the daily use of the term in popular magazines and mass media. It is not easy for anyone talking about globalization not to generalize or articulate it in stereotypes. Nevertheless, the huge and fast-growing literature on the subject demonstrates that the theoretical study of globalization is flourishing in China and abroad.

According to Hoogvelt, many of the disputable opinions on globalization arise from a confusion of globalization with its precursor movements, namely, internationalization (as processes involving the simple extension of economic activities across national boundaries) and transnationalization (as in the increasing organization of production on a cross-border basis by multinational organizations) (1997:114). Robertson's concept of globalization focuses on an intensified compression of the world and people's increasing consciousness of the world with the ever-increasing abundance of global connections and general spread of global phenomena. In his view, globalization can suitably be seen as "compression of the world" and understood in terms of the institutions of modernity. Moreover, the globality of modernity can also be interpreted as a cultural norm (1992). Following this line of thinking, one can differentiate between a view of culture as bounded, tied to a specific location and inward-looking, and one in which culture is regarded as outward-looking "translocal learning process", as Pieterse suggests:

"Introverted cultures, which have been prominent over along stretch of history and which overshadowed translocal culture, are gradually receding into the background, which translocal culture made up of diverse elements is coming to the foreground" (Pieterse, 1995:62).

Tony Spybey argues that globalization in its structural dimensions can be regarded principally as nation-state system, global economy, global communication system, cultural spreading, world military order and other internationally dispersed activities (1996:5). In different terms but essentially similar implications, Appadurai (1993) has mentioned the five important features of global conditions in contemporary era, which are termed as the "disjunctive" flows of ethnoscapes, technoscapes, finanscapas, mediascapes and ideoscapes. In other words, globalization involves the dynamic movements of ethnic groups, technology, financial transactions, media images and ideological conflicts which are not strictly controlled by one single dominant "master plan". Rather, the speed, scope and impact of these flows are not smoothly or harmoniously interrelated.

Among numerous ways of defining globalization, Anthony Giddens definition is probably one of the most well-known: "Globalization can thus be defined as the intensification of worldwide social relations which link distant localities in such a way that local happenings are shaped by events occurring many miles away and vice versa" (1990:64).

Giddens' remarks on globalization may be interpreted as that on our planet Earth it is virtually impossible for anyone to be engaged in social activities without being influenced by ideologies and institutions of global nature in one way or another. It can therefore be realized from this point of view that globalization cannot be interpreted only in terms of economic interdependence or the simple extension of economic activities across national boundaries. Rather, the process of globalization is motivated by a mixture of cultural, economic and political influences. This process transforms social and cultural institutions even in the poorest regions of the world. But, globalization as economic, social and cultural process is never even or uniform. In actual fact, different nations and different social groups have different experiences of globalization. Some countries or regions are naturally more active, more engaged and more affected than others. Specifically, the effects of globalization process, may they be positive or negative, are especially significant in developing countries, such as the People's Republic of China. The global trends in all walks of life, especially in contemporary popular cultures, reflect that China, after having shut itself against the outside world, has merged into the world society to a considerable extent.

There appears to be a gap between China and the West in the field of theoretical research on globalization. Comparatively, academic global study in the West is more active than that in China and that the quantity of literature on globalization in the West is larger. Some of the new terms such as *guojihua* (internationalisation), *yitihua* (integration), *xianghu yicun* (interdependency) (Yang & Wang, 1998) have come into fashion in China only in recent times, which indicates that more and more people have begun to know the importance and immediacies of globalization.

Probably it is unfortunate to note that although most traditional Marxist classics have carefully been studied in Chinese scholastic traditions, due attention may not have been given to the original comments on globalization by the "great teachers of the proletariat". In "The Communist Manifesto", Marx and Engels claimed:

"Modern industry has established the world market, for which the discovery of America pave the way⋯[The] need of a constantly expanding market for its products chases the bourgeoisie over the whole surface of the globe. It must nestle everywhere, settle everywhere, establish connections everywhere⋯The bourgeoisie, by the rapid improvement of all instruments of production, by the immensely facilitated means of communication, draws all, even the most barbarian nations into civilisation⋯In a word, it creates a world after its own image." (Marx and Engels, quoting from Cvetkovich & Kellner, 1997:4-5)

The driving force of the capitalist market, as Marx and Engels saw it, was the main reason of globalizing process. The imposition of the process is not only confined in economic activities, but in many other aspects. The global capitalism " generated immense forces of commerce, navigation and discovery, communications, and industry, creating a new world of abundance, diversity, and prosperity" (Ibid). On the basis of the above statement, we may question the correctness of what Lenin said about capitalism. Lenin concluded that imperialism was a decadent and dying capitalism. This conclusion is actually regarded not to be in accord with reality. Lenin is still a great teacher just like Marx and Engels in Chinese past and present, but we must not make a fetish of every word he said.

With regard to identity, it has come to the forefront of attention only in recent time as an opposing and embracing operation to globalization (Rajchman, 1995). In spite of the fact that there is no reference to identity in Raymond Williams' *Keywords* (1983), it has now become a key concept and an important field of theoretical study. As to the significance of discussion on identity, perhaps it is not so far-fetched to refer to Xunzi, an ancient Chinese philosopher, who said that men cannot but band in groups, but groups without differentiated identities shall contend. Contention brews disorder, disorder brews separation,

separation reduces their strength and results in chaos. The Chinese legacy of "harmony allowing diversity" thousands of years ago remains practical for the topical discussions on almost every aspect of the broad theme of identity at conferences and seminars, in books and articles. Generally, these theoretical studies on identity are associated with theories of postmodernism and globalization. On the one hand, as a form of resistance, emphasis on identity has emerged as a response to homogenizing global forces. On the other hand, as a generative force, ever-proliferating globalization produces new configurations of identity—national, local, and cultural. The flow of products, culture, capital, and information is accompanied by flows of people and emigration (Sarup, 1996: 1; Lash and Urry, 1994:171). A transnational diaspora from every continent involving vast migrations of peoples and individuals produces the conditions for new transnational hybridized cultures and identities. Tendencies of "blending culture and capital" with specified functions of "regulating spaces, exercising aesthetic control, and producing historical narratives and images" are in fact originated from localities (Edensor, 1997:176). Due to the fact that modern society is undergoing constant, rapid and permanent change, it is argued that there is gradual disappearance of traditional and highly valued frames of reference in terms of which people could define themselves and their place in society, and so feel relatively secure in their personal and collective identities. Traditional sources of identity—social class, national and local cultures, local communities, the "neighborhood", religion, the nation state—are said to be weakened as a result of tendencies in modern capitalism. The present debates about identity are situated "within all those historically specific developments and practices which have disturbed the relatively 'settled' character of many populations and cultures, above all in relation to the processes of globalization" (Hall, 1996:4). Mass production, marketing and distribution taking place on an international basis is seen as an important reason for the gradual erosion of these traditional sources of identity. Transnational processes erode the significance of local and national identities. Stuart Hall indicates that the old identities which have kept the social world stable for a long time are now declining while new identities are emerging and fragmenting the modern individuals as a unified subject (1996: 596). Grossberg remarks that "the modern transforms all relations of identity into relations of difference. Thus, the modern constitutes not identity out of difference but difference out of identity" (1997:93).

Today's global instantaneous electronic communication, the intensification of social activities and growing transnational exchange all contribute to "the growing immediacy of global space and time" (Strinati, 1995:226) and the reformation of new identities.

> "Capitalist reorganisation, the concentration of corporate mass media, a new globalisation of capital and communications and information technologies, and the emergence of new kinds of politics and social movements underlie the demarcation and formation of a new and multilayered cultural terrain. " (Donn, 1998:107)

As a consequence of global changes, it is believed that traditional identities have gradually passed into history while newly-emerged ones take their places. However, the relationship between globalization and localization or local identities is never harmonious. They are constantly engaged in the play of power. The global has been theorized as

> "[Matrix]oftransnational economic, political, and cultural forces that are circulating throughout the globe and producing universal, global conditions, often transversing and even erasing previously formed national and regional boundaries. But the concept of the global also includes those constituents of class, gender, and race that cut across local differences and that provide fundamental axes of power and subordination, constituting the structures around which contemporary societies are organised . " (Cvetkovich

& Kellner, 1997:14)

Therefore, the global and the local are balanced by the level of participation, inclusion and exclusion of ones over the others. Against the background of global capitalism, the logical concepts of economic mechanisms, such as "the winner is the best", "the survival of the fittest" and "natural selection and ruthless elimination", are not only applied effectively in global economy, but also in identity formation and construction. Some identities are weakened and excluded while other identities are developed and strengthened. In some cases, the whole new identities could even be created out of hybridization. Meanwhile, globalization on its own part, has served to increase the range of sources and resources available for identity construction, allowing for the production of multiple identities in the context of a postmodern society.

Discussion on cultural identity concerns the confluence of global culture with local and national culture. The global trends and local variations place a great strain on older concepts of a national and regional culture. A global media culture provides new sources for pleasures and identities that redefine gender, fantasies and new cultural experiences. These lead to the fragmentation of traditional identities, subjectivities and the construction of new identities. Obviously, the intersection of the global and the local is producing new matrixes to legitimize the production of hybrid identities. In other words, the global permeates the local and new configurations emerge that synthesize both poles, creating "contradictory forces of neocolonization and resistance, global homogenization and new local hybrid forms and identities" (Yu, 1998). Although global forces can be oppressive and erode cultural traditions and identities they can also provide new material to rework one's identity and can make people well equipped to create more new ones.

The process of globalisation keeps pace with the notion of postmodernity or "late modernity" in Giddens' alternative view. The impact of theories of globalization and postmodernist thinking, for instance, is great and far-reaching in that the discourse of globalization and postmodernity offers a new way to view the world. In Chinese context, globalization is a remarkable opportunity to update the basic questions concerning the new cultural identities and emerging cultural trends. In cultural field, there have been more changes than alterations in the official policy concerning the "mainstream", the "high" and popular cultures with a result that a general blurring appears among them (Wang, 1999). Specifically, the proponents of global and postmodern theme detect a major shift in the cultural landscape in which existing symbolic hierarchies are deconstructed and a more playful, popular democratic impulse becomes manifest. The blurring of traditional divide between serious culture and popular culture becomes most obvious. Literary and cultural study on mass culture, women literature, theme park, soap opera, internet and postmodernism is drawing more attention in China's academia. Cultural realities in the country abundantly demonstrate that the much talked-about "paradigm shift" is no longer merely a wishful thinking or hot air. They provide us with convincing examples of some new directions, subjects of investigations and reading strategies. Qian Zhongwen remarks:

> "Nowadays, interdisciplinary literary criticism not only involves the humanities but also penetrates into a large domain-social sciences, and even science and technology-where consensus and discrepancies should go alongside to combine cultural studies with literary criticism, abandon unitary literary criticism and establish multi-polar literary theories." (August, 2000)

Therefore, cultural patterns in the new era will be constructed in the process of meeting, mixing, confirming and supplementing of different culture media and norms. With the influence of the globalization of cultures and the formation of a new world system, China is witnessing a "cultural movement" characterized by one "fever" after another. Against the background of global capitalism, the above mentioned logical concepts of economic mechanism are not only applied effectively in economic activities, but also in cultural development. The hegemony of Chinese mainstream culture may still be influential, but the emerging popular culture identities have managed to make a strong presence. More and more people have changed their attitudes towards consumer culture with the result that cultural studies has recently become a fashionable interdisciplinary inquiry and multiculturalism, a much debatable theory.

The rise of popular culture in China is accompanied by globalization trends and "the market economy increasingly penetrating into all realms of social life and consumption starting to manipulate and generate desire" (Tang, 1993: 286). According to Hebdige, "popular culture" or "commercial culture" can be defined as "a set of generally available artifacts: film, records, clothes, TV programs, modes of transport, etc." (Strinati, 1995: xvii). "Popular culture" is often billed as "market culture" in Chinese context, as opposed to the "mainstream" culture—works about the State ideology, the "main theme" culture—works highlighting the leadership of the Party, the revolutionary traditions and the socialist spiritual civilization, and the 'intellectual culture' which is usually of "high-brow" works enriched with "deep thought" and "elegance" (Meng, 1997: 23). The fact that popular culture makes use of modern media such as TV, film, video, electronic print, etc. is responsible for its popularity. Popular culture as newly-emerged cultural identity is obviously achieving more and more presence in the cultural market.

In China, the emergence of new cultural identities such as the 'popular' indicates competition with the mainstream cultural values and challenges to the canon. For instance, compared with classical music and traditional drama, imported MTV and *karaoke*, are more welcome. The reason is that they not only fulfill many people's desire to sing "pop songs" but also satisfy people's need of cultural participation, and of staging and performing cultural identities in fashion. A foreign critic notes that "the *karaoke* machine, though not quite as fashionable in the West as it used to be, can be found in the centers of entertainment all around the world—even in small and remote Chinese villages. " (Spybey, 1996: 84)

What makes it fascinating is the double function of this cross-media. MTV, an imported cultural form from America via Hong Kong, is now being transformed into a propaganda device for the service of the Party and the State ideology.

"The predominant fad in popular culture was a new wave of Mao nostalgia, exemplified by the cassette album of Hong Taiyang (Red Sun) series 1 and 2, which reproduced the Cultural Revolution songs eulogising Mao the Great Helmsman, now set to a rock beat. The album sold over two million copies . " (Liu , 1998:166)

People listening to this reformed music are more fascinated by the "new style" rather than being able to arouse the "revolutionary enthusiasm" of the old days. At the same time, political nostalgia about the cultural relics of the times of the Great Cultural Revolution is also dissolved in this playful style. The political canon has in the process been secularized. The same fate has happened to almost the whole variety of Chinese classical series and the "high-brow" works, including the "red classics". [1]

Today, high culture and revolutionary literature are not so impact-making as they used to, while popular culture is gaining more strength and playing a dominant role. At present, the binary position between "high" and "low" still exists, although there is a gradual process of intermingling. As commented in an official newspaper, "with further development of market economy, essence culture re-emerges, and a lofty humane spirit is gradually seeping into popular culture. " (*Guangming Daily*, January 8, 1997) Whether the comments are of wishful thinking or popular culture is exempt from mutation still needs to prove with the passage of time.

There is a heated debate on the matter. [2] Some think that popular culture characterized by commercialization is not culture in its true sense, because it is prioritized to make a profit rather than to cultivate or educate (*New China Digest*, No. 10, 1998, pp153-56). Others believe that popular culture is a direct consequence of international cultural flows and global capitalism. In order to appreciate it, one has to take the power of social discourse, the market economy and the cultural "consumer" into consideration. The former holds the viewpoint that commercialization of culture is a form of capitalist ideology which is considered to be "spiritual contamination", especially to the younger generation. The latter considers that the function of popular culture is mainly to enrich the life of the masses and that it liberates culture from the ivory tower of the elite. Its multiple cultural forms match people's desire for variety of cultural needs. Therefore, it functions to promote social progress and cultural prosperity. However, people tend to go to extremes in the new situation. With new cultural identities approaching, some are quite worried about the degradation of traditional Chinese cultural values. As a result, they make their mind to try to assert the "crisis of human spirit". Others, seeing chances to get rich quick, so involve themselves heart and soul in culture business. They devote themselves into money-making writing, paying little or no attention to artistic and spiritual pursuit in their work. In spite of the debate and disputes, new cultural identities are being recognized and popular culture has become part of people's life.

Since global elements have entered the country, imported Western theories and practices are welcomed. Not only are they discussed in a wide range of academic fields, but the practice of the theories has the effect of directing the population towards what are perceived to be significant changes in artistic and popular cultural identities, methods of signification and modes of orientation with society and the people's lives. The current Chinese discourse of modernity and globalization is essentially co-operative but sometimes contradictory with the country's development. As a local identification of global meaning, it articulates both an anxiety over the full-blown absorption of China into the global "world-system" and desires for intervention and resistance. Internationally, with the downfall of the former Soviet Union, the balance of the global power is dramatically changed. But, due to political reasons, the discourse of the Cold War continues with a shift towards socialist China (Wang, 1999). In this respect, some are trying to foster a public image of China which can be seen as resistance to globalization though the represented image is not quite appealing generally. True to its name, China remains a socialist country despite its special characteristics. Therefore, China's ideological and political identity as a third-world country, the theory of "Socialism with Chinese Characteristics", the "main theme" highlighting the leadership of the Communist Party, the revolutionary traditions and the socialist spiritual civilization, have to be recognized and considered within the context of globalization and identity construction of the country. In economic field, the adoption of the State policy, namely, economic reform and opening to the outside world, has proved fruitful in many ways. Over the past decades, China has achieved progress attracting global attention. There is a manifold increase in the income for both urban and rural residents and enrichment in the material and cultural life of the people. Foreign observers comment that China, "after several decades of self-imposed separation from the world economy…become an immensely significant regional—and global player. " (Dicken, 1998:139)

Although China has engaged itself in economic reform and involved itself in the process of globalization to a considerable extent, its ideological and political identity as a third-world, socialist country remains. Marxism with Chinese modifications is the guiding theory for the "initial stage of socialism". To challenge such "main theme" or "master narrative" is by no means an easy task despite the current distrust of all master narratives in postmodernist endeavors. In the contemporary period, the policies of reform and door-opening can be said to have moved constantly in two directions. On the one hand, they turn toward the future and embrace modernity as an ideology for change. On the other hand, they look back to the past with ambivalence and even nostalgia. The "cultural fever" of the 1980s and 1990s was indirectly fuelled by an impassioned interest in new theories and methodologies. Western theories and methodologies were carefully and critically studied. It is obvious that changing geographies, particularly the new forces of globalization that are now shaping our times and the global themes are significant for the cultural and economic life of contemporary Chinese. It is in this global context, we believe, that we can begin to understand contemporary Chinese cultural trends and identities. It is also in this context that the mutual communication and international cultural exchange are now becoming more important than ever in this global era.

NOTE

[1] Red Classics are books and artistic works on revolution at home and abroad. The best sellers used to be such titles as *The Making of A Hero*, *My University*, from former Soviet Union and *Tracks in the Snowy Forest*, *Railway Guerrillas*, *The Song of Youth*, *Red Crag* of China, to name only a few.

[2] Referring here respectively to the debate "Forum on Cultural Industry" appearing in *New China Digest* (1998) and the "Discussion on Postmodernity in Contemporary China" in *Studies on Chinese Culture*, Autumn Vol. 1997, Beijing.

REFERENCES

Appadurai, Arjun. "Disjuncture and Difference in the Global Cultural Economy" in P. Willaiams and L. Chrisman (eds) *Colonial Discourse and Post-Colonial Theory* (1993). Hemel Hemptead: Harvester Wheatsheaf.

Cvetkovich, Ann & Douglas Kellner. "Introduction: Thinking Global and Local" *Articulating the Global and Local* (1997). Ed. Ann Cvetkovich and Douglas Kellner. Colorado: Westview Press.

Dunn, G. Robert. *Identity Crises: A Social Critique of Postmodernity* (1998). Minneapolis: The University of Minnesota Press.

Dicken, Peter. *Global Shift: Transforming the World Economy* (1998). London: Sage Publications.

Giddens, Anthony. *The Consequences of Modernity* (1990). Cambridge: Polity Press.

Hoogvelt, Ankie. *Globalization and Postcolonial World* (1997). London: Macmillan Press Ltd.

Hall, Stuart. *The Question of Cultural Identity* (1996). Milton Keynes: Open University Press.

Lash, Scott and John Urry. *Economy of Signs and Space* (1994). London: Sage Publications.

Meng, Fanhua. *Dance of Gods and Ghosts: A Study on Conflicting Cultural Phenomena in Contemporary China* (1998). Beijing: China Today Publishing House.

Pieterse, J. "Globalization as Hybridization" in M. Featherstone, S. Lash and R. Robertson (eds) *Global Modernity* (1995). London and Newbury: Park: CA Sage.

Qian, Zhongwen. "Two Dangers in the Context of Plural Cultures and the Future of Literature Theory", conference proceedings for *The Future of Literary Theory and Criticism* (August 2000), Beijing Language and Culture University.

Rajchman, John. *The Identity in Question* (1995). Ed. London: Routledge.

Robertson, R. *Globalization* (1992), London and Newbury: CA Sage.

Spybey, Tony. *Globalization and World Society* (1996). Cambridge: Polity Press.

Sarup, Madan. *Identity, Culture and the Postmodern World* (1996).

Edinburgh: Edinburgh University Press.

Strinati, Dominic. *Introduction to Theories of Popular Culture* (1995). London: Routledge.

Tang, Xiaobing. "The Function of New Theory: What Does It Mean to talk about Postmodernism in China?" in *Politics, Ideology, and Literary Discourse in Modern China—Theoretical Interventions and Cultural Critique* (1993), Durham: Duke University Press.

Williams, Raymond. *Keywords: A Vocabulary of Culture and Society* (1976). London: Fontana Press.

Wang, Ning. *Globalization and Postcolonial Criticism* (1998). Beijing: Central Compilation & Translation Press.

Wang, Jisi. "Comments on Debate on the Civilization Clash", *Studies on International Cultural Theories* (1999). Beijing: Chinese Social Sciences Press.

Yang, Xuedong and Wang, Lie. "Dialogue on Globalization and China's Involvement" *Contemporary World and Socialism*, No. 3, 1998, Beijing.

Yu, Keping and Huang, Weiping. *Globalization and Its Contradictory Interpretations* (1998), ed. Beijing: Central Compilation & Translation Press.

Cultural Identity and Ideological Space

Introduction

This is an interdisciplinary study of Overseas Chinese Town theme park (OCT) in China, based on the Western theories of tourism and going beyond. The research of the project aims to shed a cultural, political and ideological light on the "modern pleasure dome" produced and consumed in China. In view of the quantity of theme park study in the USA and Europe, a shift of orientation in the study of the theme park in China becomes meaningful and urgent as the emerging theme parks in the country are described as "springing up like bamboo shoots after a rain". In examining Overseas China Town theme park as a tourist product and business enterprise of Western style, the focus of study is placed on the interpretation of the park as an ideological tool and a space of cultural symbolism with national significance.

The theme park as a special kind of tourist landscape has become a major subject in cultural studies and has received increasing scholarly attention in the last two decades. In tourism research, perspectives have varied from American approaches which treat the American Disney theme park as the production base of the American Dream (Bryman, 1995; Wasko, 2001; Klugman, 1995; Philips, 1999) to discursive critical methodology (Smoodin, 1994; Gottdiener, 1997; Willis, 1995; Smith, 1996), audience response study (Wasko, Phillips & Meehan, 2001), to various interpretations of the tourist space in semiotic, structural and post-modern approaches (Fjeman, 1992; Sorkin, 1996; Adams, 1991). The body of research is enormous and has proved to be very beneficial in understanding the theme park as a cultural form and business unit. Other studies of the theme park have been conducted with a more practical emphasis on implications and significance for economic development and urban design for the local and peripheral surroundings (Brown, 1980; Sorkin, 1996). This research of Overseas China Town theme park aims to shed a different light on the "modern pleasure dome" produced and consumed in China. In view of the overwhelming quantity of theme park study in the USA and Europe, a shift of orientation in the study of theme parks in China becomes meaningful and urgent as the emerging theme parks in the country are described as "springing up like bamboo shoots after a rain" (Sun, 1999:2). In examining Overseas China Town theme park as a tourist product and business enterprise of Western style, my focus of study is placed on the interpretation of the park as an ideological tool and a space of cultural symbolism with national signification.

From early 1990s, the central government of China has promoted favorable policies of mass tourism in countless sites of natural and cultural heritage across the country and invested heavily in the protection and restoration of historic sites. To the surprise of not only foreign visitors but also domestic sightseers, cultural images formerly discarded as carrying feudal or bourgeois overtones have been revived, such as the "lunar calendar festivals and events, classical art forms, religious ceremonies and re-enactments of nostalgia" (Feng & Shi, 2003:80). To explain this cultural phenomenon, it may help to associate the revival of mass tourism of traditional cultural attractions embedded with new meanings rather than for circulation of old ideas, such as modernized motives of people visiting historic architectural heritage sites and attending traditional festival events. Practically, the representational recycling of history has served the double purpose of strengthening the link between the natural landscapes with the cultural identity of Chinese people and meeting the growing need for tourism.

Along with the development of large scale constructions of civil engineering and infrastructure works for the past two decades, the construction of cultural projects such as theme parks have also boomed, most of which are projects focusing on the "traditional pilgrimage and sacred sites" (Digance, 2003:146), legacy and heritage of traditional Chinese culture and dreams of globalization. Overseas Chinese Town theme park (incorporating Splendid China, Folk Culture Villages and Window of the World), Beijing Shijingshan Amusement Park, the Huangdi Emperor Tomb in Shannxi and the Giant Statue of the Supreme Patriarch Lao Zi (founder of Daoism) in Guangdong Province, as well as a mushrooming of "ethic minority villages" and "folk culture parks" have emerged. These cultural establishments and theme parks serve the purposes of remembering "the unquestioned totality of the nation", "placing the country onto the track of globalization" and "transforming local space into profitable tourism" (Feng & Shi, 2003).

Shenzhen, an Emerging Megacity

Located in Shenzhen, the largest and first Special Economic Zone (SEZ) in China, and overlooking the skyline of Hong Kong, the Overseas Chinese Town theme park has been both "a project of spiritual and material civilization of the era of the 'four modernizations'" (Yang, 2001:325). This essay analyses how OCT, a tourism product with post-modern features, was established in the cultural, social and economic environment of Shenzhen, arguing that rapid urbanization in the Shenzhen Special Economic Zone and the influence of capitalist Hong Kong serve as the catalyst for such a cultural project. In 1990s, cultural development in Shenzhen had entered a period of transition. Whilst the traditional rural or "folk" forms and genres did not completely disappear, they were being rapidly supplanted by commercial forms of popular entertainment, such as Overseas Chinese Town theme park (Zhang, 2001: 340-347; Chen, 2001:348-353).

The shift appeared to have moved decisively towards the growing urban centers. These forms did not necessarily displace such older places of historic interests as temples, museums and heritage sites. Increasing mercerization in Shenzhen led to the establishment of large-scale pleasure attractions and show business. The emerging theme parks are the product of the combination of foreign investment and local cooperation. As of foreign style, the theme parks feature a variety of non-traditional forms of " cinematically related spectacle entertainments" and "simulation rides" (Darley, 2000: 31). Although the Western-style theme parks typified by Disneyland mediate images and set a live model for this similar yet different project in Shenzhen, special Chinese characteristics are encoded at all stages of programming in the Shenzhen' theme parks. Basically, the Shenzhen's theme parks and other cultural projects for the "tourist gaze" (Urry. 1990) , to various degrees, have expressed ideologies of modernization, political propaganda, identification of Chinese identity, as well as of touristic ends.

It becomes necessary to point out that cultural advancement of Shenzhen has given birth to the theme parks and that the theme parks have consequently enhanced and contributed immensely to the social and cultural modernization of the city. Different from other cities with longstanding cultural tradition in China, the newly established Special Economic Zone of Shenzhen has cultivated an urban culture which can be characterized by contemporary Western capitalism influence and globalization trends. The process of cultural modernity of Shenzhen is accompanied by rapid speed of urbanization and the migration tide in the Special Economic Zone, which has changed the small fishing village into a modern city with a population of over five million. The advancement is a "Great Leap Forward" rather than a "Long March" (Hu, 2001: 81-83). The processes embody a thorough reconstruction from a remote and poverty-stricken village into a modernized city with most capitalist characteristics. This fast material accumulation is only a part of the story for the jump-start development of Shenzhen. It has been a series of strides towards urban civilization from rural cultivation, in alternative terms, a change from agricultural culture to industrialized and post-industrialized culture. As such, the paradigm of cultural modernity in Shenzhen SEZ has taken shape from the time of establishment of the Special Economic Zone in 1979, when the "economic reform" and open policy were adopted.

Generally, overall urbanization of Shenzhen in over twenty years can be regarded as "macro" and "micro". The former is mainly associated with the superstructure, including governmental establishments, social functionaries, administrative organs while the latter is connected with the local and regional facilities and collectives with their respective hierarchical subsidiaries. As discussed earlier, the leadership of Shenzhen and its subordinates were liberal minded and ready to learn from Hong Kong. "As long as one catches mice, it's a good cat" (Deng Xiaoping's quotation and governance strategy). In this respect, Hong Kong provides an immediate model teacher regardless of its capitalism. As a result, frequent exchanges of expertise and mutual visits between Shenzhen and Hong Kong have become a regular schedule. In the era of reform, the quantification and qualification of civil engineering were frequently measured as the yardstick of economic achievement. Shenzhen takes pride in that within a short period of time, numerous multi-storeyed estate and skyscrapers were mushrooming in the city. At the time of building, some were even the highest buildings in the country and they are still regarded as the landmarks of Shenzhen: King of Earth, New China Building, The Financial Center, "Eiffel" inside Overseas Chinese Town theme park, to name only a few.

One of striking features of urban development in Shenzhen is said to embrace post-modernity highlighted by architectural landmarks and cultural transformation of spaces with then the tallest commercial building of Earth King and Overseas Chinese Town theme park at the apex. A more thorough understanding of so-called the "Shenzhen Speed" of development needs a historical regression.

Historical Recollections

It is necessary to review briefly the history of how Shenzhen, formerly a remote place with no fame, has developed into a new city. Essentially, this is a story about the successive subsidence and re-territorialization of a rural area that, during the Ming and Qing Dynasties, was called Xin'an County (Wu, 2001: 543-547). After the first Opium War in 1840, part of Xin'an County, Hong Kong Island was taken by the British colonists. Subsequently, The Kowloon peninsula and the New Territories were incorporated into the colony by a succession of pacts and agreements between the feudal government of the Qing Dynasty and British government. The local annals recorded that the renaming of Xin'an into Baoan County by the Guomindang Government took place in 1913, neither of which is used. When the People's Republic of China was established, the border was closed for various reasons. But, the closing of the border did not prevent normal communication and business exchange. In actual fact, the flow of people and goods has never ceased before and after the closure of the border due to the spatial and geographical convenience as well as cultural dependency, including shared faith, customs, cultural values and lifestyle. On the other hand, the closing of the border marked an important transition in the articulation of China and the rest of the world. In the colonial period, the border had been invisible to the imperial influence within the traditional world order in which Great Britain had played a decisive role. Throughout the late Qing Dynasty (1616—1911) and Guomindang times (1912-1949), Hong Kong had been a small fishing town without any cultural accumulation. It was a symbol of "backwardness" and inability of the "corrupted" governments. During the Second World War, Japanese invaders attacked Hong Kong but did not win the war. But the development of the colony was greatly affected. When the Allies returned their concessions to the Guomindang government, it was not of much significance. Even after new China was founded in 1949, the question of Hong Kong's return to China remained suspended. Admittedly, Hong Kong's modernization and reputation as "a hub of the global economy" (Dirlik, 1999: 55) were achieved in the colonial period, though its political influence was limited. In the Cold War period, the colony, like Taiwan, Japan, and South Korea was integrated into the pacific strategic circle forged by the North Atlantic Treaty Organization in order to contain the potential threat of emerging socialist China, or in Napoleon's word, the "arising lion". The most important function of Hong Kong lies in world trade and global transport. Rather than Hong Kong playing a great role in world politics, Hong Kong was always an ideal place for entrepreneurship and financial development.

The spirit of economic pragmatism was pervasive in China when Deng Xiaoping took the leadership after the death of Mao Zedong in 1976. The ultimate goal aimed to launch the modernization drive, improve the quality of life of the population and repair the country after the disastrous mass movement of the Cultural Revolution. The so-called "reform and opening up" policy marked a shift in the international strategy of China. The question most concerned was the conditions under which China would modernize. The ambivalence has become that whether China should continue to follow the template of the Soviet planned economy, or to learn from the Western market economy and become increasingly capitalist or Westernized (*Xi Hua*). The central committee of the Communist Party of China has followed a more practical route of modernization which was basically geared to the same track of the Western model. Deng interprets Marxism in a creative way and advanced the theory of " socialism with Chinese characteristics", with regard to Chinese specific social and historical conditions. Far from an idealist, Deng has targeted the kernel problems of China and found a solution to them. What the " open door" policy has so far proved reflects his insightful re-interpretation of *Capital* by Karl Marx and the possibility perceived by him whether Marxism can still be applied in the reform of China and recovery of economy.

This historical mapping out of these shifts and transformations is helpful for an objective understanding of the process from pre-modernization to modernization in Xin'an to Baoan to Shenzhen Special Economic Zone. In considering the modernization of Shenzhen and post—modernity of Hong Kong, it is clear that the former has been trying to learn from the latter. But the processes and practices of modernization of Shenzhen have been different from those by Hong Kong. Further, as mentioned before, Shenzhen's mode of modernity is not seen as a negative of that of Hong Kong, precisely because it is designed and implemented under the rule of the Communist Party, which needs to be conceptualized specifically in the era of the " reform".

Special Economic Zone in the Era of Reform

When the policy of reform and opening was first implemented in some coastal cities in 1978, overall reform took place in south China, especially in the Pearl River Delta. In this region, intensive inflows of labor-intensive, foreign-investment business have had a direct and sizeable impact on local labor demand and has been a major cause of population migration to the region. Foreign-investment enterprises thus provided a large number of employment opportunities not only for local surplus rural labor, but also for migrants from other regions outside the Delta. The population movements comprise the demographic and spatial aspects of urbanization in the Delta during the period of reform and opening. Foreign investment enterprises, their industrial activities and the related supporting and servicing activities such as hospitality business, transport, entertainment and retailing in small towns and rural districts have led to dramatic changes of land use and of the shaping of physical landscape in the region. The large-scale construction of cultural entertainment projects may be attributed to a rapid growth of demand stimulated by the increasing urban population with its rising living standard and needs for diversity of cultural life. Arguing about the relationships between "the cultural power", "identity" and cultural institutions from the Western context, Sharon Zukin remarks:

"Yet the cultural power to create an image, to frame a vision, of the city has become more important as publics have become more mobile and diverse, and traditional institutions—both social classes and political parties—have become less relevant mechanisms of expressing identity. Those who create images stamp a collective identity. Whether they are media corporations like the Disney Company, art museums, or politicians, they are developing new spaces for public cultures. Significant public spaces of the late 19th and early 20th century—such as Central Park, the Broadway theatre district, and the top of the Empire State Building—have been joined by Disney World, Bryant Park, and the entertainment-based retail shops of Sony Plaza. " (1995:2)

More significantly, the production sector in the Delta is allowed to adopt "special policies and flexible measures" (Sun, 1999:135) while the government there operates under a socialist market system. It is a unique integration of socialist political ideology with the capitalist market economy. This practical combination of market capitalism and state socialism characterizes the Delta's unique institutional provision for mixed economic development and thus is chronicled as an important period in Chinese history. In about twenty years, Shenzhen and the Pearl River Delta, as the "homeland of overseas Chinese", have experienced a sea change. From the 1980s onwards, Shenzhen has been geared on a fast track of modernization. The municipality and city builders have modernized their concept and ideology and succeeded in their economic, cultural and political experiment. First, they have tremendously improved the infrastructure, including transport, energy, communication and information facilities. Secondly, they have improved services facilities such as public finance, education, medical institutions and housing. Thirdly, they have constructed and innovated a large quantity of cultural establishment such as cultural quarters, book cities and museums, which has been termed as the "spiritual food" for the citizens. The modernized "hardware" and "software" of the milieu have sufficiently contributed to the popularity of Shenzhen as an attractive and desirable place. A European broker Chen Danyan humorously commented thus when arriving in the Special Zone: "It can't be China, at least not the China as I expected. But it's definitely not a foreign country". (*EU Chinese Journal* published in London, No. 17, p17)

Initiating a Theme Park

Overseas Chinese Town theme park can be regarded as one of the largest theme parks in China measuring up to the world standards. The park consists of three major sites (Splendid China, Folk Culture Villages, Window of the World) featuring the image of rich material and spiritual culture of China and the world.

Apart from social benefits, OCT has succeeded in gaining economic benefits, accounting for a big share of the tourism in Shenzhen (*The Investigation Report of Overseas Chinese Town*, 2002). The effects of the theme park, in the sense that it has both introduced the theory and practice of modern theme park tourism in the pioneering stance, are exemplary. The idea of Overseas Chinese Town theme park took shape in 1985, when the principal, provincial and central authorities, realizing the potential benefits to be derived from tourism in the Special Economic Zone, decided to create a spectacular tourism project that will bring positive reputation and foreign investment to Shenzhen (Sun, 1999:3). Different from the original inspiration occurring to Walt Disney of the science dream and his respect of "cleanliness" (Sorkin, 1996:206), the idea for the Chinese theme park is attributed to a group of political elites from the local to the central governments, who, envisioned the special status of Shenzhen, have intended to make full use of the new-born metropolis in promoting the affairs of overseas Chinese for the purposes of economic construction of motherland and political propagandism. Realistically, they needed a physical space to implement the idea. In August, 1985, the State Council accepted the idea of the 'Overseas Chinese Town' and a designated space of 4.8 km^2 was granted in a formerly an agricultural farm in Shenzhen's Nanshan Administrative District near the Shenzhen Bay. As the name of the project suggests, Overseas Chinese Town would be made to serve the needs of "enticing more overseas Chinese; introducing funding, technology and resources from outside China; and carrying out overseas Chinese affairs more efficiently" (Sun, 1999). The responsibility of construction of the theme park was then directed to China Travel International Investment Limited, a tourism company registered in Hong Kong.

The genesis of Overseas Chinese Town theme park took place in 1985, with a more concrete proposal by Ma Zhimin, the former General Manager of China Travel Service (Hong Kong) Limited. Inspired by the expressed model of Disney and other destination parks in the West, they have accomplished in establishing

"Splendid China" and "Folk Culture Villages" with unique features. It is suggested that the following three essential factors were vital in their successful endeavors, namely, "Heaven" (favorable political atmosphere), "Earth" (the Special Economic Zone close to Hong Kong) and "People" (strong team led by charismatic leader Ma Zhimin) (Sun, 1999:17-27).

For the leadership of OCT, implementation of up-to-date management is more important than actual building of the theme park. Basically, it can also be attributed to its practice of providing quality service and "emotional care" (Zhang, 2003:39) for the park visitors. For their enjoyment or their rights of consumers, the park provides all kinds of conveniences in terms of the "consuming consciousness and choice" (Bell and Valentine, 1997), from viewing seating (for both able and disabled) to sundry amenities (restaurants, restrooms, gift shop, film sales and rent services) to interpretation (encoding and decoding of attractions). The visitors are especially appreciating the "emotional care" management, which includes providing escorts to usher out tourists around closing time (Zhang, 2003:41-42).

OCT theme park is good at seizing business opportunities. Individual themed zones have regularly presented spectacular theme activities of carnival nature: Shenzhen Beer Festival, the Water-Splashing Folk Festival, the International Italian Culture Week, Food Festival, European Week, French Fashion Show, The Sakura Festival. Karaoke Contests, weekly singing and dancing parties, and concerts presented by nationally and internationally well-known bands. The programes have provided a high degree of visitor satisfaction and made a sterling profit to the park owners.

Layout of OCT Theme Park

What is special about the theme park of Shenzhen is the geographical position and political overtone of the project. There exists considerable autonomy of self-control and independent management by the leadership of OCT as the investment of OCT comes from Hong Kong. Official policy by the local and central government can therefore be negotiated and re-conciliated. In fact, the practice of official policies and local tactics as well as "They direct, we decide", is not only uncommon in Shenzhen's cultural business but also in other enterprises. The management of OCT has succeeded in their sophisticated efforts and the result is the good profit earned and "positive social and economic benefits" achieved from opening of the theme park. It is further noticed that the foreign-local joint ownership of the theme park gives flexibility to the theme park to function independently.

It is worthwhile to emphasize generally that in the process of reform and modernization, the country's economic policy has shifted from the Soviet's template of plan economy to the Western free market economy. The State's political ideology has therefore been softened to accommodate emerging cultural identities during the process of economic reform, which is remarkable in the Special Zone. Many administrative institutions including the State-owned cultural establishments can operate in a strategically negotiable way. To a great extent, the success of Overseas Chinese Town is the result of the "invisible transformation of the State's ideology" and the exercise of "flexible political measures" (Ni, 2000:196).

Ideological Representation in "Splendid China"

In both theoretical and practical terms, an array of "themed villages and zones" within Overseas Chinese Town can be made parallel to the classification of the themed "Lands" of Disney World (Bryman, 1995). The composite theme park production of OCT reflects the mainstream discourses of Chinese political culture. Splendid China themed zone is perceived as a manifestation of cultural and natural heritage in China, as expressions of nationhood and cultural integrity. Folk Culture Villages presents the physical and spiritual life of ethnic minorities suggesting a sense of national identity and unity which conforms Benedict Anderson's classic concept of the nation as an "imagined community" (1991: 6); while Window of the World park represents such key cultural conceptions as the "global village" (McLuhan, 1968), "high modernity" (Giddens, 1991), "Occedentalism versus Orientalism" (Said, 1978), and "Dialogism" (Bakhtin, 1984) among different cultures of the world.

As part of OCT, "Splendid China" themed zone occupies an area of 3.27 km² featuring the epitome of Chinese spiritual, constitutional and mental culture. It includes some of China's most well-known historic architectures, cultural attractions and natural landscapes such as the Imperial Palace in Beijing, the Great Wall, the Terracotta Army of Emperor Qin's Mausoleum in Shanxi, the Big Buddha of Leshan Mountain in Sichuan, the Mogao Grottoes at Dunhuang, the Potala Palace in Tibet, Mt. Huangshan in Anhui, the Shaolin Temple in Henan, the Three Gorges of the Yangtse River. They consist of three categories: "Ancient Buildings", such as palaces, monasteries, temples, towers, pagodas and bridges, "Natural Scenery" including famous mountains, rivers, landforms of geographical magnificence and beauty, and "Folk Customs and Local Dwellings" which include different styles of local houses, such as the "Memorial Ceremony for Confucius", the Mongolian wrestling, archery, horse racing and so on (*Shenzhen Splendid China Development Report 2001*).

Its slogan of "Going Back in History in One Step and Traveling Across China in One Day" advertises magnetic uniqueness of "Splendid China". Super-ordination characterizes some of the most attractive sites as listed above. The replicas are arranged, more or less, according to their realistic geography in China. The philosophy behind is shown in its advertising slogan. It is proper to say that "Splendid China", with its spectacular display of China's national landmarks, represents her longstanding history, unique natural heritage and ethnic diversity. The implied emphasis of the park as a whole is on the rebuilding of a new image of nationhood in the times of modernization. China, in the search for modernity, has to negotiate between nationalism and heritage. Apparently, Splendid China has attempted to create a sense of Chineseness through territorial representation in the era of "four modernizations".

Most theme parks in the world highlight national values and spirit amidst variety and comprehensiveness of their contents. Overseas Chinese Town is no exception in this regard. It is easy to find the obvious foregrounding and emphasis on China and Chineseness, though representation of globalization and Westernization can also be seen and felt as well. However, the propaganda of "Mega-China" and "the Central Kingdom under the Heaven" (Ronan & Needham, 1978:4) is legitimate in order to enhance the great rejuvenation of the Chinese nation with all ethnic peoples taking part, a cherished dream of a strong China. Splendid China has benefited from the "deep and rich cultural and natural heritage" in order to spread political ideology, mainstream culture and consumerism.

In spite of the fact that the park planners have designed the miniatures to suggest the totality of "Chineseness", walking inside the Lilliputian spaces, one relates to the feel of boundary, distance and difference, "walling in" and "walling out" (Robert Frost), all of which can naturally be topics of debate on negotiation and reconstruction of Chinese identity. It is acknowledged that the reference system for identity is found in the framework of difference. Referring to the "norms and values" of "Chineseness" in relation to the emerging discourse of identity crisis, Nonini and Ong argues:

> "Chineseness" is no longer, if it ever was, a property or essence of a person calculated by that person's having more or fewer "Chinese" values or norms, but instead can be understood only in terms of the multiplicity of ways in which "being Chinese" is an inscribed relation of persons and groups to forces and processes associated with global capitalism and its modernities. "(1997:3-4, cited in Kong, 1999:222)

Splendid China creates a "super-fake" of China in the manner of intensified "compression of time and space" (Giddens, 1990). The guide of the park leads the visitor into a world of representation of original cultural setting of selected nationalities and the architectural monuments of Chinese longstanding civilization—a geographical shrinking of the country in an attempt to arouse amazing effect and impact on the park visitor. The park in its own right has also succeeded as a live and illustrated "textbook" for education of national culture, as the Communist Party of China (CPC) has repeatedly emphasized on education of traditional culture and patriotism for the younger generation. Evidently, the performances, festivals and display of heritage sites within the theme park are even more vivid than the multi-media teaching rooms. As the physical arrangement of Splendid China tries to promote, the Han people are in harmony with the fifty-five minority peoples in the atmosphere of Chinese multiculturalism. But it is necessary to stress that in reality, ethnic conflict and dispute remain surprisingly persistent in China, where one might have the naive thought that the "open door" and reform policy would have benefited all the nationalities equally and created new relationships among ethnic groups.

Displaying Identities in "Folk Culture Villages"

Lying adjacent to the rim of the picturesque Shenzhen Bay, "Folk Culture Villages" is an ethnic theme park where folklore ethnic arts, architecture and customs of China's minority nationalities are presented. The park contains a number of dwelling houses and other buildings including life-size mountain villages, residential quarters, streets and markets, forming relatively independent micro communities such as the Bouyei stone cottage, the Miao village, the Dong village, the Yao village, the Naxi house, the Mosuo wooden house, the Gaoshan house, the Hani mushroom-shaped house, the Jingpo village, the Li village, the Bai village, the Dai bamboo house, the Tujia water market, the Kazakstan and Inner Mongolia yurts, the Tibetan house and lamasery, the Korean cottage, the Han courtyard house, the Han cave dwelling in northern Shaanxi and the Zhuang village. Many of these villages and houses were designed and built by native people from their places of origins and the articles for daily life displayed were either bought directly from local families or made to order by local craftsmen. Apart from these life-size architectural reproductions, there are over twenty well-known scenic spots of China constructed in the Villages such as the Coconut Palm Forest of Hainan Island, Buddhist pagodas from Nanfeng, giant banyans from Xishuangbana of Yunnan, the 23-metre high statue of the Thousand-handed and Thousand-eyed Guanyin (the Chinese Goddess of Mercy), and the Yunnan Stone Forest (*Splendid China Development Report 2001*). For only a year after it opened in 1991, more than four million local and global visitors toured the park.

In order to gain the "natural flavour and authentic taste" of the minority ethnic customs and lifestyles in their source regions, the park aims to present a Utopian atmosphere where the original cultural setting of the minority groups was re-arranged in the limited fabricated space. All the dwellings and houses together with the "inhabitants" inside possess the value of display and exhibition. As to the actual construction of the houses and buildings, "Be faithful, expressive and graceful", the classic Chinese principles of translation, was coincided with the guideline of construction of this park which focuses on "extracting the essence of mundane life but avoiding its duplication, and being faithful to life but rising to a higher level" (Sun, 1999:83). Depending on specificity of the dwellings of the minorities, some were transported directly from their original places followed by re-assembly. Others houses are the buildings constructed immediately in the park but with strict criteria for the traditional construction styles, methods and materials of the originals except that the mechanical equipment such as lighting and air-conditioning is installed due to the sub-tropical climate of Shenzhen. Following the standard practice of majority theme parks in the world, the three OCT themed zones entertain the visitors on the daily basis. In Folk Culture Villages, the cast characters are the minority "villagers" inhabiting in the "Villages". The "villagers", or the actors and actresses come from their appropriate ethnicity. In order to present the daily entertainment and display of the fabricated village life in quality and quantity, hundreds of artists and other staff members of twenty-three nationalities all over the country have been recruited. The recruitment was conducted through a series of selections in order that the "authenticity" of all the appropriate ethnicities can be portrayed. Among the criteria of selection are the bilingual skills (Standard Spoken Chinese and native ethnic language), performing talents (singing and dancing their ethnic profiles and playing instruments), folk techniques (native cuisine, handicraft-making, horsemanship and so forth), and presentable appearance. The contracted actors and actresses of the "Villages" are in the ratio of 7:3. As the

"Villages" manager revealed, the star-looking actresses have more eye-catching effect, in view of the fact that the theme park are receiving more and more prosperous Hong Kong male visitors (Ni, 2000:197).

It is notable that the intention of creating the dynamic atmosphere is to invite participation and involvement of the visitors inside the Villages, in communicating with the performing 'inhabitants', in their folk singing and dancing, on-the-spot demonstrations of making handicrafts, and in cooking of local delicacies of ethnic styles. However, it is hard to rate these as 'true to life' or 'authentic' when folk shows are staged in their comparatively homogenous physical milieu within Splendid China and Folk Culture Villages, with regard to their artistic originality and traditional way of performing. Furthermore, some relentless modification and bold deformation of ethnic art forms have deprived the authenticity of value and meaning of the original, as starkly demonstrated in change of forms and contents of ethnic arts to suit the *Spectacular National Costume Show* and the *Grand Evening Parade.*

Paradoxically, as argued by some critics, the issues of "authenticity" can be classified differently. As a negotiated conception, one may argue that the theme park creates the "staged authenticity" (MacCannell, 1973: 589) or "existential authenticity" (Wang, 1999: 350) as presented by Folk Culture Villages and Splendid China. Frederic Jameson terms this as "new depthlessness" (Jameson, 1984:58). What is at stake is an understanding of the process and purpose of authentication of the theme park (Wall & Xie, 2003:374-388). With reflection on what happens in Folk Culture Villages, the explanation can be found in the relationship between the park's artificiality and consumerized actuality. Alternatively, the combination of staging, sightseeing, imagination and authenticity, has been seen by the theme park practitioners of OCT as necessary to do profitable business.

Folk Culture Villages can be described as a "semiotic system" (Barthes,

1972) whereby (in)-authentic objects and people, together with their cultures and lifestyles are deployed to spread the mainstream ideology of the "great solidarity" and the image of China being "a big happy family". Again, following Barthes' processes of de-mystification one can view a clearer picture which does not conform exactly to the implications of the park themes and activities. Although the Han is either positioned or presented centrally in the park's performing profile, the dominant ideology of the majority people can still be felt and detected like an "unseen hand". The foregrounding of ethnic minorities and their life and customs needs to be seen as both political and economic strategy and means of displacement. A variety of colorful representation of cultures, customs and practices of the selected minority groups creates the special carnival for the entertainment of the visitors, which, in a way, sweetens and romanticizes the realistic aspects of life and well being of ethnic minorities. In other words, amidst the carnivalesque atmosphere of the park, the visitor is made to forget the problems, conflicts and differences in current situation of the Han-minority groups relationship and relationships among ethnic peoples. What has left may be the pure imagination and initial assumption about the harmonious ethnic relationship in China, strengthened by the merry and light-hearted representation of life and culture of these "chosen people". Therefore, Folk Culture Villages, as a themed zone is just a fabrication space, an organic component of an overall political discourse and expression of official ideology. In such a regulated and controlled space, mainstream culture takes dominance, where behavior and speech of all participants must be watched in terms of political requirement.

In the chronicles of OCT, 1992 is special, when Deng Xiaoping, the "general architect of China's reform and modernization", made his official inspection to south China and was invited to visit Splendid China and Folk Culture Villages in Shenzhen. Deng's presence had great political implications and an instant effect for not only Shenzhen but also for the country. Deng's praising remarks on the opening and success of OCT was disseminated through the media, and further popularized the theme park. Indeed, Deng's official inspection in Shenzhen and his historic touring of OCT has aroused a great sensation in China and focused national attention on the OCT. As a matter of fact, the emergence of the boost of tourism in Shenzhen and the growing popularity of OCT theme park can be traced to that historic visitation. The subsequent visits to the theme park by heads of states of China and other countries, though also influential, were never equal to Deng's. The literal visit shows that apart from sound marketing strategies and business promotion, political elements can exercise considerable influence on the operation and development of cultural establishments in Chinese context, such as OCT theme park. This can be regarded as characteristic in the development of the theme park tourism in China.

Globalizing "Window of the World"

The comprehensive theming of OCT is supposedly completed by the opening of another theme zone of Window of the World in 1994. Different from Splendid China and Folk Culture Villages, which are viewed by many as essential expressions of Chinese culture, "Window of the World" presents a panorama of globalization dominated by Euro-centralism and Americanization. Window of the World features the famous cultural and historical attractions of the globe, natural landmarks as well as indigenous dwellings, well-known sculptures, drawings, folklore and theatrical performances glorifying cultures of globalization. In accordance with the geographical positions and categories of the sights, this park is divided into nine areas—the World Square, Asia, Oceania, Europe, America, Africa, Recreation Center of Modern Science & Technology, World Sculptures Gallery, and the International Street, totaling 118 scenic spots among which are world wonders such as the Pyramid and the Amon Temple of Karnak from Egypt, the Stonehenge from Britain, miniaturized Basulica from Italy, the Grand Canyon of America, Taj Mahal from India, L'Arc de Triomphe from Paris, the St. Peter's Cathedral of the Vatican, the Sydney Opera House from Australia, the Leaning Tower of Pisa, Borobudur from Indonesia, Serengeti Game Park from East Africa, Mount Corcovado from Brazil. Probably the most spectacular attractions are the 108-metre-tall Eiffel Tower (its top reachable by the elevator and where tourists can even see Hong Kong), the Niagara Falls (80 meters wide and over 10 meters in its drop), and the "active" Hawaii volcanoes (with glowing blazes, surging lava and fountains spurting steamy water as high as 100 meters). "Window of the World" was constructed on 1:1, 1:5, or 1:15 scales respectively, depending on the needs and specifications of the attractions. With static and dynamic layout of Window of the World as the backdrop, it is relevant to view the "condensed globalization" within the boundaries of this theme park.

The philosophy of OCT is that the world is seen as a harmonious global village where every culture and civilization meet and speak, a mock denial of Rudyard Kipling's divide of the Occidental and the Oriental (*The Wordsworth Poetry Library*, 1994). At the entrance of the World Square, with a standing capacity for over 10,000 visitors, stand six world renowned statues such as Venus, David, Tang Xuanzang, African Mother and Son and around the Square there are 108 giant pillars of different styles; six huge gates representing the birthplaces of the ancient civilizations proper: India, China, Islam, Babylon, Egypt and America, and relief between the gates on walls of 200 square meters demonstrates the world history of millions of years. The fall of the night preludes the evening entertainment of "World Rejoicing with You" show: performances of songs and dances by the "Five-Continent Song & Dance Troupe" with artists from all over the world and the Big Parade and Carnival Tour of individual national customs. A charming and exotic sentiment prevails over the park and grand entertaining performance combining multinational songs and dances creates a climax of enjoyment. By way of highlighting, the theme song goes, "Here we come along with our colorful dreams/ To this wonderful paradise we build/ Of every beautiful dream, every appealing custom/ And cream of every culture/

Whatever you are, or color of skin/ No more war and crime, nor hatred and feud/ All the people in the world/ Join together with love, joy and peace/ With hope here to realize/ Our proud dream/ To you, to all the world" (*Window of the World Video*).

If Splendid China and Folk Culture Villages represent the political ideology of China being an organic whole and the showcase of Chinese identity and cultural hegemony of the Han, with less emphasis on business consideration, Window of the World follows a more practical route with efforts towards the economic value of the "tourist gaze" (Urry, 1990). In response to a popular maxim which posits that "the more traditional, the more modernistic", one may claim that "the more global, the more local", if one makes a careful observation of what is presented in Window of the World. The enthusiasm and higher rate of repeat visitation of this theme park convince that the park planners are aware that celebrating global cultures appeals to the domestic audiences with regard to their nostalgia of the "glorious past" in history and their "adoring eyes" to the West (Chakrabarty, 2000:151). The process of selecting the global sites and scenes could have been relatively complicated, but the park planners seem to have made it much less so, which can be regarded as a reflection of both ideological favoritism for Eurocentralism and meeting touristic ends: from continental Europe and Anglo-America, they have selected thirty-two sights while representatives chosen from Africa and Asia are approximately half of the number. It is apparent that the theme park showcases intensively the "Ocean Blue Civilization" (*Lan Se Wen Ming*) (Liu, 1998:1730).

In spite of the fact that Window of the World is in stark contrast with Splendid China and Folk Culture Villages in terms of theming and exhibiting layout, political philosophy and ideological orientation across the three themed zones are interconnected and complementary to one another. Window of the World embodies collective unconscious of a "powerful empire" of China in the old days and on the "Silk Road" as well as a dream of "Renaissance" in the future. However, although the theming draws extensively upon the concrete forms of world cultures and civilization as essential to the "faithfulness of representation", unjustified trivializations and omissions are not difficult to find. The park represents a variety of cultural displays, coupled with the accommodation of cultural difference and contradiction. For the visitor, Window of the World serves the multiple purpose of "making the foreign to serve China", "broadening the scale of knowledge", "experiencing exotic and distant cultures" and "realizing the dream of going abroad" (Yang, 2001:309).

Conclusion

Overseas Chinese Town theme park is the largest theme park of international standards and one of the most successful tourist attractions in China. Its dominant position and hegemonic features remain evident among numerous counterparts and destination parks in China. Owing to the theme park's geopolitical position and its proximity to capitalist Hong Kong, which has facilitated the global-local nexus, OCT continues to claim the growing market demand though domestic and global competition for the theme park industry is getting intense. At present, the stress has been placed on the "becoming process" or sustainability of Overseas Chinese Town theme park, as the theming of the park is never static. Arguing against normal accounts of the "life circle" of the theme park typical in theme park tourism in the West, focus has been placed on the innovation and the transformational and generative aspects of Overseas China Town by looking at the destiny of OCT in the twenty-first century. As suggested previously, this research is about global trend, Chinese politics and the State ideology represented by OCT theme park in the times of modernization. What is at stake is the trend of the new tourism or post-tourism, with Disney's global expansion towards the East. Over last twenty years, the theme park tourism in China has engaged in a revolutionary process with the result that there is a general mix of global influence and local colors. In the above study of Overseas China Town theme park, an attempt has been made to account for as a symbolic space with both Chinese and Western features. It is positive to predict that China's overall favoritism for cultural establishment, continuation of flexible tourism policy adopted by the management, its political speculation and its unique branding will provide further optimism to Overseas Chinese Town.

REFERENCES

Adams, J. *The American Amusement Park Industry: A History of Technology and Thrills* (1991), Boston: G. K. Hall.

Bakhtin, M. *On Dostovesky's Poetic Issues* (1988), Beijing: The Bookstore of Three Unions.

Barthes, R. "Semiology and the Urban", *Rethinking Architecture: A Reader in Culture Theory* (1997), Ed. N. Leach, London: Routledge.

Bell, D. *Consuming Geographies: We Are Where We Eat* (1997). London: Routledge.

Brown, D. L. "Thinking of a Theme Park", *Urban Land* (1980), Vol. 39, No. 2.

Bryman, A. *Disney and His World* (1995), London: Routledge.

Chakrabarty, D. *Principalizing Europe: Postcolonial Thought and Historical Difference* (2000), Princetown University Press.

Chen, N. G. "A Study of Travel Culture and Its Trends in Shenzhen", *The Cultural Forum of the Special Zone* (2001), Vol. 2, Ed. Yu Longyu, Shenzhen: Hai Tian Press.

Darley, A. *Visual Digital Culture: Surface Play and Spectacle in New Media Genres*, London: Routledge, 2000.

Digance, J. (2003), "Pilgrimage at Contested Sites", *Annals of Tourism Research*, Vol. 30, No. 1.

Dirlik, A. "Globalization and the politics of place" in *Globalization and the Asia-Pacific Contested Territories*, Kris Olds et al (ed), (1999), London: Routledge.

Feng, J & J. Shi (2003), *Amusement Industry in China and Foreign Countries*, Beijing: China Tourism Press.

Fjellman, S. M. *Vinyl Leaves: Walt Disney World and America* (1992), Oxford: Westview Press.

Ghimire, K. B. & L. Zhou. "The Economic Role of National Tourism in China", Ed. *The Native Tourist* (2001), Krishna B. London: Earthscan Publications Ltd.

Giddens, A. *The Consequences of Modernity* (1990). Cambridge: Polity Press.

Giddens, A. *Modernity and Self Identity: Self and Society in the Late Modern Age* (1991), Cambridge: Polity.

Gottdiener, M. *The Theming of America* (1997), Oxford: Westview Press.

Hu, B. "A Brief Historical Review of Film and TV Production in Shenzhen", *The Cultural Forum of the Special Zone* (2001), Vol. 2, Ed. Yu Longyu, Shenzhen: Hai Tian Press.

Jameson, F. "Postmodernism, or The Cultural Logic of Late Capitalism", *New Left Review* (1984), Vol. 146.

Klugman, Karen. "Reality Revisited", *Inside the Mouse: Work and Play at Disney World-the Project on Disney* (1995), London: Rivers Oram Press.

Kipling, R. *The Work of Rudyard Kipling* (1994), Ed. The Wordsworth Poetry Library, Herdfordshire: Wordsworth Editions Ltd.

MacCannell, D. "Staged Authenticity: Arrangements of Social Space in Tourist Settings," *American Journal of Sociology*, No. 3, 1979, pp. 589-603.

McLuhan, M. *Understanding Media: The Extensions of Man* (1968), London: Routledge and Kegan Paul.

Ni, W. "Cultural Politics in Semiotic Consumption", *Under the Masking of New Ideology: Cultural / Literary Analysis in the 1990s* (2000), Ed. Li Tuo,

Nanjing: Jiangsu People's Press.

Nonini, D. M. & Ong, A. "Chinese Transformation as a Alternative Modernity", *Ungrounded Empires: The Cultural Politics on Modern Chinese Trandformation* (1997), Ed. A. Ong and D. Nonini, London: Routledge.

Philips, D. "Narrativised Spaces: the Functions of Story in the Theme Park", *Leisure / Tourism Geographies : Practices and Geographical Knowledge* (1999), Ed. David Crouch, London: Routledge.

Phillip, M. "The Global Disney Audiences Project: Disney Across Cultures", *Dazzled by Disney? The Global Disney Audiences Project* (2001), (Ed.) Janet Wasko, Mark Phillip and Eileen R. Meehan, London and New York: Leicester University Press.

Ronan, C. A. & J. Needham. *The Shorter Science and Civilization in China: An Abridgment by Colin A. Ronan of Joseph Needham's Original Text* (1978), Cambridge: Cambridge University Press.

Said, E. *Orientalism* (1978). London: Peregrine Books.

Smith, N. "New City, New Frontier: The Lower East Side as Wild, Wild West", *Variations on a Theme Park* (1996), Ed. M. Sorkin, New York: Hill & Wang.

Smoodin, M. Ed. *Disney Discourse: Producing the Magic Kingdom* (1994), London: Routledge.

Sorkin, M. "See You in Disneyland", *Variations on Theme Park* (1996) Ed. Michael Sorkin, New York: Hill & Wang.

Sun, Y. *The Man-made Landscapes: A Way of Success in Shenzhen* (1999), Guangzhou: Huacheng Publishing House.

Urry, J. *The Tourist Gaze: Leisure and Travel in Contemporary Societies* (1990). London: Sage.

Wall, J. & P. Xie. "Ethic Tourism in Hainan, China: Li Dancers", *Tourism Planning and Management in Developing Countries* (2003), Ed. Bao Jigang et al. Beijing: China Tourism Press.

Wang, N. "Rethinking Authenticity in Tourism Experience", *Annals of*

Tourism Research (1999), Vol. 26, No. 2.

Wasko, J. & E. R. Meehan. "Dazzled by Disney? Ambiguity in Ubiquity", *Dazzled by Disney? The Global Disney Audiences Project* (2001), (Ed.) Janet Wasko, Mark Phillip and Eile, Leicester University Press.

Wang N. *Globalization and Postcolonial Criticism* (1998). Beijing: Central Compilation & Translation Press.

Wasko, J. *Understanding Disney* (2001), Cambridge: Polity Press.

Willis, S. "Public Use / Private State", *Inside the Mouse: Work and Play at Disney World—the Project on Disney* (1995), London: Rivers Oram Press.

Wu, J. Z. "Shen-Kong Cultural Exchange and the Cultural Construction of Shenzhen", *The Cultural Forum of the Special Economic Zone* (2001), Vol. 2. Ed. Yu Longyu, Shenzhen: Haitian Press.

Yang, H. H. "Successful Exploitation of Cultural Resources: An Experience of OCT Tourism", *The Cultural Forum of the Special Zone* (2001), Vol. 2, Ed. Yu Longyu, Shenzhen: Hai Tian Press.

Zhang, Z. K. "Splendid China Phenomenon and Development of the Theme Park in China", *The 21st Century Forum for Development of China Theme Park* (2003), Ed. The Overseas Chinese Town Group, Beijing: China Tourism Press.

Zukin, S. *Landscapes of Power: From Detroit to Disneyland* (1991), California: University of California Press.

Part Two

Literary Works and Their Cultural Assumptions

Introduction

By looking at the works of a couple of Caribbean and English literary writers, an attempt has been made to demonstrate that literary writings are intimately related to the cultural and historical assumptions of literary writers. And these cultural assumptions are often unconscious ones. They tend to belie the work of authors. As a matter of fact, no writer can discuss a subject either alien or familiar to them without a sense of identity, which proves what E. Said said is quite right. Identity comes from what he or she is not rather than what he or she is. This sense of self and of other is essential to writing an individual's truth, for it is this that defines what is individually true instead of what is factually true. A literary text, be it a poem or a novel, always relies on certain cultural assumptions, either by accepting them or by questioning them. It is the basic framework of beliefs which supports writers composing their works.

In this essay a postcolonial approach is useful to discuss the works of a couple of respective Caribbean and English literary writers. The works of three Caribbean poets will come under study. These poets have a unique shared history, that of the Caribbean. The Caribbean history is one of upheaval, passing between French and English hands for many years before the English won political power. Then Caribbean writers have the option of either selecting the appropriate pre-Caribbean history (most were immigrant slaves of African or Indian origins) or to try to accept the whole history. This often proves to be too much of a task and so many Caribbean writers feel they are "de-racialized". Therefore, some powerful images of a future, and a literature, which are uniquely West Indian, have their roots in slavery. In comparison, the author will look at the works of a couple of English poets. They all have different views on what renders them English. No one poet is factually incorrect; they all look at different eras to demonstrate their nationhood. All are part of a large expanse of history, which is incomplete by nature.

Further to this two novels are to be studied in the light of cultural identity. The first novel is E. M. Forster's *A Passage to India*. This will give the view of a British person who feels they are liberal and progressive and show how non-liberal and unprogressive they are with their beliefs about the culture they have usurped. To counteract this V. S. Naipaul's *In a Free State* will be studied. Both novels look at the aftermath of the withdrawal of the British from former colonies. Naipaul's work shows that it is not easy to regain an identity of one's own when one has been "liberated" by a colonizing nation. Having been through this process himself, Naipaul is well-qualified to judge from a "native" point of view, although the views he extols do not win him many friends from amongst his contemporaries.

Contrast between Caribbean and English Poetry

According to Ian Ousby (1989) , Derek Walcott has always written courageously for a Caribbean tradition subsuming African, Indian and European cultures in the region he describes as "Our hammock swung between Americas" (Elegy). He has tried his best to "alchemize ' where nothing was / the language of a race ' (Crusoe 's Journal) out of various despised patois and metropolitan English, with which to confront Caribbean individual, historical and racial contradictions. " (1039)

Although he sometimes writes in a less Creole form, Walcott seems to be unapproachable. In *Another Life* he speaks of the past and of his childhood. It speaks of his discovery of those less fortunate than himself.

> ···Afternoon light ripened the valley,
> Rifling smoke climbed from the smalllabourers' houses,
> And I dissolved into a trance.
>
> I was seized by a pity more profound
> Than my young body could bear, I climbed
> With the labouring smoke···

He later goes on to discuss the British education he received.

> Cramming half-heartedly for the scholarship,
> I looked up from my red-jacketed Williamson 's
> *History of the British Empire*, towards

> The Barracks plumed, imperial hillsides
>
> Where canon-bursts of bamboo sprayed the ridge,
>
> Riding to Khartoum, Rorke's Drift,
>
> Through dervishes of dust⋯

These lines show that he had a relatively Westernized education, involving little education about his own past and heritage. The assumption therefore, is that he has no culture of his own, and that it must always be borrowed. He has been raised as a European and so it is a surprise for him to see poverty, as in the labourers.

Poetry detached but simultaneously skeptical, has followed through in his *Sea Grapes* (1976) and other poem collections. In *Sea Grapes* he uses even less Creole language and references.

> That sail which leans on light,
>
> tired of islands,
>
> a schooner beating up the Caribbean
>
> for home, could be Odysseus,
>
> home-bound on the Aegean;
>
> that father and husband's
>
> longing, under gnarled sour grapes, is
>
> like the adulterer hearing Nausicaa's name
>
> in every gull's outcry.
>
> This brings nobody peace. The ancient war
>
> Between obsession and responsibility
>
> Will never finish and has been the same

For the sea-wanderer or the one on shore

Now wriggling on his sandals to walk home,

Since Troy sighed its last flame,

And the blind giant's boulder heaved the trough

From whose ground-swell the great hexameters come

To the conclusions of exhausted surf.

The classics can console. But not enough.

Nostalgia can strongly be felt here. The poem is narrated in the third person. This suggests that he is speaking this from an objective point of view. There are realities and mythologies. European cultural references are abundant, such as "Odysseus", "Nausicaa", "obsession and responsibility", "the blind giant", and "exhausted surf". Interestingly, the poet pretends to be an observer, but that is hard. In actual fact, he is both "in" and "out" of the nostalgic story.

Grace Nichols was far more accessible. She is Caribbean by birth and raising, but chose to come to England in the 1970s. And many of her subjects are the differences between the two. Concern with race and gender are key topics in Grace Nichols's poems, but she treats both with a measure of comedy, particularly apparent in her second verse collection *The Fat Black Woman's Poems* (1984).

Nichols injects self-criticism and humor into some of her works and also a little nostalgia for home. In "Tropical Death" she writes,

The fat black woman want

125

A brilliant tropical death

Not a cold sojourn

In some North Europe far/forlorn.

The fat black woman want

Some heat/hibiscus at her feet

Blue sea dress

To wrap her neat.

However, some of her early poems show a strong sense of the colonial injustices perpetrated against black people and against women. In them she has cast her mind back to the miserable sugar gathering days of her ancestors. Such West Indian poets have spoken of the dead and of their heritage of slavery. But they have also written with a faith that life will continue. They have written in the language that can make hope, humor and healing possible (See Chamberlin 20-22). In fact, the cultural identity of West Indian poets often involves historical contradictions and caricatures, which is vividly represented in their language representation.

The proper comparison is with some of the well-known English poets. Specifically these are Ted Hughes, Phillip Larkin and Geoffrey Hill. They use references of their national history or some aspect of it as a muse, and translate it so that it speaks to their readers. They represent movements within English poetry shared by others but led by the above. Ted Hughes is the case in point. Much is made of Hughes's love of the dark and monolithic. Hughes utilizes many sorts of cultural deposits and capital, including the pagan Anglo Saxon and Norse elements, and he draws energy also from a related constellation of primitive myths and world views. He seems to look almost to prehistory for his truths and package them in a way that they seem romantically bleak to the reader. His subjects are often plants or animals. Modernity in his many poems is sometimes defined in terms of antiquity (Zhang 28-29) .

Phillip Larkin's work has characterized the dominant trend of English poetry of his times. The poet was acknowledged as "the effective unofficial laureate of the post-1945 England". (Easthope 184) He has great admiration for Lawrence's *Lady Chatterley's Lover*, which may partly explain the linguistic simplicity of some of his poems published in *High Windows*.

> When I see a couple of kids
> And guess he's fucking her and she's
> Taking pills or wearing a diaphragm,
> I know this is paradise
> Everyone old has dreamed of all their lives

Larkin's line ("They fuck you up, your mum and dad") serves as the beginning of the poem entitled "This Be The Verse". The poetic expressions appear to be greatly concerned with Freudian theory, but they may move into intensely private realization of human production of the people concerned (See Bennett and Royle 3):

> Man hands on misery to man.
> It deepens like a coastal shelf.
> Get out as early as you can,
> And don't have any kids yourself.

On the subject of Phillip Larkin generally, Heaney writes "⋯ his proper hinterland is the English language Frenchified and turned humanist by the Norman conquest and the renaissance, made nimble, melodious and plangent by Chaucer and Spenser ⋯" (Walder 19) His is a more modern England than Hughes's but still deeply rooted in tradition. The subjects about which he writes are more varied than Hughes's.

The final poet to be considered here is Geoffrey Hill. Such customary themes of his as history, war, English landscape, music, poetry, and faith are also concerned with dense references to the literature and the echoing voices of old histories.

It is believed that his work and his ambivalent attitude to Christianity account for his poetic reputation. His poetic writings are featured with rigor and discipline in literary comments. The first poem in *Hill's King Log* (1968) recalls the dying command of John Tiptoft that he should be decapitated in three strokes "in honor of the Trinity" (See Sanders 636):

> Processionals in the exemplary cave,
> Benediction of shadows. Pomfred. London.
> The voice fragrant with mannered humility,
> With an equable contempt for this world,
> "In honorem of Trinitatis". Crash. The head
> Struck down into a meaty conduit of blood.
> So these dispose themselves to receive each
> Pentecoastal blow from axe or seraph,
> Spattering block-straw with mortal residue.
> Psalteries whine through the empyrean···

It seems that these violent and horrified scenes and events can typically found in the history drama of Shakespeare. One may detect the fierce imagery that Hill evolves from the eventful things of the distant past is doubtlessly of his creation.

Geoffrey Hill shares the common "Anglo-Saxon base", however his language is more Europeanized and Latinate. He writes about history as if it were contemporary, mixing in the modern regularly, with references in his *Mercian Hymns* to "the citadel of Tamworth", "the overlord of the M5". "Merovingian car-dealers" and "the mythical Camelot". His attitude seems to be summed up in the title of one of his poems, "Requiem for the Plantagenet Kings". He looks back in history, although this is not entirely nostalgic. Essentially, *Mercian Hymns* is a series of prose-poems "using the historical figure Offa to connect the idea of kingship with the private responsibilities of the individual and those of the poet to his people and his time" (Ousby 461).

Unlike their Caribbean counterparts, these poets have history. It is believed that together they give a fairly accurate picture of it. It is definitely something that roots them. That is not to say that the Caribbean poets are any less valid by their fragmented history, merely that what they have to say is different. The cultural assumptions in question here are historical in nature. One culture is steeped in history and the other is very limited in it. It is this basic assumption of antiquity that underlies the poetry of all of these poem writers.

Naipaul's *In a Free State* and Forster's *A Passage to India*

In line of the above discussion but with a different genre, it is proper to look at Naipaul and Forster. V. S. Naipaul's *In a Free State*, first of all, is not a traditionally arranged novel. Chapters have been replaced with individual narratives of usually unrelated stories. This "unrelatedness" is not the case through the whole book, since the first and fifth narratives are in fact journal entries from what is indicated to be the same person, relating in the first person violent incidents which take place on two trips to Egypt. The first happens to an English "tramp". His status as tramp is in question because although he is described as somewhat scruffy his actions are those of someone who is merely eccentric. "···when he came closer we saw that his clothes were all in ruin, that the knot on his scarf was tight and grimy; that he was a tramp. " Furthermore he obviously is sufficiently solvent to pay for fairly regular trips abroad. "I've been to Egypt six or seven times. Gone around the world about a dozen times ··· Geologist, or used to be···I've been traveling for thirty eight years. I think of myself as a citizen of the world. " This issue is significant because it highlights the cultural prejudices of the other passengers. He is the only British passenger (although the narrator is somewhat unsure about his own identity) and he is distinctly odd as an individual. His status as Other threatens his fellow passengers. The epilogue (the previous narrative is a prologue) marks the return of the narrator to Egypt. A further violent incident occurs. Beggar children are thrashed for seeking food from Europeans. The narrator sees this as grossly unfair and reacts to the man whipping them. He did not react in the prologue. Has he changed his views of the victim? Is he more inclined to help because they are children or natives? Is it just that there is safety in numbers? He sees natives as less able to defend themselves than the Englishman who is so well established that he should be able to look after himself. Perhaps he feels pity for the native children as dispossessed and feels no pity whatsoever for the "tramp". It is an important point that in all of Naipaul's narratives in this novel some kind of revolution has taken place. In Egypt it is a political one, hence plenty of poverty and numerous beggars.

In his first narrative within the framework of the Egyptian journals, "One Out of Many", an Indian Hindu servant is transplanted from his home, where he is respected for the status of his employer, to Washington, USA. This is a personal revolution for him. He sees society as completely restructured. "Outside the supermarket there was always a policeman with a gun. Inside there were a couple of Hubshi guards with truncheons, and, behind the cashiers, some old Hubshi beggar men in rags." Hippies and black people (Hubshis) are equal to everyone else and there is no caste system. He faces the dilemma of whether he is superior to the black people around him as he would be at home, or whether he is inferior because they are at home there and he is not. As he spends more time there he is involved increasingly in the outside world. He has a relationship with a black woman, which would be unforgivable in his native land, he gets a job for his own sake rather than his master's and ultimately is legally naturalized. As a character, and as a Hindu, Santosh is painted as somewhat submissive. He is surprised at the aggressive attitudes of the Americans and he expects little. He is used to sleeping in a cupboard whereas his American counterparts have entire apartments. When he arrives in America he is childlike. He is an innocent who is corrupted by this new world in which he is the Other. The main corruptor is the black woman, and he despises her for this, but yet marries her. He chooses to be part of this new life, even though he prefers the old. So what cultural assumptions are there in this story and how are they treated? The narrator assumes a lot about the character of the Hindu. They are childlike and submissive, easily led astray. This may have come from the experience of the Indian Trinidadian Naipaul, a lapsed Hindu. The narrator also assumes that black people are sexually demanding and smoke cannabis. It is impossible to quantify this and it could be argued that the incidents represent individual characters rather than a race of people, but nameless faceless people who can only be represented by individual characters populate the city. The narrator seems to accept these assumptions and work with them, but this may be a clever device on Naipaul's part to make the reader question them. It may also be another example of the racism of which he has been accused.

In the second narrative, "Tell Me Who to Kill", the revolution is once again personal. Perhaps this is the device of using the first person. The narrator, whose name we are never given, is a protector. Education is a feature of the ever present Other. It is entirely alien to the environment in which the narrator and his family have grown up, but it is shown as a guiding light by a Christian relative. The youngest son, Dayo, is the most cherished member of the family and so it is he who is given the gift of education, the agent of revolution. This leads him to England, home of civilization supposedly. Once he has arrived there his brother, the narrator, feels he needs protecting and goes over to do that. Theirs is a relationship that is not easy. They need one another and somehow resent one another too. The narrator works hard and earns a 10t of money but this disappears quickly. It is ultimately Dayo who breaks away from this, marrying an English girl. The narrator then realizes how much Dayo and his needs have shaped his identity.

It is indicated, although never specified that these men are Caribbean. They have a fragmented history and feel baseless. This may make it easier to start again elsewhere, but it leaves them without an identity. This is indicated by the narrator's lack of name. It is this lack of naming that indicates that Naipaul is most closely linked to these protagonists. This, as also indicated by the title of the section, renders the narrator unstable and therefore dangerous. We meet his friend Frank, a constant companion with whom the narrator shares everything and is often annoyed. Is Frank a friend, as the words state? Is he as close as a lover? It is doubtful that Frank is another side to the personality of the narrator. He seems to put across sense when the narrator is at his least stable, and comfort him when he is worried. He is all that the narrator will have left after Dayo's marriage.

What assumptions are made, then, of where they have come from? The text states that the lifestyle is slower at home. "···but it (the village at home) is home, and on a sunny Sunday morning, nobody working. I can see my father's younger brother coming up the pitch road on his bicycle". The narrator must work two jobs to support himself and Dayo in England. Is this suggesting that

Naipaul thinks that the Trinidadian way of life is somehow lazy or that the English way of life is all hard work for little reward? The main characters' way of life is without doubt somewhat squalid. Perhaps poverty in England is less friendly than poverty in a hot climate. What assumptions do readers make? The reader is given a number of characters' names, their religions and clues to their whereabouts, but at no point does it state that they are black. But it is strongly indicated that they were.

The third narrative, "In a Free State", features a political revolution, and hints at a sexual one. It is made clear from the beginning that one of the main protagonists is promiscuous and the other is gay, although it is still a shock when he refers to himself later as "queer". This revolution, which involves everyone and so is much less personal, is represented in the third person. The other potential meaning of this change of voice is that Naipaul as the author could sympathize with the other situations and he cannot do so with this one. A journey takes place during which political activities come and go, including a beating for Bobby from soldiers and the defeat of the King by the President. Almost more important than the revolution going on around them are the discussions that take place between Bobby and Linda. They both respect and dislike the other at times, but they share a racial unity, which they protect by sticking together. Their attitudes are different but equally useless. Linda is a pragmatist who sees the chance to make the most of what is left. She is an opportunist, as her planned infidelity with a fellow traveler, Carter, proves. She seems to flirt with Bobby too, knowing that she has no chance. Bobby is a liberal. He sees himself as a friend of the African. The English are no longer in charge, yet he takes a very superior view of the African who accidentally scratches his car windscreen. This view is not limited to black people, though. It is also shown in his and Linda's joking about Doris Marshall, the South African wife of a colleague. It is not a prejudice against Africans; it is a fear of the Other. Many black people have taken to combing their hair in the "English" style. This is taken to mean that they have their independence but they do not know what to do with it, so they imitate their colonizers. This is given an ironic twist later, as the true attitude to the Colonizers is shown to be unwelcoming. This mimicry is shown to be either ironic at the English. Bobby and Linda see it only as the sincerest form of flattery though. They assume that natives want to speak English and that they require English help to establish themselves. It is this that creates the untaken opportunity for Bobby to seduce a waiter at the Hunting Lodge. This is untaken because his basic revulsion comes into play. This is another attitude he and Linda share. They see that Africans are dirty and their scent is regularly mentioned. Whilst Bobby thinks of himself as liberal and a man who would "bend over blackwards", he is as repulsed and threatened by Africans. Interestingly Bobby also thinks of Linda in terms of her smell. He notices her vaginal deodorant and sees this as a mask for her unhygienic undercarriage.

It is also interesting to compare Naipaul's Bobby with E. M. Forster's Fielding. In *A Passage to India* Forster writes about an imagined Indian response to the end of British rule in India. Indians, like Naipaul's Santosh, are submissive and childlike. The English (or Americans) are kindly benefactors the adults of the situation, although this attitude could almost be tolerated when the protagonist has gone into that situation, as with Santosh, it is hugely patronizing when the adult civilizing benefactors have invaded one's home, as in Forster's novel. In this all Indians are savages, awaiting the calming influence of the superior, British race. This is not irony by Forster but assumed of his reader. He does suggest that, as a result of the English influence, Indian natives are no longer necessarily savages. This view is merely perpetuated by the British to enhance their own sense of being depended on. The reader is asked to assess his or her own assumptions by the deliberate non-specification of Adela's attack. Do we assume that she is a weak woman who cried rape? Is this her discovery of the "real India"? Was she attacked and blamed by the nearest person. Probable is that she was attacked, however not by Aziz. The conveniently absent guide seems a much more likely culprit, although there is the absence of detail in this regard. Forster seems to be quite pro-Indian. Hence many of the Indian characters are portrayed as rather one dimensional in comparison to the English.

There are characters who have much in common in Naipaul's *In a Free State* and Forster's *A Passage to India*. The main two are Forster's Fielding and Naipaul's Bobby. They share liberal sentiments towards natives but favor their own kind in reality. Bobby's is conscious. He will side with white people over black people innately, but he makes conscious decisions to side politically with the new native government. Fielding is less conscious of his bias. He lives in India and feels awkward in English company, but he cannot fit into Indian society either. He is the Indian's white friend. He will represent the Indian as a white man to white men. His true bias is noted on his return to England, as he feels safer and safer through Europe. "The buildings of Venice, like the mountains of Crete and the fields of Egypt, stood in the right place, whereas in poor India everything was placed wrong." One could also compare Adela and Linda. They seem quite different on the surface but they share a degree of naivety towards the natives. Adela asks Aziz if he has more than one wife and he is offended. Linda sees the politics that has brought about the demise of the British rule as rather simplified and does not think to question her place in the changing society.

Some critics believe that *A Passage to India* marked a turning point for colonial literature, having had an "even greater influence on British imperial politics than on English literature" (Chaudhuri 19). Others think on the work about India becoming a book about the representation of India. This representation can be somewhat negative. It ultimately represents what the Western mind does not know about itself. Forster's image of India is of a cave. His is a seductive India, which leads to the alleged rape of Adela. There is a probability that this attack did not take place, but that Adela is hysterical and imagines it, half in hope. This casts India as erotic and desirable, yet somehow unattainable to outsiders (Forster loved the country but was always an outsider). In this situation one can consider that the narrator is Forster, since it is his assumptions of the erotic and exotic land taking over his characters.

The unique voice to be heard in passing is that of Edward Said. He wrote what is one of the most famous criticisms of Otherness, *Orientalism* (1978). He feels that Western scholars wholly bring about the study of the Orient. There are a number of implications for this as numerous "questions raised by Orientalism" (p15). The first is economic. What the West lacks it makes up for from the east. This could be in terms of gross product, or in terms of labor—it was mostly African and Indian slaves dispatched to the Caribbean. It serves the Western economic purpose to subjugate and make Others submissive Orientals. If the West feels superior to them they are able to control them. There are also social implications involved. The West defines itself and its inhabitants not in terms of what it is but in terms of what it is not. Where Europe is strong, steady, reliable, adult and masculine, the Orient is weak, unstable, savage, childlike and feminine. There is European and there is Other. Of course this is oversimplified, but it explains the concept of Imperialism well. The English poets seem to have little sense of Otherness because they seem largely to concentrate on their own culture. The concept of the other is now a cultural assumption, which does not have to be spoken about to be acknowledged.

In conclusion, it is clear that literary production is related to cultural assumptions, often unconscious ones. They tend to belie the work of authors. No writer can discuss a subject either alien or familiar to them without a sense of identity, and Said points out that this identity comes from what they are not rather than what they are. This sense of self and of other is essential to writing an individual's truth, for it is this that defines what is individually true instead of what is factually true. It is the basic framework of beliefs and histories which supports writers composing poetry and fiction.

REFERENCES

Bennett, A. and Royle, N. *Literature, Criticism and Theory: Key Critical Concepts*, Hertfordshire: Prentice Hall / Harvester Wheatsheaf,1995.

Chamberlin, J. E. "Introduction to An Anthology of Caribbean Literature", *An Anthology of Caribbean Literature*, (ed.) Zhongwen Huang, Nanjing: Nanjing University Press,1995.

Chaudhuri, N. C. "Passage to and from India", *Encounter*, June 1954, pp19-24.

Easthope, Antony. *Englishness and National Culture*, London: Routledge, 1999.

Forster, E. M. *A Passage to India*, Penguin Books,1979.

Huang, Zhongwen. *An Anthology of Caribbean Literature* (ed.), Nanjing University Press, Nanjing,1995.

Naipaul, V. S. *In a Free State*, Pelican Books,1973.

Ousby, I. *The Cambridge Guide to Literature in English* (ed.), Cambridge: The Cambridge University Press,1988.

Said, E. *Orientalism: Western Conceptions of the Orient*, London: The Penguin Group,1995.

Sanders, A. *The Oxford History of English Literature* (2nd Edition), Oxford: Oxford University Press,1999.

The Poetry Anthology, Open University Press,1991.

The Prose Anthology, Open University Press,1991.

Walder, Dennis. *Literature in the Modem World*, 1990.

Zhang, Pinggong. "Sense and Sensibility: Understanding Hughes through *Cave Birds*", *EPSIANS*, Vol. Three, 2013 (1).

Some Reflections on Frost's
Pastoral and Philosophical Poems

"A poem", Robert Frost once said, "is never a put-up job so to speak. It begins as a lump in the throat, a sense of wrong, a homesickness, a lovesickness" (*Highlights of American Literature*, p34). So is a Robert Frost poem to the reader. It is a piece of immortality, and a piece of the north-eastern United States called New England, its simple style reflecting these rural people and their lives. Robert Frost is probably twentieth century America's most famous poet. His career was long and celebrated, his voice distinctive. Because he was close to the land, and because he dealt with emotions and concerns common to people of different times and cultures, Chinese who have exposed themselves to American literature should have no difficulty in understanding and appreciating many of his works.

Joseph Brodsky, a great poet also, has this to say about Frost's life in a very condensed way,

"Robert Frost was born in 1874 and died in 1963, at the age of eighty-eight. One marriage, six children; fairly strapped when young; farming, and, later, teaching jobs in various schools. Not much travelling until late in his life; he mostly resided on the East Coast, in New England. If biography accounts for poetry, this one should have resulted in none. Yet he published nine books of poems. " (1988:5)

Indeed, Frost wrote numerous poems, but could not get them printed until at the beginning of the First World War when his works were accepted by a publisher. Soon they became popular in America. While he was teaching at universities and writing poems, he was doing farm work at the same time. Few years before his death, the young president John Kennedy warmly invited Frost to read a poem at the ceremony of President's Inauguration. "Along with recognition naturally came a great deal of envy···He was indeed a quintessential American poet. " (Brodsky, 1988:6)

As a regional poet, Frost's poetic works bear a strong sense of identity. According to Buell, several elements can be considered as criteria for matching a poet with his works or his poetic practice and regional identity. Biographically, it is through the personal history of the writer, along with the evidence of reading in attentiveness to sociality with other regionalist practitioners. Geographically, it is through the cultural and physical experiences of the writer's represented world, including rural villages with their traditional spatial quarters and boundary, together with the civic and religious rituals associated with them, local ethnical components, small-scale agrarianism, stone walls, and other folk architectural motifs and so on. Ideologically, it is realized by attitudinal traits like town-centeredness, self-sufficiency protestant religiosity, moralism, the work ethic, historical and genealogical self-consciousness. Linguistically, it is technically done by distinctive idiom, pronunciation, syntax, and tonality. Formally, it is created by employing specific literary genres and metrics, as well as figures of speech to particular works of previous generations (110-111).

Frost wrote what he knew—the landscapes and people of Massachusetts, Verment, etc. and wrote them in many moods. His farming experience tells him much about nature, its favorable and destructive power, and the hardship of solitary farmers. In face of obstacles and challenges of life, Frost was undoubtedly a strong courageous man. Commenting on the poet and locality, Derek Walcott remarks,

"Frost felt that in New England he was being offered an unexplored, unuttered theatre, away from the leaves of libraries, in a natural setting rich with stories and characters…We think of Frost's work in theatrical terms, with the poet, of course, as its central character, mocking his crises, his stopping at a crossroads, but also because of the voices in the poems. These voices are American, but their meter is not as subtly varied as the lyrical and yet colloquial power of his meditations. " (1988:101).

Frost was by no means an activist in the literary movements of the 20th century. He preferred to use conventional forms and plain language, but with a graceful style. His poems were essentially like conversations, but they turned out to be wise and pretty conversations: very carefully constructed and with a constant flow. He had the gift of using symbols from everyday country life. These symbols in his poems usually reflected deep meanings and profound thoughts.

Frost wrote all his life. When his last poem was published, he was eighty-eight years old. During his lifetime, he won many prizes including four Pulitzer Prizes and the Poetry Prize. In 1960, the American government presented him a gold medal for his contribution to American culture. Fame came late for Robert Frost, but it came long and enduring. People in the United State and abroad honored him for his fruitful 60-year literary career. Monteiro recorded thus,

"Frost's popularity with politicians running the so-called New Frontier administration ran unabated into the next year. Congress voted Frost a Congressional Medal ' in recognition of his contributions to American letters, ' which the President awarded at White House ceremonies on the poet's eight-eighth birthday. " (p227)

In a general way of classification, Frost's poetry can roughly be divided into three categories: the pastoral poems, the philosophical poems and the poems with symbols and humor. The following is some respective treatment of the main features of these three categories.

The Pastoral Poems

Pastoral should be understood as an important implication in American national culture.

"The Puritan pursuit of renewal through rebellion against ecclesiastical corruption often invokes the pastoral longing of perfection through simplicity. Thomas Jefferson's praise of the way of agrarianism echoes Greek ideals even if his prophetic fear of the destruction of agrarian life sounded prophetic Hebraic chords" (Faggen, p49).

Technically, pastoral has widely been considered as a cultural mode that

"encompasses many genres including poetry. Its mythic contents have been shown to include the search for a peaceful and beautiful landscape (a *locus amoenus*), the dialogue and singing of shepherds, and the praise of contemplation over work (*otium* over *labor*)" (Faggen, p50).

Frost would like to relate his poetic works to a traditional pastoral ideology, the praise of rural over urban life:

Poetry is more often of the country than the city…Poetry is very, very rural-rustic. It might be taken as a symbol of man, taking its rise from individuality and seclusion-written first for the person that writes and then going out into its social appeal and use. Just so the race lives best to itself—first to itself, storing strength in the more individual life of the country, of the farm-then going to market and socializing in the industrial city. (*Interview with Robert Frost*, p76)

Many poems by Frost gracefully capture a moment in nature. One might find the typical features of his writing through this "Stopping by Woods on a Snowy Evening". [1]

Whose woods these are I think I know.
His house is in the village though;
He will not see me stopping here
To watch his woods fill up with snow.
…
The woods are lovely, dark and deep,
But I have promises to keep
And miles to go before I sleep,
And miles to go before I sleep.

This is considered one of the best poems by Robert Frost. Compared with his other poems, this one is more regular and elegant. The meanings and feelings are quite genuine. The language, refined New England spoken language, is simple yet suitable. Technically the poem is of iambic pentameter, following the rhyme scheme of a a b a, b b c b, c c d e, d d d d. This light and clear rhyme scheme matches the simple pleasant language. With this perfect arrangement of images, rhythms, sounds, and syntax, the poet creates a vivid picture of the landscape.

The ground is white with snow. Everything is frozen. And the forest is silent, the cloud-cover low. But the poet is in high spirits on a night of flying snow-flakes. He enjoys the white sea of tranquillity, the peaceful sounds of the bells on the horse's harness and the easy wind. In Seamus Heaney's terms, Frost would like these "more comfortable imaginings" of the "warm-blooded image of his generally beloved horseman" (1988:63) in the poem.

Frost was very familiar with country life and farm work. That is why his writing about farm life has such poetic vividness and insight. "Mowing" is another good illustration of the pastoral theme. It shares most characteristics of Frost's poetry, namely simple language, deep implication, tidy structure, various rhythms, loose without, condensed within, and expressive wisdom. In fact, Frost is setting up an example who

"demonstrates, memorable poem by memorable poem, that the rhythms of colloquial speech can vitally coexist with normative metrical structure. If metrical writing, as it has been practiced for several millennia, is to survive in the twentieth-first century, poets will have to recover and sustain Frost's love for the dialectic between prosodic rule and individual tonality."
(Steele, p124)

Philosophical Poems

One finds great effectiveness in the way Frost writes his philosophical poems with sometimes a mocking stance. What Frost thinks about and what he prefers or questions can be found in them.

One of the best known philosophical poems by Frost is "The Road Not

Taken". Under the surface of simplicity is a deeper meaning.

> Two roads diverged in a yellow wood,
> And sorry I could not travel both
> And be one traveller, long I stood
> And looked down one as far as I could
> To where it bent in the undergrowth;
> ...
> I shall be telling this with a sigh
> Somewhere ages and ages hence:
> Two roads diverged in a wood, and I—
> I took the one less travelled by,
> And that has made all the difference.

Robert Frost liked taking excursions into the wide. This poem seems about the routine. His casual steps carry him to a fork in the road. Hesitating to go on, he stood there for moments. The road in "The Road Not Taken" is the road in the country as well as the alternatives in people's real life. Analogically, such universal dilemma does exist in actual life: One cannot have two forenoons in the same day. Today, the objects of his observation may have vanished with the changing landscape, but the sense of wonder remains.

The interpretation of the poem is twofold. Literally, the poet feels at odds in his mind about the choice of the roads, because they are both "fair" and "wanted wear". Eventually, he takes the one "less travelled by", a symbol of his choice to be a farmer and poet, rather than some other professions. Had he chosen to be something else he might never have become so famous and loved. Although the setting of the poem is in some woods, the place where choices are made is really anywhere at anytime. The dilemma is also poetic and realistic. There is nothing truly local or folksy in the language Frost uses. His message is worldwide.

The form of the poem is in classic five-line stanzas with the rhyme scheme a b a a b, each being regular in its arrangement of rhymes. Compared with "Mending Wall", this poem has fewer of personal and colloquial rhythms in the lines.

Frost is quite adept in employing humorous elements in his philosophical poetry. In "Fire and Ice", the reader's attention is obviously caught when the poet begins:

> Some say the world will end in fire,
> Some say in ice.

Then the poet compares the strong emotion of desire to fire and hatred to ice. At this, the reader may await something amusing to say afterwards:

> From what I've tasted of desire
> I hold with those who favour fire.
> But if it had to perish twice,
> I think I know enough of hate
> To say that for destruction ice
> Is also great
> And would suffice.

The parallel conclusion may possibly be drawn: while the natural disasters (fire, ice) can destroy the world, the evil feelings of man (desire, hatred) can also ruin men themselves in the same way. The poem surely sheds light in our understanding the risks and opportunities in today's world, where ecological environment is being threatened and man and nature are not getting along in harmony, let alone the relationship of humankind.

Poems with Symbols and Humor

Frost once claims that "Metaphor is the whole of poetry ⋯ Poetry is simply made of metaphor ⋯ Every poem is a new metaphor inside or it is nothing. " (Poirier and Richard, 787) The poet went even farther in claiming that metaphor is the whole of thinking, and that, therefore, to be educated by poetry. He remarks in "Education by Poetry" thus:

"The he teacher must, teach the pupil to think ⋯ We still ask boys in college to think, ⋯ but we seldom tell them it is just putting this and that together, it is saying one thing in terms of another. To tell them is to set their feet on the first rung of a ladder the top of which reaches to the sky ⋯ The metaphor whose manage we are best taught in poetry—that is all there is of thinking. It may not seem for the mind to go, but it is the mind's furthest. The richest accumulation of the ages is the noble metaphors we have rolled up. " (Ibid. 725)

According to Frost, poetic metaphors need to have the power of "radiating". Technically, words, lines, stanzas, metaphors, poems should radiate meanings outward from the page,

"becoming more than their literal selves, but never at the expense of losing their moorings, coming loose from the actual words and images that 'anchor' them, or hold them 'rooted' to the poet's text. " (Oster, p166)

It is both right and proper to say that many unforgettable metaphors and symbols in Frost's poems are well conceived, carefully organized and intelligently used. First reading some of his poems appears clear and simple, but more reflection shows them to be rich in hidden meanings. Frost likes the way of saying one thing in terms of another. One finds in his poem, a certain reticence, a kind of indirectness, a quality characteristic of his New England heritage. He often leaves the reader to search for any implied significance. On an occasion he said: "I prefer the synecdoche in poetry—that figure of speech in which we use a part for the whole" (*Highlights of American Literature*, p35).

Life, as Frost saw it, is full of apparent paradoxes. It is tragic and comic, beautiful and ugly, chaotic and unified.

Quite symbolic is the wall in the poem "Mending Wall". The wall has double meaning. It is the literal wall separating the two farms as well as the unseen obstacle separating people and hindering them from understanding each other.

> Something there is that doesn't love a wall,
> That sends the frozen ground-swell under it,
> And spills the upper boulders in the sun,
> And makes gaps even two can pass abreast.
> The work of hunters is another thing:
> I have come after them and make repair
> Where they have left not one stone on a stone,
> But they would have the rabbit out of hiding,
> To please the yelping dogs. The gaps I mean,
> No one has seen them made or heard them made,
> But at spring mending-time we find them there.
> I let my neighbor know beyond the hills;

And on a day we meet to walk the line

And set the wall between us once again.

We keep the wall between us as we go.

To each the boulders that have fallen to each.

And some are loaves and some so nearly balls

We have to use a spell to make thembalance:

"Stay where you are until our backs are turned!"

We hear our fingers rough with handling them.

Oh, just another kind of outdoor game,

One on a side. It comes to little more:

There where it is we do not need the wall:

He is all pines and I am apple-orchard,

My apple trees will never get across

And eat the cones under the pines, I tell him.

He only says, "Good fences make good neighbours."

This poem depicts the poetic persona at work with his neighbor. They are busy repairing a stone wall that separates their two farms. This causes the poet to question the purpose of walls. But his neighbor likes the walls immensely. When one finishes reading the whole poem, he realizes the walls the poet is telling about are the things that separate people from one another. These things exhibit our relationships with each other in real life. In the poem, the poet does not say dogmatically what is right or wrong. Instead, he shares observation with his fellowmen. He teaches the brotherhood of man in an interesting way. What keeps the poem from being didactic are Frost's special humor, the informality of his lines, and the story-telling style. Following his New England poetic masters, Frost favors either bound prosodic forms or blank verse. The poem is written in blank verse. It has five beats to a line, and the beat comes on every second syllable. Also, the lines do not rhyme. So Frost takes the literary form of blank verse and yet he is so flexible at using it; he makes the poem almost like everyday conversation. The point is, however, that it turns out to be a wise and beautiful conversation.

People can only surmise the number of times "Mending Wall" had been put to use in political situations and critical occasions, the typical one being the protracted controversy over the reinforced concrete wall that made a divide between East and West Germany. The probably most famous line is "Something there is that doesn't love a wall." The slightly altered lines in the poem are probably having more specific focuses and referents, such as "Old-stone savage or new-power-hungry savage," and "the good-fences-make-good-neighbors philosophy in Berlin." Upon his visit to the former USSR, Frost was reading the poem to the local audience and welcomed. Then the *Times* printed a page of photographs of the poet in audience among the Russians. Several pictures—under the title of "'Mending Wall' in Moscow"—carried a single caption:

"Some of the gentlest mockery the Soviet Union has endured came recently from the 88-year-old poet, Robert Frost, a cultural-exchange visitor. Among other things, he read from his poem, 'Mending Wall,' in Moscow: 'Before I built a wall I'd ask to know / What I was walling out. / And to whom I was likely to give offense.' The reference to Berlin seemed clear, but Frost would not interpret."

The poet, though a literary figure, was never ignorant of the international current affairs, and he shared common understanding of American official ideology that the era of the "iron curtain" should be ended. And the wall, the symbol of the political and military divide, should be demolished (See Monteiro, p236).

When reading "Birches", another well-known poem of Frost, people have a very fresh mental picture of young birches, slender and lovely white barked trees in the country. What is being said behind the scene is figuratively important. The tree is the symbol for things fresh with new life. It is suitable to compare the young birches to bright energetic youth. The poem reads:

> When I see birches bend to left and right
> Across the lines of straighter darker trees,
> I like to think some boy's been swinging them.
> But swinging doesn't bend them down to stay
> As ice-storms do. Often you must have seen them
> Loaded with ice a sunny winter morning
> After a rain. They click upon themselves
> As the breeze rises, and turn many-colored
> As the stir cracks and crazes their enamel.
> Soon the sun's warmth makes them shed crystal shells
> Shattering and avalanching on the snow-crust—
> Such heaps of broken glass to sweep away
> You'd think the inner dome of heaven had fallen.
> ...

A poem like "Birches," practically forces us to ask numerous questions: what is this poem trying to convey? Rather than telling about the main content of the poem or reference of birches, the poet is asking us to make connections and to reflect on challenges of life. The birches are obviously presenting us with a typical landscape of his hometown New England, the realistic image we get should not confined to "a static tableau of trees, but a powerful, dynamic drama of *climbing* birches, of a boy testing the limits of his daring, keeping his balance in a precarious position of his own choosing" (Oster, p160). As a country boy, he is being kept from accessing to the playing ground or convenient facilities of physical training in town or city. It is even hard for the lonely boy to find playing mates for a game. The trees and the physical actions and effective metaphors are vividly conceived and expressed here.

Frost's popularity and reputation were enhanced with the election of fellow New Englander John Kennedy to the American presidency in 1960. Kennedy, as we know, was a Pulitzer Prize winner himself, and had an appreciation of good writing. During his campaign for election he frequently quoted Frost in his speeches, particularly to college audiences. He would often end a speech with reference to his hectic schedule and his need to move on with Frost's lines, "But I have other promises to keep. And miles to go before I sleep. And miles go before I sleep."

Frost's performance was impressive at the Presidential inaugural ceremony on January 19, 1961. The glaring winter sunlight so annoyed and distracted the seemingly disorganized, somewhat disheveled old man that he gave up his attempt to read the poem he had composed for this most public of readings before his greatest audience ever. He set his new poem aside and went on to recite "The Gift Outright" from memory,

> The land was ours before we were the land's.
> She was our land more than a hundred years
> Before we were her people.

According to Derek Walcott, Frost had actually composed one dedication poem for the occasion. As it was in hot sun and the wind was blowing, he had to recite "one that many had heard and perhaps learned by heart" (1988:93). The response from President and audience was warm. Kennedy later had this to say in the speech about poet whom he so much admired:

> "I think, politicians and poets share at least one thing, that is, their greatness depends upon the courage with which they face the challenges of

life. There are many kinds of courage. Perhaps the rarest courage of all, for the skill to pursue it is given to very few men, is the courage to wage a silent battle to illuminate the nature of man and the world in which he lives. This is Robert Frost's courage".

NOTES

[1] This poem and other illustrated poems in this article are from *The Poems of Robert Frost*, New York: Random House, 1946.

REFERENCES

Bacon, Helen. "Frost and the Ancient Muses", *The Cambridge Companion to Robert Frost*, CUP. 2004.

Booz, Elisabeth B. *A Brief Introduction to Modern American Literature*, (ed.) Shanghai: Foreign Language Education Press, 1982.

Bryfonski, Dedria. *Contemporary Literary Criticism* (ed.), Michigan: Gale Research Company, 1979.

Brodsky, Joseph. "On Grief and Reason", *Homage to Robert Frost*, London: Faber and Faber Limited, 1988.

Buell, Lawrence. "Frost as a New England Poet", *The Cambridge Companion to Robert Frost*, CUP. 2004.

Collected Poems, Prose, and Plays, ed. Richard Poirier and Mark Richardson, New York: Library of America, 1995.

Faggen, Robert. "Frost and the Question of Pastoral", *The Cambridge Companion to Robert Frost*, CUP. 2004.

Heaney, Seamus. "Above the Brim", *Homage to Robert Frost*, London: Faber and Faber Limited, 1988.

Highlights of American Literature. Ed. English Teaching Division, (ed.), Washington: Information Center Service, 1970.

Interview with Robert Frost, ed. Edward Connery Lathem, New York: Holt, Rinehart and Winston, 1966.

Monteiro, George. "Frost's Politics and the Cold War", *The Cambridge Companion to Robert Frost*, CUP. 2004.

Oster, Judith. "Frost's Poetry of Metaphor" , *The Cambridge Companion to Robert Frost*, CUP. 2004.

Shipley, Joseph T. *A Dictionary of World Literary Terms*, (ed.) Revised Edition, Boston: George Allen and Union, 1979.

Steele, Timothy. "Across Spaces of the Footed Line: the Meter and Versification of Robert Frost", *The Cambridge Companion to Robert Frost*, CUP. 2004.

"Studio One: Something Like a Star". Voice of America. Jan. 29, 1983.

Walcott, Derek. "The Road Taken", *Homage to Robert Frost*, London: Faber and Faber Limited, 1988.

(This is the largely revised version. The original article was published in *Journal of Foreign Languages*, Shanghai International Studies University, No. 4, August 1992.)

Towards an Understanding of Said's
Re-constructed Orientalism

At least two important works written by Edward Said, *Orientalism*: *Western Conception of the Orient* (1978) and Orientalism Reconsidered (1980), one extremely lengthy and the other considerably brief, are considered as key texts in cultural and literary studies. Since their publication, the influence has been enormous and marked a turning point.

Evidently, *Orientalism*, as its complete title indicates, is not about oriental cultures in its usual sense, but about the Western representation of cultures in the "Near East", which is particularly associated with a scholarly discipline entitled Orientalism. Supported by abundant references and illustrations, Said demonstrated how this discipline was created alongside the European penetration into the "Near East" and how it was nurtured and "proved" by various other disciplines such as history, anthropology, philosophy, literature, etc. Referring to the invisible divide of Occident and Orient, Said has this to say,

"As a department of thought and expertise Orientalism of course refers to several overlapping domains: firstly, the changing historical and cultural relationship between Europe and Asia, a relationship with a 4000 year old history; secondly, the scientific discipline in the West according to which beginning in the early nineteenth century one specialized in the study of various Oriental cultures and traditions; and, thirdly, the ideological suppositions, images and fantasies about a currently important and politically urgent region of the world called the Orient. The relatively common denominator between these three aspects of Orientalism is the line separating Occident from Orient and this, I have argued, is less a fact of nature than it is a fact of human production, which I have called imaginative geography . " (1980 : 14)

It is considered that the division is not static or unchanging between Orient and Occident. Though in a sense the divide is not quite realistic, it is certainly not fictional. According to Said, the Orient and the Occident are not imaginary and they are actually produced by human beings, and as such must be studied as organic social components, and not the divine or natural, world. As social world is associated with specialized persons and special subject matters being studied, it is significant to " include them both in any consideration of Orientalism for, obviously enough, there could be no Orientalism without, on the one hand, the Orientalists, and on the other, the Orientals. " (14)

A few introductory remarks about Edward W. Said should be necessary before we approach his representative works. Edward Said was born in 1935 in Palestine with Arabic heritage. He received almost all his higher education in the United States. He received his BA from Princeton in 1957 and subsequent MA in 1960 and Ph. D. in 1964 from Harvard, both in English. He has lectured at Harvard, Johns Hopkins and Yale. From 1989 to 1992 he held the Old Dominton Foundation Professorship in the Humanities at Columbia University where he chairs the doctorial program in Comparative Literature. He is also editor of *Arab Studies Quarterly*. Said is most widely known for his tireless representations on behalf of the cause of the Palestinian people. His writings span the areas of literary criticism, politics and music. Because of his Arabic family background, a childhood spent in Palestine and Egypt and his subsequent emigration to the USA he generally restricts his focus to an examination of American, English and French imperialism and literature of the cultures of the Near East and Palestine.

According to Said, "Orientalism" can be interpreted in a number of ways. An orientalist can be anyone who makes systematic study of or teaches the Orient; Orientalism may be an ideology based on ontological and epistemological distinction made between the East and the West. Many literary figures, philosophers, cultural theorists have accepted this distinction as the standard for their literary creations and social and political descriptions; Orientalism can be discussed and analyzed as an instrumental system for treating the Orient in various ways, namely, "making statements about it, authorising views of it, describing it, teaching it and above all, ruling over it" (1978:43).

Orientalism sets out to treat the reconstruction of European and Euro-American discourse about civilization, cultures and peoples in some eastern countries, by redefining such "Oriental" studies against the background of Western imperialism. Therefore, Western studies of the East can only be understood when examined as a discourse of power, the theory advanced by Michel Foucault. The European and Anglo-American discourse of Orientalism, Said maintains, enables

> "the enormous systematic discipline by which European culture was able to manage—and even produce—the Orient politically, sociologically, militarily, ideologically, scientifically, and imaginatively during the post-Enlightenment period".

The primary argument remains focused on the power relationships of such discourses relative to essentially political agenda. No Western discourse, literary or political, about a nation, culture and people can be on the passive end within the context of imperialism and colonization because all participants maintain a cultural sovereignty. As remarked by Mao Zedong, wherever there is oppression there is resistance. For Said, "the history of Orientalism has both an internal consistency and a highly articulated set of relationships to the dominant culture surrounding it". Literary and historical texts are constructed within these political contexts, creating a discourse about the East as the cultural " other ". Commenting on Oriental history, Said thinks that Oriental history for Hegel, for Marx, later for Burkhardt, Nietzsche, Spengler, and other philosophers of history, was useful in portraying a region of great age and what had to be left behind. Literary historians have further noted in all sorts of aesthetic writings and plastic portrayals that a trajectory of " Westering", found for example in Keats and Holderlin, customarily saw the Orient as ceding its historical preeminence and importance to the world spirit moving westwards away from Asia and towards Europe (1980:17).

Being a Palestinian of Western educational and professional background, Said uses the discourse analysis to deal with colonialism—an experimental approach. It examines how the formal study of the "Orient", in combination with key literary texts, firmly formulated certain viewpoints and ideologies which in turn contributed to the exercises of colonial power, i. e. the " Western style for dominating, restructuring, and having authority over the ' Orient ' ". (1985: p3). In discussing about the hegemonic canonization of Western literature, particular about literary texts by Shakespeare, Said remarks,

> "Each age, for instance, re-interprets Shakespeare, not because Shakespeare changes, but because, despite the existence of numerous and reliable editions of Shakespeare, there is no such fixed and non-trivial object as Shakespeare independent of his editors, the actors who played his roles, the translators who put him in other languages, the hundreds of millions of readers who have read him or watched performances of his plays since the

late sixteenth century. On the other hand, it is too much to say that Shakespeare has no independent existence at all, and that he is completely reconstituted every time someone reads, acts, or writes about him. In fact Shakespeare leads an institutional or cultural life that among other things has guaranteed his eminence as a great poet, his authorship of thirty-odd plays, his extraordinary canonical powers in the West. The point I am making here is a rudimentary one: that even so relatively inert an object as a literary text is commonly supposed to gain some of its identity from its historical moment interacting with the attentions, judgments, scholarship and performances of its readers. "(1980:16)

However, due to the unbalance of cultural exchange and tilted flux of occidental culture, the spread and standardization of Western canons have more been experienced in the orient. The canonization and wider recognition of oriental literature in the East have been confronted many "natural" obstacles. As Said realistically admitted, "I discovered, this privilege was rarely allowed the Orient, the Arabs, or Islam. "(Ibid) Surveying *Orientalism*, the major argument in the book is that the discourse of Orientalism can create not only knowledge but also the very reality which they appear to describe—political and cultural power of the discourse. On the one hand, Said suggests that Orientalism consists of a representation, a European representation of the Orient that is far from being accurate or objective about the Orient, while on the other hand he argues that the knowledge of "Orient" could be put in the service of colonial conquest, of occupation and administration. According to Said,

"Orientalism, therefore, is not airy European fantasy about the Orient, but a created body of theory and practice in which, for many generations, there has been a considerable material investment. Continued investment made Orientalism as a system of knowledge about the Orient, an accepted grid for filtering through the Orient into Western consciousness, just as that same investment multiplied—indeed, made truly productive—the statements proliferating out from Orientalism into the general culture. " (p67)

It is proper to say that *Orientalism* initiates a new kind of study of colonialism and postcolonialism. Said maintains that representations of the "Orient" in European literary texts, travelogues and other writings contributed to the creation of a dichotomy between Europe and its "other", a dichotomy that was central to the creation of Euro-centralism as well as to the maintenance and extension of European hegemony over other lands. Said presents that this dichotomy or opposition is crucial to the self-establishment of Europe: if colonized people are irrational, Europeans are rational; if the former are barbaric, sensual, and lazy, Europe is civilized, with its sexual appetites under control and its dominant ethic of hard work; if the Orient is static, Europe can be seen as developing and marching ahead; the Orient has to be feminine so that Europe can be masculine. This dialectic between self and other, derived in part from deconstruction, has been greatly influential in subsequent studies of colonial discourse in other places. Some critics have traced it as informing colonial attitudes towards Africans, Native Americans, and other non-European peoples. Further, this dichotomy can lead to cultural bias in that instead of "seeking truth from fact" (Deng Xiaoping) and "harmony allowing diversity" ("*qiu tong cun yi*" , Confucian legacy), the attitudes towards the Orient were "a political vision of reality whose structure promoted the difference between the familiar" (Europe, the West, "us") and then strange (the Orient, the East, "them") ⋯ The result is usually to polarize the distinction—the Oriental becomes more Oriental, the Westerner more Western—and thus to limit the human contact and cross-cultural exchanges between different cultures, traditions, and societies.

It would serve the reader well to not only keep the great positive influence of *Orientalism* in mind but to take notice of disputes as well as criticism on the book from numerous commentators the world over. Some criticize *Orientalism* for adapting a view of colonial power as all pervasive, for Said claims to have based much of his work in *Orientalism* on the theoretical framework by Foucault and has "found it useful here to employ his notion of a discourse, as described by him in *The Archaeology of Knowledge* and in *Discipline and Punish*, to identify Orientalism." Foucault suggests in his works that power manifests itself not in a downward flow from the top of the social hierarchy to those below but extends itself in a capillary fashion. He also discusses how dominant structures legitimize themselves by allowing a controlled space for dissidence—resistance, in this view, is produced and then inoculated against by those in power. Following Foucault, Said tries to connect individual authors to structures of thought and to the workings of power. He further connects specific discourses and their distributions to the agents and institutions of colonialism themselves. Consequently, he brings together a large number of representative writers, statesmen, political thinkers, philologists and philosophers who contributed to the Orientalism as an institution which then provided the scale by which the "Orient" would be considered and weighted; but equally these consideration and measurement in turn governed these ways of knowing, studying, believing and writing the "Orient". Therefore, knowledge about and power over colonized lands is related together. Several other recurring critiques focus on the "binary opposition model", "exclusive concentration on canonical Western literary texts", "neglect of the self-representation of the colonized", "static model of colonial relations" and so forth. Despite all these sharp criticisms, some scholars nevertheless acknowledged that Said's project inspired and coincided with widespread attempts to write "histories from below" or "recover" the experiences of those who have been somehow "hidden from history". Chinese critics attach much emphasis on *Orientalism* and regard it as a pioneer work with a universal appeal. They feel that some non-white and the "Third World" scholars in residence of the West (Said himself included) have voiced strongly and criticized Western cultural hegemony, thus making a unique contribution to literary studies and cultural criticism. As a path-breaking work in the analysis of colonial discourse and cultural studies, Edward Said's *Orientalism* is capable of challenging fundamentally peoples' habitual ways of viewing the world.

Therefore, the significance of the work is great and far-reaching.

In recognizing Said's central contribution to the large body of knowledge on Orientalism and its critique, we should take into consideration many other impulses and works by other cultural thinkers and theorists. In *Orientalism Reconsidered* Said himself gives generously a list of such multiple writers and writings. Linda Nochlin's experimental studies on the 19th century Orientalist ideology as working within major art historical contexts; the great attempts of Hanna Batatu in his immense re-structuring of the terrain of the modern Arab state's political behavior; Raymond Williams's talented and systematic treatment of such essential concepts as structures of feeling, communities of knowledge, dominant, residual and emergent cultures, subculture and regional culture; Talal Asad's account of anthropological analysis about the works of mayor theorists, as well as his own contributions in the field; Eric Hobsbawm's reformulation of "the invention of tradition" and other related practices studied by other historians as an important reference system both of the historian's craft and of the invention of new emergent nations; the work produced in re-examination of Japanese, Indian and Chinese culture by the group around Ranajit Guha (Subaltern Studies), the representatives of which being Masao Miyoshi, Eqbal Ahmad, Tariq Ali, Romila Thapar, Gayatri Spivak, and younger scholars like Homi Bhabha and Partha Mitter; the freshly imaginative reconsideration by Arab literary critics—the Fusoul and Mawakif group, Elias Khouri, Kamal Abu Deeb, Mohammad Bannis, and others. Their academic purpose is to redefine and invigorate the reified classical structures of Arabic. Literary efforts, and as a parallel to those above, some creative works of Juan Goytisolo and Salman Rushdie whose fictions and criticisms are expressively written against the cultural stereotypes and representations commanding the field. Further, They should also be included the pioneering efforts of the Bulletin of Concerned Asian Scholars, such as American Sinologist (Benjamin Schwartz) and Ideologist (Ainslee Embree) who have reflected seriously upon what the critique of Orientalism means for their fields; still further, there is the critical project carried out by Noam Chomsky in political and historical fields, an example of independent radicalism and uncompromising severity; or in literary theory, the powerful theoretical articulations of a social, in the widest and deepest sense, model for narrative put forward by Fredric Jameson, Richard Ohmann's revolutionary definitions of canon privilege and institution in his recent work; Richard Poirier's revisionary Emersonian perspectives formulated in the critique of contemporary technological and imaginative, as well as cultural ideologies; and so forth (1980: 24-25). The above-mentioned is significantly regarded as nothing less than innovative types of knowledge, new directions of humanistic ideology, new patterns of theory. Along with Said, they have provided new horizons for critical understanding of world society and human culture.

Practically, in doing the critique of Orientalism, the practitioner should be prepared to cross boundaries of knowledge, for the simple fact that Orietalism and its critique involve necessary acquaintance of "a plurality of terrains, multiple experiences and different constituencies" (1980: 25) in the East and West. A strong sense of history and dialectical materialism remain functional for a sound interpretation of cross-disciplinary endeavors by Oriental and Occidental scholars and critics. Keen interventionism and commitment is required in order that the dismantling of dominant systems could be possible. Besides, some strategic methods such as mutual siege, war of maneuver and war of position deem to be usefully reflective in locating a study context and engaging criticism. The scholarship of Orientalism as well as its critique, in a long run, will envisage a complicated landscape and require prolonged dedication by practitioners in the lands of their creation and development.

Technically, *Orientalism* falls into two halves: the first part is concerned with the scope of the thought and action covered by the word Orientalism through European concrete experiences of and with Near Orient, Islam, and Arabs. The invention of the Orient by Europe, and its construction as a representation are in the foreground; the second is about the time when this representation and academic knowledge that was manipulated around it, became an instrument in the service of colonial power. Throughout the book, Said makes a series of judgment, according to which each writer is identified in the process of intellectual hierarchy with the West above the East.

Said's style in both *Orientalism* and "Orientalism Reconsidered" is elaborate and distinctive. The book comes off as meticulously researched masterpiece that makes a fruitful, thought-provoking reading experience. For those involving themselves in cultural studies and comparative literature and related subject matters, *Orientalism* has enormous resources and inspiration.

NOTE

Said's quotations in this essay are taken from his *Orientalism: Western Conception of the Orient* (1978) and "Orientalism Reconsidered" (1980), by Routledge.

REFERENCES

Bhabha, Homi K. (ed.) *Nation and Narration*, Routledge,1990.

Loomba, Ania. *Colonialism / Postcolonialism*, Routledge,1998.

"Orientalism and After—An Interview with Edward Said" (Interviewed by Anne Beezer and Peter Osborne), *Radical Philosophy*, London, Spring 1993.

Qian, Zhongwen and Cao, Shunqing (ed.), *Chinese—Foreign Culture & Literary Theories*, Vol. 2, Sichuan University Press,1996.

Lu, Jiande. "Edward Said's Orientalism and Postcolonialism", *Comments on International Cultural Theories*, Beijing: China Social Sciences Press,1990.

Wang, Ning and Xue, Xiaoyuan. (ed.) *Globalization and Postcolonial Criticism*, Beijing: Central Compilation & Translation Press,1998.

Studying Ted Hughes's
Poems: An Appreciative Survey

It is widely recognized that Ted Hughes is an original, skilful and inventive poet of modern times. His world-view has immense cultural ramifications. The literary creation of his is an outcome of his intellectual orientation having no faith and hope in the heritage of Enlightenment. His poetry is an sharp criticism of the dominant culture of his times. His poetry is remarkable for its radical interpretation of the modern context of mankind. In fact, the radicalism of Ted Hughes appears to fall in the line of resistance that in literature and contemporary thought that begins with the character of active combat and struggle against the dominant culture and culminates with a mystic and spiritual withdrawal into the realm of subjectivity.

Ted Hughes as witnessed in the discussion of his poems, generally projects his own set of subjective responses and perceptions as the objective truths of human existence in the contemporary Western world. His world-view is characterized by an unflinching adherence to a thematic territory and intellectual orientation which in the course of his poetic growth makes innovative expansions. His poetry is an attempt to identify the real character and forms subjugation that the hegemonic culture of modernity and Enlightenment humanism threatens the individual with. Unfettered by the possible limitations of his ideological orientation, Ted Hughes contends that the dominant cultural discourse that valorizes rationalists, and Enlightenment heritage actually inhere a gross suppression of the true character of the socio-historical conditions. His poetry is highly liberating as it constantly exhorts the reader to re-examine the role and place of the Unconscious and Nature in contemporary Western life. His poetry has a genuine urge to foreground the images, symbols and mythical connections that may inspire individuals and communities to resist the truly oppressive character of the hegemonic culture of Western world. The unconventionality of his world mainly lies in its allegiance to an ecological vision. His poetic sensibility is so singular in its sources of inspiration that it fails to find any positive substance in the progressive potential of mankind in general and the Western culture in particular. From the beginning of his literary creation, Ted Hughes transforms poetry into an act of redeeming mankind by providing an alternative mode of existence outside the established patterns of contemporary life.

The stylistic forms in Ted Hughes' poetry are inter-related with the subtle variations that characterize his projection of the contemporary human situation. His ideological antagonism towards modernity and the heritage of Enlightenment is evident in some of his early poem collections. The intensity of his quarrel with the fundamental character of the intellectual-orientations and life-forms that have evolved due to the predominance of the Enlightenment heritage, makes him look closer to the trends in thought and literature generally associated with postmodernism. But his constant search for a "closure" through adherence to an alternative existence in the form of primitivism, the constant presence of a strong subjectivity in his works, an unfailing awareness of a real and oppressive world to which his poetry responds and his serious treatment of the cultural crisis in late twentieth century Western world, bespeak of his distance from the postmodern sensibility. Despite the overtly repetitive continuity at the ideological, the poetic journey of Ted Hughes is basically characterized by a remarkable enlargement of his general thematic territory. His firm conviction that the present cultural crisis in the Western world is caused by the hegemonic instrumental rationality and humanism is powerfully expressed in his first three collections, *The Hawk in the Rain* (1957), *Lupercal* (1960) and *Wodwo* (1967).

Mainly establishing an oppositional relationship with the dominant forms of feeling and thought in a highly urbanized and industrialized society, the poems in these collections exhibit an underlying tendency to subvert the rationalistic conditioning of the modern man. Ted Hughes's obsessive recourse to animal imagery is central to his critique of rationalist humanism in his early poetry. At this stage, it is the most reliable tool for discrediting and disapproving the rationalistic tendencies of the civilized modern man. His celebration of the instinctual mode of existence as represented by the animals always works as a point of contrast to the condition and behavior of the modern man. The critique of rationality and humanism is expressed either through the over-conscious persona's response in the given dramatic situations or through the mention of human attributes or artifacts that are always referred to with an overt or implicit tone of satire and derision. Depicting the animals vastly superior to the persona living a de-energized existence, through highlighting the victimization of animal caused by human beings, the poems in the first three collections form a coherent ideological framework that inculcates strong distrust in the fundamental character of rationalist humanism. But this critique of rationalist humanism is mainly implied in the subtle and complex variations of animal imagery. The poetry of this phase is quite rich in its innovative expansion of the scope of Nature poetry in English language. The poetic imagination decodes its deeply felt receptions through a use of irony, satire, selective fantasy. There are poems like "The Horses", "A Dream of Horses", "Wind", "Bull Moses" and "The Jaguar" that implicitly expose the inadequacies of rationality and humanism. Mainly dwelling upon a structural dichotomy between the civilized and natural mode of existence, these poems express a genuine concern over the increasing gap between the rational and the irrational and the human and the non-human in an urban and industrialized society. These poems transport the reader into a poetic reality where romantic celebration of the undaunted mode of existence of the animal world makes us familiar with an "other" within and outside of persona. These poems make an implicit appeal to the modern sensibility to experience and respect a real or imaginary affiliation of the symbolic world of animals and Nature. Without attacking the persona directly in some of these poems the critique of rationalist humanism is achieved with a balanced tone.

However, it is noted that the world-view of Ted Hughes has its own internal logic that corresponds to an external reality which is oppressive, dehumanizing and grossly unimaginative towards the "other". It adds ambivalence to the available symbolism of animal imagery. Anti-humanist streak is given a consolidation and retaliation and violence are imagined as inevitable reactions from the "other" or non-human world. That is why, the dichotomy between the civilized modem man and the assertive animals gains alarming connotations. The poet relegates the whole civilized society to an insignificant level with satire and ironic fantasy. "Thrushes", "Hawk Roosting" have aggressive overtones. The poet's approval of the predatory nature of these animals emerges as a precondition to an authentic state of existence. At one level such poems subvert the established order by providing an alternative outside. But the cultural implications of this symbolic recourse to an alternative are totally inimical to evolved consciousness of the modem man.

With the publication of *Crow* (1970) Ted Hughes initiates a new phase in the strategy of subverting the dominant value system of modernity and the heritage of Enlightenment. Here the poems are governed by a poetic consciousness and ideological orientation where the quarrel with the optimistic and affirmative potential of the modem world has taken a hostile and reactionary turn. Treating the complex issues of progress and modernity with a relentless intellectual aggression, Ted Hughes in this collection of poems intends to persuade the reader to negate these ideals and values. But this programmatic dislocation of the positives does not make him a postmodernist. The mood of attack and faith in an alternative set of values is essentially not consistent with the mood of cheerful and

167

relaxed skepticism which is usually present in most versions of post-modern sensibility. The ideological antagonism towards science, instrumental rationality and humanism which characterized Ted Hughes's world-view in the first three collections takes a new form in the disturbing reality of *Crow*. The placing of "Two Legends" and "Lineage" at the beginning of the collection is highly strategic; both these poems set the uneasy tone of the whole collection. Here the emphasis on "blackness" is not merely rhetorical. It heightens a sense of irremediable crisis in the collections. It is implied in the dark imagery of *Crow* poems that these primitive energies cannot be erased or suppressed since they form an integral part of the whole creation. It is quite significant that in both these poems "light" which in Ted Hughes' symbolism represents the Enlightenment-oriented achievements and commitments of the present day Western culture is totally absent. Throughout *Crow* poems, it is part of the poet's strategy not to keep the crow a static or consistent character. It is deployed in remarkably different ways in varied contexts. There are a number of poems in which the crow is endowed with sharp intelligence and other human traits. It parodies human situations of the modern world. Unlike his early collections where rationality and humanism were unsettled through a dichotomy of the animal and human world, in the poems of *Crow* Ted Hughes's imagination digs deep into the cultural distortions of modern West. Through irony and satire, Ted Hughes in these poems disapproves the dominant attitudes of the modern world. The tone and intensity of subversion varies from poem to poem ranging from contemptuously playful to devastatingly hard-hitting. "The Black Beast" and "Crow Improvises" are direct assaults on rationalist humanism. His quarrel is not merely with the theoretical constructs of modernity and Enlightenment. All those forms of behavior and thinking that emanate from them are denatured. He finds science and rationality totally inadequate even deconstructive.

Many poems in *Crow* utter a protest against the de-humanizing conditions of Western society, such as "Crow Tries Media", "Crow Goes Hunting", and "A

Disaster". The crow in these poems represents the ordinary human consciousness in a consumerist culture. In these poems, Ted Hughes questions the established views on language, violence and ideology. He exposes the inadequacy of the consumerist culture as a whole in terms of sensibility and attitudes. Unlike the crow of "Crow Tries media" who like the poet is skeptical about the expressive potential of the present-day language, the bird in "Crow Goes Hunting" is an everyday common man fully conditioned by consumerist culture. Ted Hughes's notion of the means of communication or language in these poems is basically different from that of the post-modernist. His contention is not against language as such. Neither does he blur the difference between language and reality. But he is aware of the limitations that contemporary culture has imposed on language and its relationship to consciousness. Here, the actually nostalgic for a language that in some remote past used to crystallize human thoughts and feelings. "A Disaster", "In Laughter" and "Crow's Account of Battle" are the poems where Hughes's inner urge to re-invert a new humanism survives his anger. His longing for a pre-Christian pagan world is central to his subversive designs in a large number of *Crow* poems. But the treatment of the theme is characterized by subtle ideological variations in different groups of poems. His inversion of the established Christian myths assumes wider implications in poems such as "Crow's First Lesson" and "Crow Communes". Through the dramatic encounter the poet appears to contend that crow and the conventional God are basically irreconcilable. The defiant crow refuses to be humanized and thus remains true to his being. What love signifies at this level of crow-consciousness is something totally against the laws of Nature of which the crow, in these poems is a representative. The poet in "Crow's Theology" and "Crow's Playmates" contends that religions created by mankind are actually aberrations from the truly divine which resides in the mystery of the elemental processes of Nature. But there are a number of poems in *Crow* which have prophetic overtones and make emphatic assertions regarding the culmination of the constantly increasing gap between man and Nature. Among such poems are "Crow's last Stand", "Crow and Stone", "Crow Paints Himself Into a Chinese

Mural", "Crow's Elephant Totem Song", "The Smile", and "King of Carrion". Here Ted Hughes appears to make his final judgments about the limitations of humanism. An implicit thread of argument that links these poems is his belief that mankind has no future in a narrowly humanistic vision.

In addition to presenting a critique on modern value-system of humanism, his poetic venture is an outstanding attempt to locate specific forms of "closure" that can redeem the spiritual crisis of modern man. *Gaudete* (1977) and *Cave Birds* (1978) project an alternative mode of existence which is claimed far superior to the present-day mechanistic forms of behavior generated by the instrumental rationality. While making a vehement attack on the dominant moral order of the civilized modern world, both these books may appear to legitimize the evasion of history and culture as an essential condition for achieving a harmonious unity of the subjective and the objective world. Both these collections foreground a tension-free but imaginary state of existence where the meaningfulness and dignity of human life is inseparable from an assertion of a non-rational and unfamiliar mode of consciousness. Whereas *Gaudete* conveys this through mystifying the phallic reality, *Cave Birds* dramatizes Jung's "process of individuation". This state of consciousness as witnessed in the discussion of the poems, subsumes the individual into a larger collectivity which itself does not change with time or place and retains the freshness of a primal community prior to man's social existence in history when man felt himself to be an integral part of Nature.

Ted Hughes is essentially obsessed with sexuality as a theme. But this urge to expose the inherent weakness of modern attitude towards sex has to be seen in the broader context of Hughes's vision of life. The women figures are either dissatisfied wives seeking alternative satisfaction in Lumb-like sexual perverts, or merely innocent sacrificial agents towards the realization of the mysteries of "phallic reality". The projection of the females as a point of contrast to the males deceptively gives the impression that Ted Hughes has some special reverence for them. As contrasted with the sheer psychological activism of the rationalist husbands, the women figures seem to be bold and initially convinced of the rightness of their physical relations with Lumb. Unlike the chaotic and disruptive attitude of the males, they have consented to be active participants ensuring the birth of a "messiah". But all of them are described as bodies and not as thinking human beings. Janet, Betty, Pauline Hagen, Mrs. Westlake and Mrs. Dunworth—all live at a state of consciousness where the "sexual identity" is their collective obsession. The way Ted Hughes describes them limits their humanity and reduces their self-image of "subject hood". The subversion of the female role in the modem world assumes a complex character in *Gaudete* when Lumb-Felicity relationship comes at the centre of the narrative. Having unequivocal and mystic reverence for Lumb's immoral acts and pseudo-spiritual designs, Ted Hughes mystifies the exploitation of the innocent girl. With evolution of their relationship the narrative advances with strategies of fantasy, violence and ritualism.

Felicity, a typical product of a patriarchal system, has a personal and special relationship with Lumb. But she refuses to be just another woman in Lumb's life. With a most conventional kind of conditioned response in a male-dominated society, she suggests elopement and marriage with Lumb, a proposal to which the priest remains inhumanly indifferent. This formal cementing of relationship is projected by the poet as an unwarranted desire causing enormous destruction and disorder. The lake episode which is characterized by fantasy is functional in this particular aspect. Here Lumb is indirectly warned against his increasing intimacy with Felicity, and possible surrender to her ordinary demands. Lumb himself has no regards for such plans or feelings of Felicity. Full of resentment, when she puts before Lumb his photo with Evan's wife and insists on immediate elopement and marriage, Lumb, ignoring all her psychic trauma, tries to "unzip" her. The final episode of the main narrative of *Gaudete* that takes place in the Women Institute is characterized by ritualistic methods. It brings out the real character of the kind of ritualism which is constantly projected as an alternative mode of existence. The ritual begins with an extraordinary evocation of music. The women respond to it with an ecstatic state of mind as received in training from here. The climax of the action occurs when all of them are sexually aroused to have a physical union with Lumb whose choice of the partner will be spontaneous and unplanned. But in this final episode his decision to have sexual relation with Felicity is seen by Maud and other women as an evidence of his growing digression from the code of conduct established by himself as an honest representative of the forces of Nature.

The subsequent violence and deaths are not as important in understanding the poet's attitude towards women as are the patterns of sexual and ritualistic imagery in this episode. The phrases like a "sacramental thing" and "sacred doll" are emblematic of the flaws in the treatment of Felicity in particular and the women characters in general. Reducing the female characters to an abstraction, the poet tries to impress upon the reader that they are basically imbued with an organic wholeness of being and thus, have achieved the fullness of subjectivity. But their passivity, their mindlessness, their lack of independent initiative, are the sub-human status to which they have been pushed in a world dominated by Lumb. The other important dimension of this ritualistic rehearsal in *Gaudete* is to affirm a wholeness of being which Ted Hughes seems to contend. In *Gaudete*, The role and status of woman that the recent feminist movements have defined is totally incomprehensible and unacceptable to Ted Hughes. That is why his treatment of women in *Gaudete* is undoubtedly governed by rigidly patriarchal ideologies.

As an introduction of new changes in the conscious of Ted Hughes, *Cave Birds* (1978) serves as a continuation of the relaxed and exploratory tone of the verse pieces of the epilogue of *Gaudete*. This book experiments with novel methods of subverting the established value-system of the rationalist and secular humanism. Through an internal drama of an individual's transformation, the poems in this sequence defamiliarize the theme of Nature in Ted Hughes's poetry; The Jungian model of the "individuation" process or development of wholeness of being seems to provide the poet with a new mode of responding to the present day cultural crisis in the Western society. The individual to be regenerated through this "alchemical process" is a Socratic ordinary man, a modern sensibility who is confident of the "hegemonic" status of modern values.

Cave Birds is characterized by a distanced poetic consciousness that corrects supplements and sometimes even overturns the meanings projected through the persona. Nature as a regenerative force is represented by varied symbols and the recurring "she" in the sequence. But it is noteworthy that in this sequence Nature is largely non-violent. Instead, it emerges as a force giving to solve the persona coming into contact with it. Poems such as "The Scream", "After the First Fright", "In These Fading Moments", and "The Accused" initiate the ironic tone of the whole of *Cave Birds*. Exposing the spiritual and moral bankruptcy of instrumental rationality and arrogant humanism, these poems express the urgency of a humility and reverence before the forces of Nature. The mind is a "sacred assassin" without any redemptive potential. In most of these poems the falsity of the persona's claims, whether expressed with overt humility or arrogance, generates irony. As the action of the sequence evolves, irony becomes more subtle and penetrating. The regeneration of the persona in *Cave Birds* is dependent upon the benevolence of an ambivalent force in whose mode of working death and birth, violence and peace are simply indivisible and unavoidable, both as means and consequence. It is noteworthy that violence in these poems occurs only as an attribute to a metaphysical and symbolic entity. "The Green Mother" and "The Executioner" implicitly make the reader feel the vastness and virtual inaccessibility of the deity, some aspects of whose being had been partly communicated in the preceding poems. The forces being metaphorically celebrated in both these poems are essentially foreign to the modern consciousness. "The Green Mother" is a powerful and exceptional celebration of the heterogeneity and richness of the life that earth offers to man. The patterns of imagery in the poem and the inherent elements of mysticism and transcendentalism put Nature at a single metaphysical plain of an alternative religiosity.

In the penultimate poems of *Cave Birds* the wholeness of being or the authenticity of existence made impossible by the dominance of the rationalistic thinking and the civilized coverings of the persona's consciousness is achieved. Here the recovery of a mystic reverence for Nature residing in the human as well as the non-human world characterizes the persona's behavior. These are the poems where Ted Hughes appears to have resolved the tension between the subjective and the objective world. Unlike *Gaudete* episodes where ritualism was predominant, in many poems of *Cave Birds*, the "flawless" entry into an intimate and mystical relationship with the internal as well as external Nature is more pointed in its emphasis on the human element. In *Gaudete* and *Cave Birds* Ted Hughes is clearly at odds with Christianity and other conventional religions. But he also makes affirmation to a vibrant religiosity emanating from his faith in Nature. As evident in the discussion of Hughes' poems, the alternative mode of existence based on the revival of a harmonious relationship between man and Nature, will be reinstated either by a fundamental transformation in the state of "consciousness" that the modern sensibility represents or by some fatalistic and violent overturning of the scheme of things as implied in some poems of *Crow*.

REFERENCES

Books by Ted Hughes

The Hawk in the Rain, 1957.

Lupercal, 1960.

Wodwo, 1967.

Crow, 1970.

Gaudete, 1977.

Cave Birds, 1978.

Others

Bell, Charlie. *Ted Hughes*, London: Hodder and Stoughton, 2002.

Feinstein, Elaine. *Ted Hughes: the Life of a Poet*, New York: W. W. Norton, 2004.

Hadley, Edward. *The Elegies of Ted Hughes*, Palgrave Macmillan, 2010.

Roberts, Neil. *Ted Hughes: a Literary Life*, London: Palgrave Macmillan, 2006.

Sagar, Keith. *The Art of Ted Hughes*, Cambridge: CUP, 1978.

An Interview with Professor
Shaun Richards on Irish Drama

About Shaun Richards: Shaun Richards is Professor of Irish Studies and one of leading scholars of Irish drama in the UK. He is a member of the editorial board of *Irish Studies Review* and a founding member of British Association for Irish Studies and Chair of the Strategy Sub-committee of the Association. He is the European representative on the Council of the International Association for the Study of Irish Literature. He has supervised Ph. D students in Irish drama in the UK and has been an examiner in Irish literature from BA to Ph. D candidates in universities of the UK and Ireland. He has published dozens of essays on Irish theatre and Irish cultural studies in a range of journals including *Modern Drama*, *Theatre Research International*, *Irish Review*, *Irish Studies Review*, *Literature and History*, *Irish University Review*, *Canadian Journal of Irish Studies*, *History Workshop Journal and Etudes Irelandaises* (a French Journal). He has given plenary speeches at international conferences on Irish studies held in France, Germany, Portugal, Sweden, Holland, Czech Republic, Hungary, in addition to the UK and Ireland. His most recent works include the latest volume in the well-established *Cambridge Companion* series, *The Cambridge Companion to Twentieth-Century Irish Drama*, published by Cambridge University Press (2004).

I was pleased to be allowed to have a recorded talk with Professor Shaun Richards on October 12, 2004, which focuses on his latest edited book *The Cambridge Companion to Twentieth-Century Irish Drama*, theatrical criticism, current trends in Irish literature research and some related topics on Irish Studies in Britain and elsewhere.

Zhang: Professor Richards, please accept my congratulations for your new book *The Cambridge Companion to the Twentieth Century Irish Drama*, published by Cambridge University Press in 2004. In view of the fact that there had been a few Cambridge companions to such individual classical and well-established writers and literary critics as Swift, Oscar Wilde, Bernard Shaw, Beckett, your work is regarded as one of comprehensive guides of Irish drama in the twentieth century. It is true that the writings of Irish drama have been among the most provocative and original in the colonial and post-colonial literary studies. Could you comment on the companions on Irish literature previously published and on your edited volume specifically?

Richards: The study of Irish Literature is worldwide. Not only in the English-speaking countries of the Irish diaspora such as Australia, the USA and Canada—and, of course, the UK—but also in Europe, Japan, even Brazil. In some countries there might be only one university which has a special interest in Irish Studies while in the USA there are hundreds of universities which have specialist Irish courses. Given this wide-range of interest the aim of the companion series as a whole is to provide critical companions which, while being the "text of choice" for undergraduates studying various authors and periods would also provide provocative material for postgraduates and lecturers. However the decision about the content is made by the editor, he or she invites others to participate and broadly dictates the content and direction of the collection. So when a writer is Irish, as in the ones you mention, it's not necessarily the case that the "Irish" aspect of their work will feature highly—if at all. This, of course, is because so many Irish writers are and have been taught simply as English-language authors, even as English ones. What I wanted to do in the Companion was to keep the Irish focus to the fore—even with writers such as Wilde, Shaw and Beckett who might not immediately be read in that context. Consequently the Companion should cover all major playwrights and issues which students and lecturers of Irish drama should need for their studies.

Z: The broad theme of Irish theatre as a cross-disciplinary or interdisciplinary subject is always rooted in Irish historical and present realities. Constant debate on Irish theatre mainly focuses on colonisation, nationhood and cultural policy and institution. As one of leading specialists in Irish drama and Irish literary studies, how do you perceive the role Irish art plays in the longstanding relationship between England and Ireland?

R: This is difficult because it is so dependent on specific historical and political circumstances. If we go back to Shakespeare's *Henry V* we find the character of McMorris—who is Irish-in the English army along with Welsh and Scots soldiers: this, of course, confirms their nations' incorporation within the English state. They all speak English but with accents which are supposed to be comical and so of lower status. And later, in the 18th century, in Sherridan's *The Rivals*, we have an Irish character, Sir Lucius O'Trigger, who again is a "comic". In the nineteenth-century, as has been famously examined by L. P Curtis Jr. in his book *Apes and Angels* (1968), Irish men were imaged as simian—and so lower on the Darwinian scale of evolution than the English. If the Irish were presented positively, as they were in nineteenth-century work such as Matthew Arnold's *On the Study of Celtic Literature*, then it was as a poetic, rather than practical people. For Arnold, as for the French writer Ernest Renan, the Irish were "essentially feminine" rather than masculine which, in the nineteenth-century scheme of things, again located them as subservient to the male, i. e. England. The theoretical means to examine this were—certainly for me—provided by Edward Said's *Orientalism* (1978). Especially his central thesis that what is presented in a culture is not "truths" but "representations". And having political power gives you the power to represent those over whom you have power—this is a characteristic of the role of Ireland as far as much "English" literature is concerned. Said hasn't written that much on Ireland but his influence has been crucial in focusing attention on the political implications of writing, and so representing, the "Other". And so it's within this framework that we can see that those with whom we are now most familiar as Irish writers, particularly Yeats and Synge, were dedicated to changing these centuries-long misrepresentations, what they termed "buffoonery". And this artistic movement focused around the Abbey theatre was also linked to the activities in the 19th and 20th century Ireland for political independence. So again there is a political dimension. Now, of course, both Ireland (the Republic) and the UK are part of the EU, there is less political antagonism—although the North is still an issue— and so the role of art in the relationship changes. Seamus Heaney is published by Faber (London), Irish playwrights prefer their work to be premiered in London, Irish critics teach in UK universities and so forth.

Z: Indeed, issues of the Abby Theatre in Dublin are significant in this regard. It is apparent that regardless of individual state or specific race, theatre is universally linked with the destiny of a nation. The establishment of the Abbey Theatre may possibly be seen as something echoing the movement of Irish political independence from Britain in the early twentieth century, which has almost identical implications brought by the Chinese drama and theatre in China in the Anti-Japanese War period. It seems that theatrical efforts in Ireland and China are similar in the critical times of history. My next question is: To what extent, does the Abbey Theatre represent the wishes and desires of Irish people from the time of its establishment and in its subsequent years? How do you evaluate and critique its evolutionary stages against the backcloth of commercialisation and consumer culture in modern periods?

R: After what we might call its early "revolutionary" period the Abbey literally became the national theatre of Ireland—it received government subsidy in 1925, only three years after the founding of the Irish Free State. To a large extent it became a very conservative theatre—for a very conservative state—and that lasted through very much into the 1980s. Some would still argue that it is still "conservative", perhaps not only politically but also artistically in that it wants to "play safe" and stage plays which will attract tourists and, moreover, stage them in old, rather than innovative and new styles. All theatre is an industry, part of the culture industry, and Irish theatre is no exception to that—and the current Abbey has experienced particular problems because of the costs of production and has had to cancel some show—and this in its centenary year.

Z: It is widely claimed that Ireland is a "country of art" and Dublin one of most significant capitals of theatre in Europe. Or, adequately in your words, "Ireland had already enjoyed theatre as an art form and entertainment for several centuries". It would be of help to both ordinary audience and researchers of Irish Studies in China if you could talk specifically and differentially about some of the well-known theatre companies in Ireland, such as, The Abbey, the Druid and the Gate. You know, the Gate company visited Beijing in May 2004 and successfully performed Beckett's "Waiting For Godot", which is labelled as "Theatre of the Absurd".

R: The Abbey was very concerned to present an "authentic" picture of Ireland and its dominant style was realist; the dominant set that of the peasant cottage of the west of Ireland; all this at a time when realism was being contested in Europe by symbolism and expressionism. And this essentially conservative style and subject dominated the Abbey even when the moment of political revolution—of which "representation" was such a crucial part—was over. So the Gate theatre was established in 1928 specifically to engage directly with European experimentation applied to Irish plays and to European plays themselves. Druid is a far more recent development and dates from the 1970s when students at the University in Galway established the theatre. It's become best known for its commitment to breathing new life into "established" playwright like Synge, reviving forgotten playwrights like M. J. Molloy, or staging new playwrights like Tom Murphy and, most recently Martin McDonagh. But what all of these playwrights have is a west of Ireland setting in their work.

Z: In a sense, the Abbey Theatre is central in discussing the revolution and evolution of Irish drama. It is apparent that questions on the issue of the Abbey Theatre are always related to the political atmosphere and ideology before and after its construction on one hand, and to the well-known Irish figures on the other, such as W. B. Yeats, Lady Augusta Gregory and the Irish Marxist James Connolly. How do you consider political and theatrical orientations in the early twentieth century's Ireland and the Abbey Theatre?

R: The main issue around the Abbey was that it was established and run by people of an Anglo-Irish background; in other words they were Protestant and came from English speaking background. That is, they were in Ireland because of the conquest of the country by England. The other group in the country were Irish-Irish, that is ,they were Catholic and from a Gaelic speaking background. While both groups might have wanted independence for Ireland, the kind of independence they envisaged differed, as did their ideas as to who should run that independent country. So most of the discussions and debates are around that essential difference. When the Abbey staged something which it was felt misrepresented Ireland, portraying the country in what was felt to be a bad light then it was denounced by the Irish-Irish as not being an Irish national theatre at all; merely a continuation of the influence and dominance of England. As I've noted above, a characteristic image of the Irish in nineteenth-century England was of them as ape-like. The Irish counter to this was to argue for Irish perfection and so any staging of the Irish as less than angelic was regarded as perpetuating English insults. The plays of J. M. Synge are a good example of this tension. In his 1903 play, *Shadow of the Glen*, the wife leaves her old husband and goes away with the tramp. This was denounced as a slur on Irish women, and hence on Ireland. In his *The Playboy of the Western World* in 1907 the plot centres around a village's glorification of a man who has supposedly (but not actually) killed his own father. This seemed to be perpetuating English images of the Irish as brutish and the audience actually rioted in protest; the disturbances lasted several nights. What the audiences saw in this was that while the Abbey was supposedly a "national" theatre it was actually a national insult—something they interpreted as being a consequence of the fact that Synge and the Abbey managers were Anglo-Irish.

Z: It is positive to note that Marxism, as both theoretical approach and analytic instrument, has widely been adopted in literary and cultural research in the West and China. Obviously, however, the trajectory of development or strategic adaptation of Marxism is by a long chalk different in their respective context. In your view, how is Marxism related to Irish theatrical studies and which orientation thereof is most attached to the application of Marxist theory?

R: Because of the social divide within Ireland between the Anglo-Irish and the Irish-Irish, and the role of writers in the period of the Literary Revival to create a radical national consciousness then the Marxist writer who certainly influenced my reading of Irish Literature was Antonio Gramsci, particularly his theories of hegemony and the role of the intellectual. The work of Gramsci on the "subaltern" and the influence of his thinking in this area on the work of the Indian "Subaltern Studies" group has had an impact on a significant contemporary critic, David Lloyd and his work such as *After History* (1999). Indeed much of contemporary critical work by people such as Lloyd, but also Luke Gibbons (*Transformations in Irish Culture*, 1996) has been working around the idea that Ireland's was a "failed revolution"; namely that it gained political freedom but did not seek to make social changes. This current tendency is also trying to get criticism to engage with these issues, to recognise that to focus simply on an undifferentiated "Ireland" to be set against colonial England is to ignore issues of class and inequality. As far as drama is concerned a work which does address the period of the Literary Revival and its theatre in this light is Ben Levitas' *The Theatre of Nation* (2002). And it's because of this concern with social change in much contemporary Irish criticism that the writers of the Frankfurt School—Walter Benjamin, Herbert Marcuse, Ernst Bloch are also very relevant. Declan Kiberd's *Inventing Ireland*, for example, is very influenced by Bloch.

Z: Drama may have to be regarded as both similar and different from other literary writings or literary genres as it involves theatre production, drama and theatre arts. Would you make some comments or suggestions on the methods and approaches for studying drama from an academic position?

R: Theories of studying drama are far less developed in the UK or Ireland than they are in France and I often find that it's to France that I look for theories that help my analyses—the work of Patrice Pavis, or Anne Ubersfeld for example. Basically that's because the approach I take is broadly historical so I want to read the dramatic text "back" into its original moment of production. Questions then become broadly cultural rather than specifically theatrical: after all, it is the most "social" of the arts. More recently I've been looking at contemporary Irish plays in London, particularly at the Royal Court Theatre where many new Irish plays such as those by Conor McPherson and Martin McDonagh have been staged. Here I've been trying to examine the successes of various kinds of Irish plays: are they all popular, or only some of them, and which kind. This has involved looking at newspaper reviews and also finding out the box-office capacity they've played to. In think that within a global context, when Irish plays are translated and performed across the world that we have to engage with that wider context of what these plays mean now, not simply doing endless and repetitive studies of why audiences rioted at the *Playboy* in 1907.

Z: It is true that Irish Studies in China is gathering momentum. The problem, however, may be that there are perceived inadequacies of exchange between China and abroad. Insufficient research condition and information may be accountable for the problem otherwise. In view of this, could you discuss the major directions and trends in Irish Studies in Britain and in the Irish Republic?

R: As far as Britain is concerned, Irish Literature, and Irish studies more broadly—and I include history, literature, sociology, film and cultural studies in this—have become legitimate areas of study in their own right; that is, Irish writers are read in an Irish context and not simply subsumed within "English Literature". That was an important move. And across the area—and this is true of Ireland, and, I think, the USA—the dominant critical approach has been post-colonialism and debates as to its appropriateness as an approach to Ireland. That's still probably the major critical position. However I can now see that changing—or developing—into an interest in globalisation. It's still, I think, to do with issues of power and representation. But perhaps now there's an engagement with the power of trans-national corporations, not simply with nation states: this is what Anne McLintock refers to as "imperialism-without-colonies". A focus, some would say, more on Ireland's present and future rather than Ireland's past.

Z: In China, to talk about Irish studies would be of something trendy. Unfortunately, a reasonably good collection of Irish literary works or a volume of selected works of Irish playwrights is hard to find even in the local British bookstore. Can you kindly provide a short list of such works on Irish literature and recommend some relevant titles on Irish studies?

R: The best general introduction to 20th century Irish society and culture is: Terence Brown, *Ireland: A Social and Cultural History* (1985). Coverage of Irish Literature from the Gaelic society to the 20th century is Seamus Deane, *A Short History of Irish Literature* (1986). A wide survey of modern Irish literature is Declan Kiberd, *Inventing Ireland* (1995). A very good study which focuses on Yeats, Joyce, O'Casey and Synge is G. J. Watson, *Irish Identity and the Literary Revival* (1978). In the wider field of Irish cultural studies Luke Gibbons, *Transformations in Irish Culture* (1996) provides a good sense of the field.

Z: In the UK, you are one of the most devoted scholars of Irish Studies, having had dozens of books and articles published and involving heavily in the working with other international scholars of the first rank. Would you talk briefly about some of your latest research projects and plans?

R: I have a long-standing commitment to complete a book on modern Irish drama, which I must do. Currently I'm returning to a long-standing interest in Tom Murphy for a chapter in a book on Irish and British playwrights to be published by Blackwells. The next publication, I think, will be a study of the Field Day Theatre in a special Irish issue of *Modern Drama*.

Note: The Chinese version of the interview was published in *Contemporary Foreign Literature*, No. 4, 2005.

(Interviewed by Zhang Pinggong)

Literary Theory Keywords

Accent. Accent usually refers to differences of pronunciation—deviations from "the standard"— by which the speaker might be socially and /or culturally categorized (in terms of class, region, ethnicity). These deviations are implicitly seen as "inferior". For many writers—particularly working class, regional and post-colonial writers—accent or dialect is an important strategy in their work, acting to assert an identity different from and resistant to the "standard" by which they feel themselves marginalized, e. g. Tony Harrison, Robert Burns, Derek Walcott, Mo Yan, Roddy Doyle, Irving Welsh.

"Against the grain". Walter Benjamin, in his *Theses on the Philosophy of History*, writes: "There is no document of civilization that is not at the same time a document of barbarism. And just as such a document is not free of barbarism, barbarism taints also the manner in which it was transmitted. A historical materialist therefore dissociates himself from it as far as possible. He regards it as his task to brush history against the grain. " In particular, cultural materialist critics, in reading texts against the grain, seek out the social, ideological "unconscious" of the text—its gaps and silences—thereby resisting the work's naturalization.

Agency. Literally "activeness". In cultural-political terms, the notion of agency usually refers to the subject (or person) acting to determine an event—taking cntrol for themselves. As such, empowerment is a central issue—whether or not that subject is in a position of power and therefore agency.

Alienation. In addition to the general modernist or existential sense of alienation as a feeling of exclusion, unbelonging and loneliness, the term has a quite specific Marxist usage. Here, the concept of alienation refers to worker's relation to the product of his or her labor—that which s/he produces, but does not own and which becomes a commodity. Marx suggests that this relation is "as to an alien object."

Alterity. An absolute Otherness which cannot be incorporated by the (more powerful) Self. Poststructuralism sees binary oppositions as a "violent hierarchy", in which the Self seeks to neutralize the Other by incorporating, assimilating or domesticating them. Alterity is the recognition of a radical, unassimilable difference.

Androgyny. Technically referring to the union of both sexes in one individual, this term is often equated with hermaphrodism. Feminist writers and critics, though, use it to refer to the culturally, rather than biologically, determine characteristics. Androgyny is sometimes celebrated as a liberating vision of wholeness through the blurring or break down of false gender categories. See, for example, Angela Carter's novel *The Passion of New Eve.*

Aporia. From the Greek meaning "unpassable path" or "impasse". Term is particularly associated with deconstruction and the work of Jacques Derrida, and is used to describe moments when meaning cannot be satisfactorily decided—moments of "undecideability".

Arche-writing / Archi-trace. Jacques Derrida uses this term in reference to Sigmund Freud's notion of the "mystic writing pad"—a children's writing pad consisting of a wax slab covered by a double top sheet. Messages would appear when inscribed with a hard stylus, and seem to disappear when the top sheet was detached. However, the writing would always remain imprinted on the underlying wax and for Freud, this was analogous to the unconscious, where memories remain invisibly. For Derrida, no perception or expression is virginal, but is always structured by a pre-existing realm of signification.

Author. Michel Foucault points out that one cannot become "an author" by writing any old thing—a letter, for example. "The Author" is a cultural construction. Equally, as Roland Barthes argues, "the author" is seen to be a special kind of person—the apparently settled, whole, rational self which post-structuralism has sought to undermine. "Author", significantly, is etymologically linked to "authority", "authorize", "authoritarian", etc. .

Base / Superstructure. Think of an elaborate statue on a sturdy base. In Marxist analyses of how societies work, the *base* refers to the economic system and relations within that society—its so-called "mode of production". The *superstructure* of the society, then, is the elaborate statue. This is society's institutions—its education system, church, legal system, political system, arts. Clearly, the base *supports* the superstructure. Indeed, Marxists argue that economic systems and relations determine the society's institutions. Importantly, these institutions then (sometimes unknowingly) function to normalize the prevailing economic system and relations. The superstructure, then, is the realm of *ideology*.

Binary Oppositions. The structuralist name for opposed terms which are structured into a power relation, (or "violent hierarchy", for Derrida) e. g. self/other, masculine/feminine, black/white, civilian/barbarian. The notion derives from the work of Ferdinand de Saussure, who pointed out the relational features of language.

Biological Determinism. The idea that certain characteristics and differences—between sexes, genders, "races", classes—are innate or natural. This is one of the main targets of cultural theory which, broadly speaking, seeks to promote notions of social and ideological determinism.

Bourgeois. The Marxist term for the middle classes whose interest it is to preserve the status quo. The term has therefore come to stand for conventionality *per se.*

Canon. The literary canon is the body of texts conventionally considered to be worthwhile or even "great". But whose judgment counts as to what constitutes "great literature", and whose interests are served by this choice?

Capitalism. An economic system built upon the profit motive. Capitalism depends upon private individuals or companies investing money in order to make profits. In Marxist analysis, these profits are secured by exploiting workers who provide their labor.

Closure. Language, for poststructuralists, functions according to différance—an interplay of the difference and the deferral of meaning. Meaning is never even present, so how can it ever be fixed or closed? It can't, says Derrida.

The Cogito. Shorthand for the 17th century French "rationalist" philosopher Rene Descartes's famous assertion: "I think, therefore I am" (*"cogito ergo sum"*). For Descartes, his thought-processes proved his own existence beyond doubt. Recent critics have shown that, despite his attempts to escape all assumptions and arrive at "pure", indubitable truth, Descartes's philosophy is based upon a dubious notion of identity as whole, rational, coherent and essential.

Commodity. An article which exists primarily for economic exchange.

Commodification. The process by which an object or person becomes a commodity. Capitalist society, which is structured around economic exchange, is seen by many critics to commodify the whole world.

Commodity Fetishism. Fetishism is the unconscious attempt to fill a "lack" by displacing that (usually sexual) desire onto something else—often an object. In Marxist theory, commodity fetishism occurs because the worker is alienated from the product of his/her labor. The worker then confuses the "use value" of an object with the "exchange value" placed upon it in capitalist society (i. e. its economic value). This is knowing the price of everything but the value of nothing. See also the psychoanalytical notion of fetishism.

Connotation / Denotation. If denotation is the dictionary definition of a word—its precise meaning—then connotation is the word's meaning *by association*—those meanings which are conventionally related to it. For example, a red rose connoting "love".

Context. Everything surrounding the text, e. g. the social, cultural, political, historical, artistic, financial, publication factors surrounding the texts production. And equally, the factors surrounding the reception of the text as it is read—your context as reader.

Creole. Hybrid language forms which have developed, usually in colonial contexts. Creoles differ from "pidgin" language forms because they have developed all the major features and functions of a language, and have native speakers. Many Afro-Caribbean Englishes are creoles, carrying traces of other languages of empire Spanish, Portugese, French and Dutch as well as of many native, non-European languages. Creoles are languages palpably in the making, much as the European vernaculars formed after the Roman Empire.

Cultural Capital. According to Pierre Bourdieu, this is what you are acquiring at university: cultural capital is the value which even dog-eat-dog capitalist society attaches to education.

Cultural Materialism. A form of Marxist criticism, most associated with Raymond Williams, and centered around a socialist critique of literature, culture and the institutions which maintain them. Cultural materialists see language and texts as sites of ideological struggle, and emphasize the subversive and revolutionary aspects which can be highlighted by reading texts "against the grain". See also New Historicism.

Deconstruction. Deconstruction refers to the critical approach suggested by the work of "poststructuralist" philosopher Jacques Derrida. Deconstruction can be seen to dismantle the assumptions and presuppositions around notions of identity which circulate in society. By attending closely to language, deconstruction seeks to problematize all notions of knowledge, meaning and identity—showing these to be falsely constructed, and bound up with structures of power and exclusion.

Defamiliarization. The Russian Formalist critics believed that what made literature "literary" was its ability to "defamiliarize" the world—to present it in radically new ways and thereby to disrupt habitual reactions.

Desire. Desire refers to an unconscious driving force. In psychoanalytic theory, the process of socialization is characterized by *lack* of fulfillment in various respects. This lack produces desire.

Diachronic / Synchronic. Terms used by Ferdinand de Saussure in his linguistic study. Diachronic means across time. So, a diachronic study of language is one which concentrates on its historical evolution. A synchronic study, on the other hand, for example, is static rather than evolutionary, and would take a particular moment and concentrate on the structures of language at that moment.

Dialectics. As distinct from "dialect", the term is derived from the Greek term meaning a process of debate or argument which gives rise to a truth— especially when contradictions are exposed in one's opponent. Dialectical philosophies see the things in the world as existing in dynamic relationships and containing internal tensions and contradictions. The dialectical philosophy of Hegel (where a *thesis* is opposed by an *antithesis*, and the result of this clash is a *synthesis*) was built upon by Marx and Engels, who viewed class struggle and capitalism in terms of these dialectical tensions and contradictions.

Dialectical Materialism. A branch of philosophy which prioritizes matter over mind (as distinct from idealism), and which stresses that this material reality is in a constant state of tension, struggle and transformation. Marxists, for example, see history in these terms.

Dialogism. Refers to Russian theorist Mikhail Bakhtin's conception of the fundamentally multiple character of language, meaning and identity. For Bakhtin, meaning is not created within a single, sovereign consciousness, but is always produced in-between. In a conversation, for example, all utterances contain the trace of the other, are generated with the other in mind. Central to the notion of dialogism is the existence of equal, independent otherness—

"another consciousness, with the same rights, and capable of responding on an equal footing, another and equal *I* (*thou*)". As a result of this, the theory has been very influential in a number of fields—post-colonialism, for example, where it is interpreted as a theory of cultural identity.

Diaspora. A term for mass migration, used particularly in post-colonial studies to denote the scattering of peoples away from their homelands under pressures such as colonization or slavery.

Diegesis. Roland Barthes and Gérard Genette use this term to describe description or narration which appears to be judgment-free.

Différance. Jacques Derrida's pun on "difference" and "deferral", which is how language or meaning is seen to function. For Ferdinand de Saussure, meaning is not inherent in any linguistic sign, but is generated as a result of differences between signs. Furthermore, there is no necessary connection between the signifier and the signified. That they *seem* to "meet" is simply a matter of social convention. In fact, the signifier can never fully *represent* the signified, and meaning is never as stable or fixed as we might like to believe. Meaning rests upon a *lack*. There is always the potential for slippage, and this is something which many critics delight in exploiting.

Discourse. Michel Foucault saw a discourse as a system of ideas or "knowledge", inscribed in a specific vocabulary (e. g. psychoanalysis, anthropology, cultural/literary studies). The important thing, for Foucault, was that such discourses were used to legitimate the exercise of power over certain persons by categorizing them as particular "types".

Displacement. Freudian term for the replacement of one psychic figure with a tangentially related image: for example, a dream about seeking to get a novel published by Penguin Books resulting in a dream about Penguins. Jacques Lacan likens metonymy in language and literature to displacement.

Dissemination. Jacques Derrida's term describing the endless play of signifiers in the absence of concrete attachment to signifieds: "the seed of meaning that neither inseminates nor is recovered by the father (the "author"), but is scattered abroad."

Dream Interpretation. For Freud, a dream is like a piece of literature, containing various "literary" devices, e. g. condensation (condensing various meanings into one image), displacement (metonymy, tropes, allusions), regressive transformation (replacing ideas and feelings with images), secondary revision (making everything fit into a story). The dreamer is therefore an "author".

Ecriture Féminine. This term refers to a concept of women's writing, associated with French feminist critics such as Hélène Cixous and Julia Kristeva, and often seen to be indirectly derived from Virginia Woolf. This writing resists the "phallogocentric" characteristics of conventional, "rational" language use and is associated with unconscious drives—with "irrationality", jouissance and the energies of the body. Paradoxically, perhaps, Cixous cites James Joyce as the best exemplar.

Ego. Freud divides the psyche into three parts: the ego, the id and the superego. The ego is the "rational" part of the psyche.

Empiricism / Empirical. Branch of philosophy which sees all knowledge as being based in experience, for example, the experience of the senses, as distinct from theory or logic.

Epistémè. Based on the Greek word for knowledge, this term refers to an epistemological era—the beliefs, assumptions, categorizations which come to dominate a particular period.

Epistemology. The theoretical study of knowledge—what knowledge is; how it might be assessed; what the grounds/assumptions for an idea might be; what claims to truth might be made; whether true knowledge can be achieved.

Essentialism. This term is at the crux of the politics of identity and refers to a particular way of thinking about what it means to have an identity. At its crudest, essentialism is biological determinism and sees identity as a pure, unchanging essence of race or sex or class rather than something which is socially or culturally constructed. A particular "category" of people can therefore be located as "just naturally" better at, say, athletics, or government, or digging roads, or banking. See also Biological Determinism.

Etymology. The history and derivation of words, and their study.

Eurocentrism. As the name suggests, the privileging of European culture, beliefs, values, religions, to the extent that these have been naturalized—often through imperialism.

False Consciousness. Marxist term for the effects of ideology. See ideology.

Feminism. Toril Moi distinguishes between "femaleness" (sex—a biological category), "femininity" (gender—a set of culturally defined characteristics) and "feminism" (a political position).

Fetishism. Fetishism in psychoanalysis refers to an over-investment in a strangely ("unnaturally") attractive object, person or practice. For Freud, this desire is driven by a significant but unconscious absence or lack, which is then displaced onto something else. As always with Freud, the lack of the phallus is significant for women, the castration complex for men. See also the Marxist notion of Commodity Fetishism.

Formalism. The Russian Formalists of the early twentieth century sought to foreground the "literariness of literature". Critics such as Roman Jakobson, Boris Eichenbaum and Victor Shklovsky focused on the formal aspects of the text which functioned to "defamiliarize" normal, everyday experience. See also "Defamiliarization".

Frankfurt School. A group of left-wing, Jewish thinkers including Theodor Adorno, Herbert Marcuse, Max Horkheimer and Walter Benjamin. Based in Germany during the 1930s before fleeing to America with the rise of the Nazis. Their focus was upon problems of culture and ideology, in particular the mass media and the problem of commodity fetishism. Mass culture, for Frankfurt School critics such as Adorno, encourages conformity with the status quo.

Gaze. The concept of the gaze is derived largely from the psychoanalytic work of Jacques Lacan concerning the formation of subjectivity ("The Mirror Stage"). The gaze represents power: the one who looks is in the position of power over the one who is looked at. Feminist film critics have used this term to analyze ways that mainstream films maintain patriarchal norms. Laura Mulvey, for example, points out that the audience is positioned as *male* through identification with a male protagonist, and is encouraged to accept representations of women from this male perspective.

Gender. As distinct from "sex" (which is biological), gender usually refers to socially/culturally constructed (invented) characteristics which are then attributed to the different biological sexes. If sex is "female and male"; then gender is "femininity and masculinity".

Genealogy. A term Michel Foucault (after Nietzsche) uses to describe a process of historical interrogation, tracing the discourses that have produced knowledge over time.

Genre. A category of cultural practice: "drama" or "poetry" is referred to as genres; equally, so is "the psychological thriller" or "vampire novel".

Globalization. The Marxist critic of postmodernism Fredric Jameson argues that American capitalism, in the form of huge multi-national corporations backed by the Western media, is (re) colonizing the world. This "coca-colonization" of the globe is seen to result in a cultural homogenization as "native" cultures are swallowed up by Western values.

Grand Narrative/Master Narrative. Terms associated with postmodernism. The grand narrative is usually a "totalizing" ideological system (religious fundamentalism or patriarchy or Nazism, for example). Grand narratives are usually self-legitimating—they purport to contain all answers to everything (transcendental truth). The grand narrative is seen to be characteristic of modernity.

Hegemony. The word hegemony derives from the Greek term egemonia or emenon, meaning leader, ruler of political predominance. The Italian Marxist Antonio Gramsci developed this concept as a refinement of Marxist notions of ideology, demonstrating the psychocultural aspects of control, and the role of cultural institutions within this. True control, Gramsci believed, is achieved not by coercion but by gaining the people's *consent* for this control. This is not done by the army but through the social and cultural realms where it is more effectively invisible, more pervasive. Hegemony "saturates" even what we think of as "common sense" as it becomes part of our lived system of meanings and values. The concept is central to Althusser's Gramscian redefinition of ideology in the 1970s.

Hermeneutics The "science" or practice of interpretation. It assumes that the text remains as written, painted, or recorded but that its interpretation changes between historical periods, across cultures, etc.

Heterogeneity / Heterogeneous. Multiplicity or variety, as opposed to homogeneity.

Heteroglossia. A term used by Mikhail Bakhtin to describe the many-voicedness of language. Although languages (e. g. English) present themselves as unified and homogeneous (monoglossic), Bakhtin shows that they are actually always fractured and stratified (heteroglossic). For example, they include traces of other national languages (English is made up of archaic Norman, German, Latin, contemporary French, American English, etc.). Equally, language is split along social, cultural, professional lines: "scouse" or "estuary english", for example, or estate-agent-speak, academic English, military or police idioms, etc. No language, and no identity, is as unified and homogeneous as it claims.

Hommelette. Lacan's dodgy pun ("little man") for the pre-Oedipal unformed *pre-subject*, who has no sense of self distinct from not-self.

Homogeneity/Homogeneous. Sameness, as opposed to heterogeneity.

Homology. A structural parallel. In literary works, similarities and correspondences might establish a pattern or structural repetition. Similarly, critics finds homologies between, for example, the structure of a language and the structure of the unconscious (Lacan).

Homosocial. Eve Kosofsky Sedgwick uses this term to describe single-sex relationships usually between men. For Sedgwick, the term refers to the homoerotic impulses which, she argues, are often concealed behind an overt "homophobia" (fear or hatred of homosexuals).

Humanism. The object of much critique, humanism is a description of a position which believes human identity is the result of the individual's human essence, rather than the influence of social or cultural factors. Humanism is thus an idealist, even essentialist, philosophy, rather than realist or materialist.

Hybridity/Hybridisation. Most associated with postcolonialism, hybridity is a description of the inevitably mixed, interpenetrated condition of cultures, languages, etc.. The critic Stuart Hall suggests that "we are all mongrels", especially after colonialism, and that any notion of "authentic", essentialist identity is untenable. For example, any right-wing English recourse to a notion of "pure" Anglo-Saxon culture would seem to be disproved by the very compound status of that description. The novelist Salman Rushdie argues that there is nothing lost in translation, but always something to be gained.

id. For Sigmund Freud, the psyche is divided into three parts (the ego, the superego and the id). The id represents pure instinct—basic drives to fulfill instinctual needs and desires. The new-born child is all id, Freud argues. During socialization, however, the psyche splits, adding ego and superego.

Idealism. A branch of philosophy which stresses the role of the mind in our acquisition of knowledge about the world. In extreme, "solipsistic" versions, idealism becomes a theory where reality is seen to be nothing more than the activity of one's own mind—nothing exists but oneself. More usually, however, idealists point out that the way we experience the external world is necessarily affected by the activity of the mind.

Ideology. A complex term, but in short, ideology refers to a belief system or world-view; a coherent structure of thinking which obscures incongruous elements in order to uphold a particular social order.

Imaginary/Symbolic. Jacques Lacan distinguishes between a time before the child is socialized, and the time after entry into society and language. The imaginary is the former—a condition remembered as one of wholeness and identity when the child is at one with the mother's body. The "Symbolic Order", on the other hand, is society—the domain of language and power relations. After the "mirror stage", and having "acquired" an identity within society's network of power relations, the subject can never feel the fulfillment or wholeness which is nostalgically "remembered" from the Imaginary.

Intentional Fallacy. This term is used by W. K. Wimsatt & M. C. Beardsley to describe the dubious critical practice of seeking to decipher a text's "meaning" by determining the author's intentions. For them, the author's intentions can never be properly determined, but even if they could, a text should in any case only be analyzed in its own terms, ignoring any extra-textual information. Roland Barthes's notion of the "Death of the Author" provides a very different set of reasons as to the fallacy of intentionality.

Interpellation. When Louis Althusser seeks to describe how ideology actually works, he argues that we, as "subjects", actually subject ourselves to the power of ideology. This is because we *identify with* subject positions or categories of identity which are predetermined within ideological frameworks. Our process of identification with these "identities" is called interpellation—a process of (mis)recognition with an "identity" offered in society. Althusser uses the example of being hailed by an authority figure: a priest, an educator or a policeman, for example, might "hail" me, by saying "Hi, you!". I might then turn around and see myself as the addressee. Thus Althusser hopes to show how ideologies either "recruit" people to particular, acceptable subject positions in society, or else transform individuals into subjects who learn to identify with certain representations.

Intertextuality. Texts exist in cultural and aesthetic contexts alongside other texts. They influence one another and often refer to one another overtly, this being a particular characteristic of postmodernist writing. In fact, all language is itself "intertextual", since language always pre-exists the "speaker": words and meanings are always "second-hand" in some sense.

Langue and Parole. Ferdinand de Saussure distinguishes between "langue" (the whole language *system*—the rules) and "parole" (the actual, specific instance of individual's language use).

Liberal Humanism. A cultural-political position which holds to the essential decency of human beings and which promotes democracy, individualism, tolerance, rationality, civilized values, etc.. Over the past thirty years, liberal humanism has been shown to rest on a series of generalized assumptions about humanity which in fact *hide* distasteful realities and differences of power and wealth. The promotion of Western values "abroad", for example, can be seen to be complicit with the brutalities of imperialism; the notion of individualism can be seen at the very basis of capitalism with all its inequalities "at home".

Liminal. A term favored particularly by post-colonial critics, and which refers to the thresholds, boundaries and borderlines of binary constructions (black/white, masculine/feminine, Englishness / Irishness). These oppositions are often false, producing blurring and gaps which might be exploited in order to deconstruct these oppositions.

Lisible/Scriptible. Roland Barthes distinguishes between two types of text the "readable" and "writerly" respectively. The former are "transparent" or "realist" texts where the reader does not have to "work" at reading, and becomes merely a passive consumer. The more difficult "scriptible" texts (such as modernist writing), on the other hand, make the reader work and therefore disrupt conventional meanings.

Logocentrism. Logos is Greek for "word", "speech" or "reason", terms which can connote law or truth. Thus Jacques Derrida sees Western culture as inherently logocentric in that it revolves around a central set of "truths" which are purported to be universal principles.

Manicheanism. A dualistic view of the world—seeing things simplistically in terms of black/white, good/evil, etc. .

Marginality. The position of being on the margins of the dominant culture.

Marxism. Marxism is a term used to refer to a hugely diverse set of social, economic, historical, philosophical and cultural theories, only some of them derived from the thought of German philosopher Karl Marx. Broadly speaking, Marxist theories focus upon the inequalities of wealth which the capitalist economic system brings, and point to the effects of this exploitative system upon people and cultures. The Marxist analysis of this situation and its products is ultimately designed to bring about its replacement with a fairer, socialist system.

Master/Slave Dialectic. Hegel's abstract "drama" of master versus slave stands at the basis of many contemporary theories of subjectivity. Hegel shows the human search for identity as an interaction between two "beings", each of which is battling for recognition of their status as an independent Self. For Hegel, self-consciousness depends upon such recognition. It is therefore likely that the stronger of the two beings will enslave and objectify the other, using this Other merely as a "mirror" to certify the superior identity of the Self. However, the recognition provided by this "object" will prove unsatisfactory. It needs to be an equal, independent consciousness who does the recognizing. For Hegel, then, true self-consciousness can only exist in being recognized by another, autonomous individual. See also Dialogism.

Medium. The material vehicle for communication—speech, writing, paint, ink, film, photography, etc.

Metaphor and Metonymy. A metaphor is a comparison in which one linguistic sign is substituted by another: "He was a terrier in midfield". (A simile, on the other hand, is a comparison which is signaled: "He was *like* a terrier."). Metonymy is the substitution of a concept by a part of it, e. g. reference to the world of boxing as "the ring", reference to a car as "a motor". Poststructuralist theorists emphasize the way in which *all* language is in fact a kind of metaphor and metonymy.

Metaphysics. A branch of philosophy exploring the nature of reality or being, and usually finding the answers outside the physical world in God, for example.

Mimicry. The postcolonial critic Homi Bhabha suggests that one of the ways in which the colonized "writes back" to the center is through an adoption, incorporation and subversion of the dominant cultural code. This might be seen, for example, in the use of non-standard forms of English. For Bhabha, the colonizer experiences this as a mimicry which undermines the foundations of its constructed superiority.

Mirror Stage. Jacques Lacan argues that the moment when a child first recognizes its own reflection in a mirror represents its socialization—its entry into the Symbolic Order of language and power relations. Prior to this moment the child had almost believed itself to be part of its mother's body, but now begins to develop a sense of self-identity. However, Lacan sees this recognition of itself in the mirror as a *misrecognition*, because the mirror image (the identity adopted) was merely an image or sign of the self. This is never at one with the actual experience of self (which is far more fragmented than the unified mirror image). Like a linguistic sign, which is always an unsatisfactory representation of something in the world, our identities are built on unstable foundations.

Mode of Production. The Marxist term for the economic system of a society. See Base/Superstructure.

Monologism. See Dialogism.

Multi-accentuality. Mikhail Bakhtin sees all signs as inherently multiple, hybrid, *multi-accentual* in that they always carry within them a variety of possible meanings.

Nation. The act of drawing up borderlines—defining a nation-state and a national identity—is deeply problematic. On what criteria do you define "a nation"? Who belongs and who is excluded, and who decides? Nations like to see themselves as natural phenomena, but are in fact "imagined communities", to use Benedict Anderson's term. National identities are always defined, and serve the interests of, the most powerful group in the nation-state. Therefore, the act of defining a national identity is necessarily an act of excluding, marginalizing or scapegoating minority groups.

Nationalism. Frantz Fanon saw the nationalist resistance of colonized groups against the imperial power as a "beautiful" and "splendid" necessity. The nationalism which Gandhi mobilized against British rule in India, for example, was designed to counter what was seen as unjust government by a foreign power. Fanon was also one of the first to warn against its dangers and inadequacies (see *The Wretched of the Earth*). Nazism stands as the most brutal of many expressions of nationalism in the 20th and towards the 21st centuries.

Nativism/Négritude. The belief in the importance of asserting an "authentic" ethnic identity in the face of imperialism, often linked to the practice of producing an indigenous literature. Associated with Aimé Césaire, Frantz Fanon, and Léopold Sédar Senghor.

Neuroses. Psychic disorders which, according to Freud, can be obsessional, hysterical or phobic and which may be cured through psychoanalysis.

New Criticism. This refers to a group of American critics of the 1930s and 1940s, and their English counterparts I. A. Richards and William Empson. For the New Critics, a literary text should be approached as a unified whole. Attention to historical context was less important than the aesthetic features, the interrelation of verbal features and the ensuing complexities of meaning. The task of the critic, therefore, revolved around close attention to ambiguity, paradox, irony, poetic imagery, etc. , in order to show the contribution of each element to the overall unified structure of the text.

New Historicism. A form of Marxist criticism. New historicists such as Stephen Greenblatt often focus upon texts from far-removed historical contexts, e. g. Renaissance drama. Their aim is to highlight the power relations at work not only at the text's moment of production, but also at the moment of the text's "reproduction", i. e. the moment at which we, in the present, read texts from our own particular position in history and society.

Normativity. The privileging of socially constructed "norms", against which deviations are classed as "abnormal", e. g. heterosexuality/homosexuality.

Objectification. The positioning of "Others" as objects for the benefit of the "Self". See Hegel's Master / Slave dialectic.

Oedipus Complex. In *Oedipus Rex*, the Aeschylus play, Oedipus unknowingly kills his father and sleeps with his mother. Freud believes that this dramatizes a primal human desire because the process of a child's socialization revolves around the development of an unconscious libidinal attachment to the mother, alongside a jealous rivalry with the father. In Freud's theories, the unsatisfactory working-through of the Oedipus Complex lies at the root of many neuroses. Freud is really only interested in men, and although he did draw up a corresponding theory to explain a similar primal desire in females (the Electra Complex), this is pretty unconvincing.

Ontology. A branch of philosophy focusing upon the origins, essence and meaning of being.

Orientalism. Edward Said's term for an entire discourse through which "the colonial Other" is represented by "the West" as subordinate, thus providing an intellectual foundation for material domination, i. e. for imperial and economic exploitation.

The Other. The relationship of "Self" to "Other" is a relationship of "normality" to "marginality", and is always a power relationship—a binary opposition or violent hierarchy. The Other can be different from "the Norm" in a variety of senses: race, ethnicity, gender, sexuality, class, religion, etc. .

Patriarchy. Male dominance: literally "the rule of the father"; technically "government" by men, either in the family or in society, with authority and materialities such as land being passed from father to son.

Phallus. The phallus—the metaphorical penis—signifies power. See Oedipus Complex and Phallocentrism.

Phallocentrism. Critics such as Lacan and Derrida argue that in patriarchal Western culture, the Father represents the Law. The power associated with masculinity is symbolized by the phallus (that which femininity *lacks*). Women, and femininity, are defined *in relation to* men, become the Other to the norm of the male Self. See Logocentrism and Phallologocentrism.

Phallogocentrism. Jacques Derrida's combination of phallo- and logo-centrism. The term suggests that Western culture is obsessed with origins and centers, and that the specific origin and centre around which it revolves is bound up with both the phallus and the logos (masculinity as the Law, as God, as reason, as the true Word).

Phenomenology. Branch of philosophy which emphasizes that meaning is generated through the influence of a person's consciousness upon perceptions.

Positivism. Branch of philosophy which emphasizes the observable and "factual" over the theoretical or metaphysical.

Post-colonialism. A term used to describe the study of cultures who have emerged from colonial rule and who are undergoing the processes of decolonization. This, as post-colonial theory makes clear, is far more complicated than merely gaining political independence. Colonized cultures will be saturated with the influence of the imperial power—from language, through its education system to the economic and political systems imposed during colonization. The question of how a former colony makes the best of a situation in which it may never be able to escape the legacy of colonialism remains.

Postmodernism. Not so much a stage " after" modernism, more an impulse to deconstruct "totalizing" systems of knowledge, meaning or belief— "grand narratives" in the terminology of French philosopher Jean-Franois Lyotard (religions, for example, or grand political theories such as capitalism or communism, or nationalisms, or humanist theories of identity). The postmodern "condition", for Lyotard, is that of living without such systems or myths; for Derrida this is about celebrating this "advent" of an open future. The emphasis here on the fragmentation of identities has been very controversial. Fredric Jameson terms postmodernism "the cultural logic of late capitalism", and many critics have seen postmodernism as running counter to the common contemporary need for collective identities which resist the workings of power. See also Grand Narratives.

Post-structuralism. Like structuralism, post-structuralism rejects the notion of the human subject as *cogito* and emphasizes the slippery, linguistic basis of all identity, meaning, knowledge and power. The centrality of language to poststructuralist conceptions of subjectivity and culture is shown in Derrida's famous dictum: "there is no outside-text", or there is nothing outside context. Because everything is part of an unstable language system, post-structuralists draw attention to the radical instability at the foundation of textual and social meanings which appear "natural".

Primal Scene. In Freudian psychoanalysis, this refers to a moment in a child's development when significant desires, fears, needs and anxieties are generated, thus structuring that child's psyche.

Psychoanalysis. Psychoanalytical theory has had a huge impact upon literary studies, mainly through the work of Sigmund Freud and Jacques Lacan. Psychoanalysis is variously a mode of interpretation, a theory about the formation of the subject (a theory of identity and language), an apparatus through which to understand the workings of ideology in culture.

Race. "Race" is often seen to be an arbitrary, socially constructed category. This is not to say that there are not differences between people, but that the means by which certain peoples have been distinguished, categorized and subordinated across history, are usually spurious.

Rationalism. Branch of philosophy which emphasizes *reason* or intellect, rather than observation or sensory perception, as the basis for knowledge and truth.

Reification. In Marxist theory, reification refers to the process of depersonalization and alienation which capitalism induces.

Representation. The power of representation is the power to survey, define, categorize, stereotype and assert power over the represented.

Repression. For Freud, unwanted or taboo thoughts, desires, fears, anxieties get repressed into the unconscious. They do not disappear, though, and the "return of the repressed" may take a variety of forms—dreams, slips of the tongue, etc. , as well as neuroses, psychoses and compulsions.

Semiotics/Semiology. The term semiology refers to the "science of

signs", and derives from the Greek *logos* ("words") *semeion* ("about signs").
In *Mythologies*, Roland Barthes develops a study of social semiotics— the
connotations which social and cultural signs carry in popular culture and
especially advertising. Confusingly, Julia Kristeva also uses the term "semiotic"
to mean something quite different. For Kristeva, "the semiotic" is a kind of
language which is associated with the Unconscious, or more accurately Lacan's
realm of the Imaginary. This language is "jouissance" and carries the incoherent
desires, drives and pulsions of the uncoordinated pre-subject, then. There is a
link to *ecriture feminine*.

Sexuality. The term generally used to refer to sexual orientation. In
Freudian psychoanalysis, sexuality is formed in the gradual organization of the
libidinal drives to focus upon a particular object. The character of that object
depends upon the subject's particular path through the various stages of psychic
development.

Signifier/Signified. For Ferdinand de Saussure, the "sign" comes in two
parts. The *Signifier* is the vehicle for meaning—i. e. a sound or series of lines on
a page which form a "word", or it could equally be a logo. The *Signified* is that
which is denoted by the signifier, i. e. the object or concept or person which the
signifier sought to represent. Saussure argues that any meaning occurs through a
combination, a "meeting" of the two. But this is a combination which is
arbitrary.

Solipsism. The notion that it is impossible ever to know another person, so
why bother? This ends up in an absolute egotism—a refusal to acknowledge the
needs or even existence of others.

Standard. A standard is a flag—it is therefore a symbol of centralized,
uniform identity and power, and also a benchmark of quality. In Britain,

"Standard English" is supposedly the "correct" form of English, and "RP" (Received Pronunciation) the "proper" accent. It has this status because it has historically been associated with the dominant social and cultural groups in this country. Other forms have historically been associated with subordinate classes (working classes), ethnicities (minority and colonized groups), regions (anywhere that isn't the south east of England), and are devalued by being classed as a deviation from "the norm".

Stereotype. A politicized myth which has been generated through discourse and which serves to maintain conventional power relations.

Subaltern. The Indian critic Gayatri Spivak borrows this term from Antonio Gramsci to describe dominated, subordinated and marginalized groups—especially those who are "doubly oppressed", such as colonized women.

Structuralism. A school of thought which built up around a group of French thinkers in the 1950s and 1960s. Figures such as Claude Lévi-Strauss (in anthropology), Roland Barthes (in literary and cultural studies), Jacques Lacan (in psychoanalysis) and Louis Althusser (in Marxist theory) were influenced by the work of Ferdinand de Saussure, and pursued an interest in how meaning is produced. Rather than focusing upon consciousness (of an author, for example) as the locus of meaning, the structuralists analyzed underlying structures such as those of language, of the psyche, and of society. These, it was argued, were crucial in the development of meaning.

Subject/Subjectivity. The subject is seen to be that which acts and speaks, which says "I". Humanist notions of personal identity as natural are critiqued in recent theory, and replaced by the notion that identity is formed when individuals are *subjected to* forces outside themselves-ideology, for example.

211

Superego. The third part of the Freudian model of the psyche, the others being the id and ego. The superego is involved with conscience and the imposition of morality upon the wild id.

Superstructure. See Base and Superstructure.

Symbolic Order. See Imaginary / Symbolic.

Synchronic. See Diachronic and Synchronic.

Teleology. From "telos" which means an ultimate end or conclusion. Teleology refers to any "grand narrative", such as the idea of history as "progress" (an idea shared by both European imperialism and Marxism) towards an end when one idea will dominate, or be "totalized" (Western civilization, for example, or Marxist communism). Teleological theories tend to privilege one narrative (that of Western values, for example, or that of class), to the exclusion of all others.

Text / Textuality. From the Latin texere, meaning "to weave", and the term "text" implies the fabric of culture itself—the complex network of contexts, threads and traces which combine to generate meanings when we read. We ourselves are as much a part of this text as the book.

Transference. In psychoanalysis, as the patient talks to the analyst, he or she transfers his conflicts onto analyst. This creates a controlled situation, a form of repetition of the conflict, in which the analyst can intervene. What is repaired in analysis is not quite what is wrong in real life, but the patient is able to construct a new narrative for herself, in which she can interpret and make sense of the disturbances from which she suffers.

Typology. A system or method by which people or things can be classified as a particular "type". See also Discourse.

Unconscious. Freud argues that aspects of our conscious life which are socially/culturally taboo or forbidden, or which are traumatic, become *repressed*. The Unconscious is thus constructed out of repressed instincts, desires, fears and anxieties. Although our Unconscious is completely unknowable to us, it does manifest itself in disguised form—for example in Freudian slips, neuroses, compulsions and dreams. Jacques Lacan argues that the Unconscious presents itself in metaphorical and metonymic form, i. e. it uses literary devices. These, Freud and Lacan argue, must then be "read" and decoded by a psychoanalyst in order to reveal their "true meaning".

Universalism. This refers to a "humanist" tendency to generalize about human nature as if all humans have essentially the same experience of being alive regardless of, for example, economic, gender or racial differences.

(Composed by Zhang Pinggong)

Appendix (*Literature Translation*)

A

Drama from Ibsen to Brecht (1973)
Raymond Williams
INTRODUCTION

(i)

It is now just over a hundred years since Ibsen published *Brand* and *Peer Gynt*. The drama written and performed in the intervening century is by any standards a major achievement. There has never been, in any comparable period, so much innovation and experiment, and this has been related, throughout, to a growth and crisis of civilization which the drama has embodied, in some remarkable ways. For much of the century, and especially for its first seventy-five years, the play was overshadowed by the novel, as a major form. Yet it is still impossible to understand modern literature without the work of at least eight or ten dramatists, or, in another way of putting it, without a critical understanding of dramatic naturalism, dramatic expressionism, and certain related movements. At the same time, since Ibsen published *Brand* and *Peer Gynt* rather than submitting them for performance, there has been a very complicated and difficult relationship between literature and the theatre: a relationship which at times obscures and always affects the achievement of this drama. The crisis of performance, and of the theatre as an institution, itself affected by new means of dramatic performance in the cinema, in radio and in television, has made the continuing problem of dramatic form especially acute. Certain orthodoxies have hardened, and many damaging gaps have appeared and continued to appear. But also, through and within these difficulties, the energy and power of dramatic imagination have continued to create some of the essential consciousness of our world. Without this drama, we would all lack a dimension, and to study and understand it is then a major critical challenge.

When I came back from the army in Germany in 1945, I began to read Ibsen and went on until, for a few necessary weeks, I had in effect to be stopped, to complete the rest of a university course. I went back to the plays as soon as I could, and have been reading and seeing them performed, with the many hundreds of plays that succeeded them, as a central interest ever since. The studies in this book come mainly from that experience: I was moved by the plays before I even saw the critical problems. Yet as the experience continued, and as I read accounts of it, I began to see problems which are still, I think, of the utmost difficulty: problems which eventually resolve themselves as theoretical, and which raise many radical questions in fields other than drama. I have gone on working on these, and in fact almost continuously redefining them and changing the emphasis of my conclusions. I suppose and hope that this will go on, but in the last few years a phase, at least, of that original impulse has seemed to complete itself, and I have felt able to get back again to trying to draw together, in a general account, its particular experiences.

The studies of plays and dramatists which make up most of this book have been written and revised over some twenty years. They stand, in that sense, on their own: as direct and considered responses. But as I have become more aware of the theoretical problems, and of their changing definitions, I have used certain ideas and a certain vocabulary which run through the particular studies. It is then necessary, in this brief introduction, to describe these directly, for the convenience of the reader, though the general critical position to which, in the end, they relate is best reserved for the conclusion, in which there are the many readings of plays to draw on. What I need mainly to explain here, in relation to a critical question of dramatic form, is what I mean by "convention" and by a "structure of feeling".

(ii)

In a period as various, as experimental and innovating, as modern drama, the problem of conventions is necessarily central. Indeed the idea of convention is basic to any understanding of drama as a form. Yet it is always a difficult idea, and especially so in a period in which certain basic conventions are changing. It is worth, then, looking at the idea of convention directly.

The ordinary dictionary senses provide a useful starting point. Thus, *convention* is the fact of coming together; an assembly; union; coalition, specially of representatives for some definite purpose; an agreement previous to a definitive treaty; a custom. *Conventional*, similarly, is: settled by stipulation or by tacit consent; as sanctioned and currently accepted by tacit agreement; agreeable to accepted standards; agreeable to contract. As we go through these senses, and through those of the various derived words, we see an ambiguity which is important both because it indicates a possible source of confusion, which requires discussion, and because it indicates an important point of entry for an analysis of the place of conventions in drama.

The possible source of confusion is the fact that convention covers both *tacit consent* and *accepted standards*, and it is easy to see that the latter has often been understood as a set of formal rules. Thus it is common in adverse comment to say that a work is just *conventional*; *a familiar routine*; *old stuff*; *the mixture as before*. We use the word in the same way in adverse comment on people and actions that we find dull, or narrow, or old-fashioned, or unoriginal, or unreceptive to new ideas. To explain the development of *conventional* as an adverse term in criticism would take us a long way into cultural history. Briefly, it is the result of the controversy that was part of the Romantic Movement, in which emphasis fell heavily on the right of the artist to disregard, where he saw fit, the rules that had been laid down by others for the practice of his art. This was an essential emphasis, from which we have all gained. But it is then unfortunate that *convention* and *conventional* should have been so heavily compromised. For an artist only leaves one convention to follow or create another; this is the whole basis of his communication. Yet when *conventional* carries the implications of old-fashioned, or narrow, and when it is used, as it is now often used, as an easy and adverse contrast with *realistic*, it is difficult to use the word at all without being misunderstood. Yet it is possible to think of the ambiguity as the means of an important insight; and it is this that must now be discussed.

Convention, as we have seen, covers *tacit agreement* as well as *accepted standards*. In the actual practice of drama, the convention, in any particular case, is simply the terms upon which author, performers and audience agree to meet, so that the performance may be carried on. *Agree to meet*, of course, is by no means always a formal or definite process; much more usually, in any art, the consent is largely customary, and often indeed it is virtually unconscious.

This can be seen most readily in the conventions of our own period. In a naturalist play, for example, the convention is that the speech and action should as closely as possible appear to be those of everyday life; but few who watch such a play realize that this is a convention: to the majority it is merely "what a play is like", "the sort of thing a play tries to do". Yet it is, in fact, a very remarkable convention that actors should represent people behaving naturally, and usually privately, before a large audience, while all the time maintaining the illusion that, as characters, these persons are unaware of the audience's presence. The most desperate private confession, or the most dangerous conspiracy, can be played out on the stage, in full view and hearing of a thousand people; yet it will not occur to either actors or audience that this is in any way strange, because all, by the tacit consent of custom, have accepted this procedure as a convention.

Not long ago, and perhaps still in some places, it was, however, thought very strange if a character spoke in soliloquy, whether this was thought of as "thinking aloud" or directly addressing the audience. The complaint would be that this was "artificial", or "not true to life", or even "undramatic"; yet it is surely as natural, and as "true to life", when one is on a stage before a thousand people, to address them, as to pretend to carry on as if they were not there. As for the soliloquy being "undramatic", this is the kind of conditional statement, elevated into a "law", which continually confuses dramatic criticism, since it is well known that the soliloquy, in many periods, has been a normally accepted part of dramatic method.

The various conventions which have been used in drama are too numerous to list. A two-day battle between considerable armies may be represented by the passage of a few soldiers in a few brief scenes, lasting no more than a few minutes. The last hour of a man's life may be played out on a stage, with deliberate emphasis on the tension of waiting, and yet the dramatic "hour" may be no more than five minutes. A man may walk on to a bare stage, hung only by curtains, and from what he says we will agree that he is in Gloucestershire, or Illyria, or on a mythical island. He can be a Roman general, speaking to us in English blank verse from a wooden step that we take to be a rostrum in the Forum of Rome. He can be a ghost or a devil or a god, and yet drink, answer the telephone, or be wound off the stage by a crane. He can put on a grey cloak, and we will agree that he is invisible, though we continue to see him. He can speak to us, acknowledging his most private thoughts, and we will agree that while we hear him from the back of the gallery, he cannot be heard by a man a few feet away from him, or waiting in the wings. With the slightest of indications, we will accept that the events we watch are occurring four thousand years before Christ, or in the Middle Ages, or in a flat in Paris on the same night as we are in a theatre in Manchester. The men whom we see as inspector and criminal we recognize as having seen last week as criminal and inspector, or as butler and peer, but we do not challenge them. We accept; we agree; these are the conventions.

Since the use of conventions of this kind is inherent in the process of drama, it is at first surprising that when the basic convention, that of acted performance, has been accepted, there should be any difficulty in particular instances. Yet it is obvious that such difficulties are acute and recurrent. We will agree that the person on the stage is a spirit, and that, quite unaware of our intent presence, he is talking privately to his widow, in the year 1827; but if the widow attempts to address us in an aside, we can become uneasy. We will agree that a murderer may hide behind a door (where we can still see him), and that he may look down, with an expression of agony, at his hands (which we at once agree are stained with innocent blood); but if he should come forward to the front of the stage, and in twenty lines of verse, or in recitative or song, or in dance, express (if more fully and more intensely the same emotion, we at once, or many of us, feel uneasy, and are likely to say afterwards that it was "unreal". We may even, if we accept the phrases of the journeymen, conclude that the play was highbrow or surrealist, or pretentious (an increasingly common word among those professional and doubtful pretension is normality). And while we may be able to reject this kind of simplification, we shall not be able, merely by taking thought, to create an alternative convention.

This, indeed, is the central difficulty; for while it is true that the average audience is more open-minded than the average entrepreneur, so that the basis for change and development in convention always potentially exists, it is only academically true that a dramatist may use any convention that suits his material and intention. A convention, in the simplest sense, is only a method, a technical piece of machinery, which facilitates the performance. But methods change, and the techniques change, and while, say, a chorus of dancers, or the cloak of invisibility, or a sung soliloquy, are known dramatic methods, they cannot be satisfactorily used unless, at the time of a performance, they are more than methods; unless, in fact, they are conventions. Dramatist, actors and audience must be able to agree that the particular method to be employed is acceptable; and, in the nature of the case, an important part of this agreement must usually *precede* the performance, so that what is to be done may be accepted without damaging friction.

Ultimately, however, we judge a convention, not by its abstract usefulness, and not by referring it to some ultimate criterion of probability, but rather by what it manages, in an actual work of art, to get done. If in fact it were not historically true that certain works have been able, by their own strength, to modify old conventions and to introduce new ones, we should have had no change at all, short of some absolutist decree. We accept, with a common and easy sentiment, such triumphs of the past. We read, sympathetically, the biographies of an Ibsen or a Stanislavsky. But the sympathy is merely sentimental unless it can be made active, and creative, at our own point in time.

Ibsen and Stanislavsky have won, as Aeschylus won when he introduced the second actor, or Shakespeare when he transformed the tragedy of blood. Yet the history of art is not one of continual evolution into higher and better forms; there is debasement as well as refinement, and a novelty even a transformation, may be bad as well as good. It would be absurd to imagine that our own contemporary segment from the great arc of dramatic possibility is, because the latest, necessarily the best. Yet, because of the nature of convention, because of the dependence of any dramatic method upon this particular type of agreement, it is not possible, in any age, to go very far from the segment which is that age's living tradition, or to begin from anywhere but within or on its borders.

Thus we have the necessity of tradition—convention as tacit consent—and at times the equal necessity of experiment, from the development of new modes of feeling, and from the perception of new or rediscovered technical means—convention as dramatic method. It is to the interplay of these two senses of convention that we must now turn.

If we think of a dramatic convention as a technical means in an acted performance, it is clear that there is no absolute reason why any means should not be employed, and judged by its dramatic result. But we have seen that, in practice, this absolute freedom of choice is not available: a dramatist must win the consent of his audience to any particular means that he wishes to employ, and while he may often be able to do this in the course of a work itself, by the power of the effect which the method makes possible, he cannot entirely rely on this, for even if the audience is sympathetic, too great a consciousness of the novelty or strangeness of the means may as effectively hamper the full communication of a play as would open hostility. It seems probable, when we look back into the history of drama, that the effective changes took place when there was already a latent willingness to accept them, at least among certain groups in society, from whom the artist drew his support. But while it is possible to see this in retrospect, it could never have been easy, and it is not easy now, to see such a situation, with sufficient clarity, in the flux of present experience. It is here that we find ourselves considering the very difficult relations between conventions and structures of feeling.

(iii)

All serious thinking about art must begin from the recognition of two apparently contradictory facts: that an important work is always, in an irreducible sense, individual; and yet that there are authentic communities of works of art, in kinds, periods and styles. In everyday discussion, we succeed in maintaining both ideas at the same time, without real consideration of the relations between them. We see a particular play, and say, often genuinely, that in this speech, this character, this action, a particular dramatist makes himself known; it is for this specific achievement that we value his work. But then, sometimes in the next breath, we look at the speech, the character or the action and say: this is characteristic of a particular kind of drama, in a particular period. Each kind of observation is important; each helps us, every day, to understand drama better. But the difficulty raised by their apparent contradiction—here pointing to a single hand, there to a group or period—must in the end be faced. For the contradiction cannot be resolved by saying that we are in each case pointing at a different kind of fact. It is true that in some works it is possible to separate out different elements, and to say: here the dramatist is simply following the conventions of his genre or period, but here he is contributing something entirely his own. Yet in many important works it is not possible to do this: the individual genius and the particular conventions through which it is expressed are or seem inseparable. In pointing to what a particular man has done, in a particular style, we are often in the position of learning what that style is, what it is capable of doing. The individual dramatist has done this, yet what he has done is part of what we then know about a general period or style.

It is to explore this essential relationship that I use the term "structure of feeling". What I am seeking to describe is the continuity of experience from a particular work, through its particular form, to its recognition as a general form, and then the relation of this general form to a period. We can look at this continuity, first, in the most general way. All that is lived and made, by a given community in a given period, is, we now commonly believe, essentially related, although in practice, and in detail, this is not always easy to see. In the study of a period, we may be able to reconstruct, with more or less accuracy, the material life, the general social organization, and, to a large extent, the dominant ideas. It is often difficult to decide which, if any, of these aspects is, in the whole complex, determining; their separation is, in a way, arbitrary, and an important institution like the drama will, in all probability, take its colour in varying degrees from them all. But while we may, in the study of a past period, separate out particular aspects of life, and treat them as if they were self-contained, it is obvious that this is only how they may be studied, not how they were experienced. We examine each element as a precipitate, but in the living experience of the time every element was in solution of inseparable part of a complex whole. And it seems to be true from the nature of art, that it is from such a totality that the artist draws; it is in art, primarily, that the effect of a whole lived experience is expressed and embodied. To relate a work of art to any part of that whole may, in varying degrees, be useful; but it is a common experience, in analysis, to realize that when one has measured the work against the separable parts, there yet remains some element for which there is no external counterpart. It is this, in the first instance, that I mean by the structure of feeling. It is as firm and definite as "structure" suggests, yet it is based in the deepest and often least tangible elements of our experience. It is a way of responding to a particular world which in practice is not felt as one way among others—a conscious "way"—but is, in experience, the only way possible. Its means, its elements, are not propositions or techniques; they are embodied, related feelings. In the same sense, it is accessible to others—not by formal argument or by professional skills, on their own, but by direct experience—a form and a meaning, a feeling and a rhythm—in the work of art, the play, as a whole.

We can often see this structure in the drama of the past. But then it follows, from the whole emphasis of the term, that it is precisely the structure of feeling which is most difficult to distinguish while it is still being lived. Just because it has then not passed, or wholly passed, into distinguishable formations and beliefs and institutions, it is known primarily as a deep *personal* feeling; indeed it often seems, to a particular writer, unique, almost incommunicable, and lonely. We can see this most clearly in the art and thought of past periods, when, while it was being made, its creators seemed often, to themselves and others, isolated, cut off, difficult to understand. Yet again and again, when that structure of feeling has been absorbed, it is the connections, the correspondences, even the period similarities, which spring most readily to the eye. What was then a living structure, not yet known to be shared, is now a recorded structure, which can be examined and identified and even generalized. In one's own time, before this has happened, it is probable that those to whom the new structure is most accessible, in whom indeed it is most clearly forming, will know their experience primarily as their own: as what cuts them off from other men, though what they are actually cut off from is the set of received formations and conventions and institutions which no longer express or satisfy their own most essential life. When such a man speaks, in his work, often against what is felt to be the grain of the time, it is surprising to him and to others that there can be recognition of what had seemed this most difficult, inaccessible, unshared life. Established formations will criticize or reject him, but to an increasing number of people he will seem to be speaking for them, for their own deepest sense of life, just because he was speaking for himself. A new structure of feeling is then becoming articulate. It is even possible, though very difficult even by comparison with the analysis of past structures, to begin to see this contemporary structure directly, rather than only in the power of particular works. Many such expositions are too early, too superficial or too rigid, but it remains true that discovery of actual contemporary structures of feeling (usually masked by their immediate and be tter recognized predecessors) is the most important kind of attention to the art and society of one's own time.

The artist's importance, in relation to the structure of feeling, has to do above all with the fact that it is a *structure*: not an unformed flux of new responses, interests and perceptions, but a formation of these into a new way of seeing ourselves and our world. Such a formation is the purpose of all authentic contemporary activity, and its successes occur in fields other than art. But the artist, by the character of his work, is directly involved with just this process, from the beginning. He can only work at all as such formations become available, usually as a personal discovery and then a scatter of personal discoveries and then the manner of work of a generation. What this means, in practice, is the making of new conventions, new forms.

It is in this respect, finally, that I see the usefulness of "structure of feeling" as a critical term. For it directs our attention, in practical ways, to a kind of analysis which is at once concerned with particular forms and the elements of general forms. We can begin, quite locally, in what is still called practical criticism, with direct analysis: to discover the structure of feeling of a particular play. This structure, always, is an experience, to which we can directly respond. But it is also an experience communicated in a particular form, through particular conventions. There is indeed always a critical relation between the form and the experience: an identity, a tension, at times, in effect, a disintegration. It is not at all a question of applying an external form, and its rules, to a particular play; it is how the experience and its means of communication relate, by a primary internal criterion. The first study of a structure of feeling is then always local, particular, unique. But what is being drawn on, in the means of communication, is already wider than the particular work: in a language, in methods, in conventions. As we collect our experience of particular plays, we see the structure of feeling at once extending and changing: important elements in common, as experience and as method, between particular plays and dramatists; important elements changing, as the experience and the conventions change together, or as the experience is found to be in tension with existing conventions, and either succeeds or fails in altering them. Slowly, what emerges is much wider than particular work: it is a problem of form, but also, crucially, a problem of experience, for many dramatists, and in effect for a period and for successive periods. In any real analysis, the relationships are usually very difficult to sustain, but there is the possibility, which I am especially testing in this study of modern drama, of substantial connections between the most particular and the most general forms. What the analysis often shows is a change in dramatic method, but the point of my argument, through the relation of conventions and structures of feeling, is that we can look at dramatic methods with a clear technical definition, and yet know, in detail, that what is being defined is more than technique: is indeed the practical way of describing those changes in experience—the responses and their communication; the "subjects" and the "forms"—which make the drama in itself and as a history important.

(iv)

The most persistent difficulty, in the analysis of structures of feeling, is the complexity of historical change and in particular, as is very evident in modern drama, the coexistence, even within a period and a society, of alternative structures. These facts determine the arrangement of the essays in this book, though the arrangement does not point to any simple conclusion. It is a fact that there is a general historical development, from Ibsen to Brecht, from dramatic naturalism to dramatic expressionism. This indicates a general chronological arrangement, so that, for example, I start with Ibsen and end with plays of the 1950s and 1960s. But then it is not only that we have to get beyond the descriptions of naturalism and expressionism to their often more significant crossings and variants. It is also that, throughout the period, certain forms are in effect rediscovered, or go through a particular development in some intense local situation. Following the real experience through, yet at the same time trying to present it in a critically significant way, I have, within the overall historical development, followed particular kinds and areas of work through to their own conclusions, before resuming their order in time. I begin, in my first part, with the three major dramatists who seem to me to establish the importance of this period: Ibsen, Strindberg and Chekhov. They were not actual contemporaries—Ibsen was born twenty-one years before Strindberg, and thirty-two years before Chekhov—but they were all writing in the 1880s and 1890s, and it is in the substance and range of their work that modern drama, essentially, came into existence. I turn then, in my second part, to one remarkable national tradition: that of the Irish dramatists, from Yeats in the 1890s through Synge and Joyce to O'Casey in the 1940s. This tradition, as it happens, includes most of the major modern dramatic forms, but in a particular national and historical situation which requires emphasis. In my third part, I turn to an area of experiment which has been of major importance: the dramatic uses of illusion, as in Pirandello, and of myth, as in several dramatists from O'Neill to Giraudoux, Anouilh and Sartre; and I have considered, alongside these, the contrasting experiments in poetic drama, as in Lorca and Eliot, and in a range of British dramatists. In my fourth part, I have brought together, for particular emphasis, a range of writers and methods in social and political drama: beginning with a retrospect to Büchner, and his relation to Hauptmann, and going on through the contrasting figures of Shaw and Lawrence, Toller and Miller, to Brecht. In my fifth part, I discuss ten recent plays: by O'Neill, Ionesco, Beckett, Genet, Frisch and Dürrenmatt; and, among British dramatists, by Whiting, Osborne, Pinter and Arden. There are problems in this arrangement, and I have been very conscious of them. But since, finally, all the studies are related, the arrangement may be acceptable; it has certainly enabled me, while staying close to particular work, to follow certain themes and kinds through. What I then attempt, in my conclusion, is a more general statement, based on the particular studies, of the history and significance of the main dramatic forms—the conventions and structures of feeling—of this remarkable hundred years.

戏剧:从易卜生到布莱希特(导言)

[英]雷蒙·威廉斯　著

张倩玉　译

一

从易卜生的《布朗德》和《培尔·金特》出版至今不过一百年的时间，在这一个世纪里创作出和上演的戏剧可谓成就斐然，在任何时期都没有过那么多改革和实验，而且它们与文明的进步和危机自始至终息息相关，并非凡地体现出这一过程。在这个世纪的大部分时间，尤其是前七十五年里，主要的戏剧形式受小说影响深重，但若不参考至少八到十个剧作家的作品，或者换一种说法，若没有对戏剧中自然主义、表现主义及其他一些运动的深入理解而想要了解现代文学也是不可能的。与此同时，自从易卜生出版了《布朗德》及《培尔·金特》而不是将它们搬演于舞台，文学与剧场之间的一个复杂而难解的关系便产生了，这一关系常常是隐蔽的，但是影响着这种戏剧的进展。以剧场为机构的表演的危机，自身被电影院、广播和电视中新的戏剧表演形式所影响，固有的戏剧形式问题已变得非常尖锐，这种正统的压力使问题趋于严重，破坏性的裂痕纷纷出现了。然而，伴随着这些难题，戏剧的想像的能量和力量仍然持续地创造出了一些对于这个世界关键性的认知。若没有这些戏剧，我们将缺少一个看世界的维度，从而给我们从事戏剧研究带来严峻的挑战。

1945 年，当我离开军队从德国回国，我开始阅读易卜生，后来被迫停止了几个星期，用来完成余下的大学课程，之后我又回到戏剧中，读剧本，看演出，其中的几百部戏剧成为我此后的兴趣所在。这本书中的研究对象主要就从那些经验得来：我先是被这些戏感动了，然后才在其中看到重要的问题。而随着经验的积累，随着我阅读的增多，我开始看到那些仍然是最要紧的问题，它们被最终当作是理论问题加以解决，却在戏剧领域之外带出了很多根本性的问题。我一直为这些问题努力着，事实上几乎是不停地重新赋予它们定义，不断修改我的结论的细部。我认为并且希望这一过程可以继续，但最近几年，这一研究带着它的原初冲动似乎想要完结自身，同时我感觉已有能力重新回头检视，试图将这些独特的经验整合成一个基本的研究报告。

构成这本书的大部分内容的是关于剧作和剧作家的研究，我用了大致20 年的时间撰写和修订。它们在某种程度上是一种直接却是深思熟虑后的反映。但当我了解更多的理论问题并看到它们的定义不断变化之后，我开始在具体的研究中使用特定的观念和特定的词汇；为了读者的方便，有必要在这个导言中对它们进行描述，但要注意与此相联系的基本批评立场最终是为结论预备的，即那个依靠大量剧本阅读才能作出的结论。我在这里主要想阐释的，是一个关于戏剧形式的问题，也就是我所谓的"传统"及"情感结构"。

二

在现代戏剧的这样一个多样的、实验的、改革的时期，传统的问题是其核心，传统问题对于任何关于戏剧形式的认知都是首要的，然而这一问题总是难解的，尤其在这个基本传统不断变化的时期，所以，有必要直接了解一下关于传统的问题。

普通的辞典释义为我们提供了一个有用的起步，即"传统"是一个集合的行为；收集；联系；联合体；尤其指一些明确目的的代表；默认的清楚的协定；一种习俗。"传统的"的意义与此相类：被规范树立的或成规体现的；条例一样的以及当前可用的；符合标准的；和约定的。透过这些解释及派生出的词语，我们看到了一种暧昧，它的重要性首先体现在它暗示出为了避免混乱，讨论是必须的；同时它还暗示了重要的一点，也就是分析戏剧中的传统这一领地的进路。

产生混乱的可能原因是传统包括了"成规"和"标准"，而且显然后者经常被当作一种普遍的规则。因此批判一个作品时往往说它是"传统的"；"熟稔的套路"；"老调重弹"；"古董大杂烩"。这个词也被用来批判一些我们认为无趣、狭隘、过时、不原创以及不接受新观念的人或行为。若要解释"传统的"作为一个反面的概念在批评中的发展需要考察很多文化史；简单地说，这是浪漫主义运动中的一场争论导致的，艺术家的权力曾极大地被强调，他可以在他认为适当的情况下忽略他人在创作中定下的规则。这是一个关键性的强调，我们都从中获益，不幸的是"传统"和"传统的"就要自此做出极大的让步。一个艺术家要么遵循一种传统，要么创造出一种，这是他进行交流的全部基础。但当"传统的"带有了一种过时或狭隘的内涵后，它在今天经常被用作一种和"现实主义"相对的简单的反面概念，想要不被误解地使用这个词变得无比艰难。然而把这种暧昧性当作取得一种重要洞见的方法进行考察是可能的；这也是现在要讨论的。

我们已经看到，传统包含了"成规"和"标准"。在戏剧实践的任何个例中，这种传统是作者、演员和观众共同遵守的条约，如此演出才能进行，"共同遵守"无疑保证了一个正式而明晰的程序。其他艺术形式亦是如此，人们对条规更习以为常，以致经常意识不到。

这一点在我们所处时代的传统中更为明显。举个例子，在一个自然主义的剧里，传统体现为言语和行动必须尽可能地接近日常生活；但看这种戏的观众极少有人意识到这其实是一种传统：也就是说他们仅仅看到"一个戏是怎样的"，"一个戏试图做到这样"。事实上这却是一个重要的传统，它要求演员应该在大庭广众之下表现人们自然的且通常是私密的行为，同时全程保持一种幻觉，即作为角色的人对观众的在场毫无知觉。最绝望的隐密告白，最险恶的阴谋都可以在一千人的视界里和听觉范围内被呈现于舞台上，而不论演员或观众都不觉得这有何奇怪；由于已成为习惯的成规在起作用，他们已把这一过程当作传统接受下来。

不久之前，若一个角色进行独白，人们会觉得很奇怪，不管它被称为"出声地想"或"直接对观众讲述"。在有些地方或许现在仍然如此。人们会抱怨这太过"人为"或"不符合生活真实"，甚或"不像戏"。而被认为顺理成章的或"符合生活真实"的却是一个人站在舞台上，面对一千名观众，向他们演讲，同时假装他们并不存在。当说独白"不像戏"时，这是一种有条件的陈述，它被放在了一种"戒律"里考量；而一直以来戏剧评论家们很疑惑，因为众所周知独白在很多历史时期曾是一种广为接受的戏剧表演方法。

戏剧所使用的各种传统不能尽数。上规模的军队之间为时两天的战役可以用很少的士兵和一些很简洁的场面表现，只需几分钟。一个人临终前的一小时可以通过审慎地强调他等待的压力而被表现在舞台上，而戏剧上的"小时"可能不超过五分种。一个人走过除了挂着的窗帘之外空无一物的舞台，从他说的话里我们知道他身处格洛斯特郡，或伊利里亚，或一个神秘的岛上。他可以是一个用生硬的节奏向我们念着英语白话诗的罗马将军，我们会把这当成古罗马广场的演讲台。他可以是一个鬼魂或魔鬼或上帝，同时却喝酒，打电话，或被吊在舞台上方转圈。他可以披上一件灰斗蓬，我们会认为他消失了，即使我们仍看得见他。他可以对我们说出他最隐秘的想法，而我们会认为当我们从走廊的背面听到他说话时，离他几步远的人或在幕旁等候的人听不见他说话。只需一点微小的暗示，我们就会接受我们观看的事件是发生在基督诞生之前四千年，或是中世纪，或在今夜巴黎的一幢公寓里，和我们在曼彻斯特的剧院里同时进行着。舞台上的警官和犯人可以是我们上星期才见过的犯人和警官，管家和贵族也是一样，我们不质疑他们。我们接受，我们同意，所有这些都属于传统。

在戏剧发展中这一类的传统应用是固有的，让人惊奇的是既然这些表演上的基本传统已被接受了，一些特例却遇到了障碍。而这些困难显然是尖锐和反复出现的。我们会同意站在舞台上的是某一种精神的化身，他对我们的密切注视毫不在意，正在 1827 年的某地对着他的寡妇说私密话，而如果寡妇试图向我们作一个旁白，我们会不自在。我们会认为一个谋杀犯可能藏在门后（我们仍能看到他），同时他也许会带着痛苦低头看他的双手（我们马上知道它们沾满无辜者的血）；但是如果他走到舞台前部，用二十行诗，或用朗诵、歌唱，或用舞蹈来表达同样的情绪（即使更热情饱满），我们或我们之中的一部份人，会马上感到不舒服，随后多半会说这是"不真实的"。如果我们接受老练的人的说法，就会说这个戏高级，或超现实，或矫饰（一个在那些对自身又专业又可疑的虚饰习以为常的人之中正变得越来越常用的词）。然而，就算我们能够拒绝这一类的简单化，我们却不能，创造或设想出另一种传统。

这就是最核心的问题：一般观众比一般的经纪人更为头脑开放，所以改变和发展传统一直有潜在的基础。戏剧家可以随意使用任何适合他的素材和意愿的传统——这只在学术上成立。一种传统，最简单地说只是一种方法，一种可以使演出像机器一样运转的技术支持。但是方法会变，技术会变；然而，比如说一队舞者，一件隐形斗篷或一段独唱，这些都被认为是戏剧方法，然而它们在演出时却不能被好好利用，除非它们不仅是方法而实际上属于传统。戏剧家、演员和观众必须认同特殊方法的使用是可接受的。而且这个协议的重要部分应该是演出的前提，这是自然而然的。只有这样，发生的事情才会被接受而不产生破坏性的摩擦。

最后，我们评判一个传统不是通过抽象的有用性，也不是考虑某种最终的理论上的可行性，而是看它在一个艺术作品里运用得如何，能否成功。如果事实上这些尝试不能用它们自己的优势历史性地改造旧有的传统，介绍新的，我们就将失去机会，达不到某些绝对标准。我们用一种简单朴素的心情接受过去的胜利。我们热心地阅读诸如易卜生和斯坦尼斯拉夫斯基的传记。然而若不能使它在我们自己的时代变得活跃和有创造性，这种热情只不过是多愁善感。

易卜生和斯坦尼斯拉夫斯基曾经取胜，就像埃斯库罗斯引进了第二个演员，就像莎士比亚曾使血腥的悲剧改变面貌，然而艺术史不是一个不断变革从而进入更好更高级形式的历史，在这里有进步也有退步；同时，一个新鲜事物，甚至一种改造的出现可能是好的也可能使情况变糟。设想我们当代这一阶段的戏剧在戏剧殿堂里可能是最佳的——就因为出现得最晚——是荒谬的。另外，因为传统的规律，因为任何戏剧方法都要仰赖这一特殊协议，远离现阶段这个时代的传统，以及从边界或之外开始，这在任何时代都是不可能的。

于是我们需要已被默认的传统作为一种习俗，在传统作为戏剧方法的时候，我们同样需要那些从新的感觉模式发展而来，以及从对新出现或再发现的技术手段的认知而来的经验。我们现在必须面对传统这两个方面的相互影响。

如果我们在演出中将戏剧传统当成技术手段，不去使用某种手段或不用戏剧效果检测它们是说不过去的，但我们已经看到，在实践中这一理所当然的选择自由并没有实现：一个戏剧家必须为他想使用的任何手段赢得观众认可。运用新方法所产生的力量使他能够在过程中独立完成作品，而他却不能完全信赖自己，因为即使观众很热心，太明显地让人意识到手段的新鲜与陌生，不仅会阻碍戏的整体交流，还会造成抵触。若我们回顾戏剧的历史，有效的改变似乎有可能发生在已经有一种接受它们的意愿存在的时候，至少存在于支持艺术家的社会特定团体之间。但历史是不容易看清的，而在经验融汇的现今，想充分看清现状也不易。正是在这里我们发现自己考虑的就是传统与多种情感结构之间难解的关系问题。

三

　　所有对艺术的严肃思考必须从承认两个明显矛盾的事实入手：一方面，一个重要的艺术品毋庸置疑总是个性化的；另一方面，又有艺术品的种类、时期和风格的确凿分类。在日常的讨论中，我们成功地同时持有这两种看法，而没有真正去思考两者之间的关系。我们看了一个特别的戏，然后通常是真诚地说：这台词、这角色、这演出使一个独特的戏剧家为人所知，这时我们通过特殊的成就评价他作品的价值。然而有时我们从另一角度看这台词、角色和演出，然后说道：这是某个特定时期某一类戏剧的特征。这两种观察都重要，都在每一天帮助我们更好地了解戏剧，但它们之间明显的矛盾使问题突显——一会儿说一个方面，一会儿又说一个群体和一段时期——这个问题必须面对。声称我们在每种说法中指涉了不同种类的事实并不能解决上述矛盾。在某些作品中区分出不同元素，然后说戏剧家在遵循他的类型和时期的同时又贡献了一些完全属于他自己的东西，这是可能的。但在许多重要的作品中这样做却不可行：表达出个性化的天才的和特定的传统的作品似乎确实是不可分割的。涉及一个独特的人用独特的风格所做的东西时，我们通常是在判断这个风格是什么或什么是可行的。个性化的戏剧家做到了这些，而他所做的恰是我们稍后认定为某个时期或风格的一部分。

　　正是在探索这一关键性的关系时我使用了"情感结构"。我试图形容的是一个特殊的作品通过它独特的形式被当作一种基本形式认可的经验过程，以及这一基本形式与一个时期的关系。我们可以首先用最普通的方式来看这一过程。我们现在通常相信所有既定种类与既定时期的创造物都是紧密相连的，即使在实践中和从细节处并不容易看出这一点。不管够不够精确，我们在研究某一时期时可以重组物质生活、基本社会组织，很大程度上还可以归纳出主流思想。通常要认定在复杂整体的众多方面中哪个是决定性的——如果有的话——是困难的。它们的划分在某种程度上是武断的，而且一个像戏剧一样重要的机制会穷尽一切办法从所有方面撷取深浅不一的色彩。但即使我们能在对过去时期的研究中将生活的不同方面分开，将它们看成是自足的，显然这也只证明它们可以怎样被研究而非怎样被经历的。我们把每种元素当作沉淀物研究，但在时代中活的经验的每种元素是融合的，是复杂整体一个不可分割的部分。似乎在艺术的法则里，艺术家就是这样从整体中取材的。正是在艺术中，整个现时经验的影响首先被表达和体现出来。将一种艺术品和上面所说的整体联系起来或多或少可以说明问题，但在分析中出现了一种共识：即把作品与整体的其他部分相对立，仍有一些元素由于没有外部对应部分而留下来。这就是我所谓"情感结构"的第一个例子。它像一种结构一样确凿，但它又是基于最深刻且通常最不确实的体验的元素。它是一种对特定世界做出回应的方法。虽然在实践中，和其他方法相比这不像是一种可感知的"方式"，但在体验中它才是唯一可行的。这意味着它的元素不是观念或技术，相反它被充满感情地体现出来。与此同时，它是可感知的——并非通过关于它的正式讨论或专业技巧，而是通过直接经验——一种形式和意义，一种情感和韵律——贯穿于整个作品，作为一个整体的一出戏。

我们经常能在从前的戏剧中看到这种结构，但随之而来的关键问题在于，恰恰是情感的结构难以被分辨出来，因为它正在形成。就因它还未或者未完全过去，变成可以区分的模式、理念和制度，它首先被认为是一种深层的"个人"情感；对一个独特的作家来说，他似乎确实是独一无二，几乎无法沟通和孤独的。在过往时期的艺术和思想里可以最清楚地看到这种情况：当它被创造时，作者似乎经常是孤立、与世隔绝和难以理解的，对作者本人或他人都是如此。可是当情感结构被接受之后，那种联系、一致性甚至同一时期的相似性变得一目了然，这种情况也不断发生。在过去曾是一个未被分享的活的结构，现在被记录下来，成了可以观测、定义甚至归纳的结构。而在上述情况发生前，一个人在他的时代里，知道如何使用新结构，对新形式了如指掌，比其他人更早地获得属于他们自己的经验，这也是可能的。就像是有什么把这种人和其他人隔离开来，其实他只是与那些不再能表达或满足他们最重要生活的一系列既定模式、传统和制度隔开了。当这样一个人在他的作品里说着与那个时代的本质通常感觉上是对立的内容时，这种似乎是最复杂，不可接近和分享的生活竟然能被认

235

可，这对他自己和其他人来说同样令人惊讶。已建立的模式会批评和拒绝他，但对于一群数量不断增加的受众来说，他好像成了他们的代言人，说出了他们对生活最深刻的感受，而这却是因为他说的是他自己的心声。一种新的情感结构遂逐渐成型。不与对过往结构的分析作比较（这样做已很困难），也不依靠具体作品的力量，而是直接观察这种当代结构，这样做甚至也是可能的。大量这样的说明显得为时尚早，太肤浅和死板，但我仍要说对真实的情感结构（它经常被离它最近的或知名度更高的前一种所掩盖）的探索是对一个时代的艺术和社会最重要的一种关注形式。

一个艺术家对情感结构的重要性首先在于他贡献了一种"结构"，不是新反映的不成形的融合，或兴趣和领悟，而是一种由这些所形成的一种观察我们自己和世界的新方式的固定模式。这种模式是所有可靠的现代活动的理由，而且它在艺术以外的领域也获得成功。艺术家由于工作的性质，从一开始就直接地参与到这一过程中。只有当这模式可用的时候，他才能完全地开展工作。一般先是个人探索，然后散布开来，最后成为一代人的工作方法。所有这些表明了一个新传统、新形式在实践中是如何形成的。

就是在这个层面上我最终肯定了"情感结构"作为一个批评术语的作用。因为它引导我们在实践中把注意力放在一种注重特殊形式与普遍形式之元素的分析上。我们可以用直接而本土化的分析开始名副其实的批评实践：发现一个具体剧作的情感结构。这种结构总是一种我们可以直接回应的经验。但它同时也是一种在特定传统中用一种特定形式传达的经验。诚然，在形式和经验中总有一种重要关系存在：一种身份，一种紧张关系，有时在相互影响上还是一种分裂。将一种外来的形式和它的规则运用到一个戏里是没有问题的，但在一种首要的内部准则之下，经验和交流方式怎样结合起来更值得关注。对情感结构的研究应该是本土化、具体和独特的。但交流方法总是比具体作品涵盖更广：不论在语言、方法还是传统上。只要收集一下我们对具体的戏剧的经验，我们会看到情感结构在扩大和变化：在具体作品和戏剧家之间，重要元素作为经验和方法，是平常的；而当经验与传统一起改变，或当经验与现存的传统关系紧张，前者不一定能改变后者，这时重要元素就会改变。渐渐地，比具体作品更宽泛的问题显露出来：这不仅是一个形式的问题，更严峻的是，对很多戏剧家来说，这是一个经验的问题，它影响着一个时期或整个历史。在任何切实的分析中，这些关系通常很难证明，但仍有可能。我正在从事的着眼于最特殊和最普遍的形式之间确实联系的现代戏剧研究说明了这一点。分析经常表明，变化的是戏剧方法，但我的论点是，通过传统和情感结构的关系，我们可以得到更清晰的戏剧方法的技术解释，并且详细了解到更多技术以外的阐释：可操作的用来形容经验变化的方法——反响与交流，"主体"与"形式"——也即戏剧本身和它作为一种历史的重要性所在。

四

在分析情感结构时，最顽固的困难在于历史变化的复杂性，尤其在现代戏剧中，甚至在同一时期同一个社会，显然是多种结构共存的。这一事实决定了这本书的构思，虽然我本不打算得出任何简单结论。从易卜生到布莱希特，从自然主义戏剧到表现主义戏剧有一个基本的历史性的发展，这是一个事实。这暗示了一种基本的逻辑时序，因此我从易卜生开始，写到 1950 和 1960 年代的戏剧为止，作为一种举例论证。但我要做的不仅是超越自然主义和表现主义之间显著的交叉和变体的描述，而且要在事实上重新发现在某一时期的一些特定形式，或在特别的地域条件下产生的特殊变化。在重新整理它们的顺序之前，我已在整个历史发展的框架下将不同类别和区域的作品归入它们自己所属的结论——跟随着真实的体验，同时试图把它用相当明确的语言呈现出来。在本书第一部分，我用三位重要的剧作家开头，对我来说他们是奠定了这一时期戏剧重要性的基础：易卜生，斯特林堡和契河夫。他们实际上不是同时代的——易卜生比斯特林堡早出生 21 年，比契河夫早了 32 年——但他们都在 1880 年和 1890 年代进行创作。而且，正是他们作品的内容和范围使得现代戏剧得以确立。接下来在第二部分，我聚焦于一种非凡的民族戏剧：从 1890 年代的叶芝和 1940 年代的沁孤、乔伊斯和奥凯西的爱尔兰戏剧，这一传统从一开始就包括了大部分主要现代戏剧形式，但由于是在某种具体的民族和历史观照之下，所以需要被更多地强调。在第三部分，我转向一种很重要的实验领域：对幻觉的戏剧化运用，像皮兰德娄的作品，以及从奥尼尔到吉罗杜、阿努伊和萨特的许多剧作家对神话的使用。除此之外，我还考察了与之相对应的诗剧实验，像洛尔卡和艾略特，以及一系列英国剧作家。在第四部分，我将与社会和政治相关的戏剧家和戏剧方法放在一起进行详述：从对毕希纳的回顾开始，及至霍普特曼与他的联系，然后是特征与之相对的肖伯纳和劳伦斯，托勒和米勒，直至布莱希特。在第五部分，我将讨论十部新剧，作者包括奥尼尔、尤涅斯库、贝克特、日奈、弗里希和迪伦马特，以及英国剧作家怀廷、奥斯本、品特和奥登。这种构思安排有它的问题，而我对此是意识到的。但既然所有研究最终都有所关联，这种构思或许可以被接受；它让我在细读具体作品时遵循特定的主题和分类。然后，在具体研究的基础上，我尝试得出关于这非凡的一百年间主要戏剧形式的历史和重要性的一个普遍的观点——传统与情感结构。

（张平功　校）

B

Poems by Robert Frost

罗伯特·佛罗斯特诗歌

张倩玉　译

RELUCTANCE

Out through the fields and the woods
And over the walls I have wended;
I have climbed the hills of view
And looked at the world, and descended;
I have come by the highway home,
And lo, it is ended.

The leaves are all dead on the ground,
Save those that the oak is keeping
To ravel them one by one
And let them go scraping and creeping

Out over the crusted snow,
When others are sleeping.

And the dead leaves lie huddled and still,
No longer blown hither and thither;
The last lone aster is gone;
The flowers of the witch-hazel wither;
The heart is still aching to seek,
But the feet question "Whither?"

Ah, when to the heart of man
Was it ever less than a treason
To go with the drift of things,
To yield with a grace to reason,
And bow and accept the end
Of a love or a season?

不 甘

出门穿过田野和树木，
在我行走的城墙之上，
我曾爬山赏景，
看这个世界，下山；
取道公路回家，
现在看吧，都结束了。

所有叶子落了铺了满地，
除了橡树上还有一些，
把它们一片片摘掉，

让它们粉碎然后，
在积雪上匍匐，
当别人睡觉时。

落叶挤挤挨挨，安安静静，
不再被吹到东吹到西；
最后一颗星已不见；
榛树的花枯萎了；
心仍为寻找而疼痛，
脚却问了"向何处去？"

啊，对于人的心来说，
这难道不相当于背叛
和物体的消亡一道离开，
优雅地屈服于理性，
弯腰接受一个爱或者
一个季节的结局？

THE PASTURE

I'm going out to clean the pasture spring;
I'll only stop to rake the leaves away
(And wait to watch the water dear, I may):
I shan't be gone long. — You come too.

I'm going out to fetch the little calf
That's standing by the mother. It's so young,
It totters when she licks it with her tongue.
I shan't be gone long. — You come too.

放 牧

我去清理牧场的泉，
只将落叶耙走便了，
（或者再等等，看水变清）：
我不会离开太久——你亦将至。

我去牵回那头牛犊，
它正站在母牛身旁。那么小，
母牛舔它时蹒跚了几步，
我不会去太久——你亦将至。

MY NOVEMBER GUEST

My Sorrow, when she's here with me,
Thinks these dark days of autumn rain
Are beautiful as days can be;
She loves the bare, the withered tree;
She walks the sodden pasture lane.

Her pleasure will not letme stay
She talks andI am fain to list:
She's glad the birds are gone away,
She's glad her simple worsted grey
Is silver now with clinging mist.

The desolate, deserted trees,
The faded earth, the heavy sky,
The beauties she so truly sees,

The thinks I have no eye for these,
And vexes me for reason why.

Not yesterday I learned to know
The love of bare November days
Before the coming of the snow,
But it were vain to tell her so,
And they are better for her praise.

我的十一月的访客

我难过，当她和我一起呆在这，
觉得这些秋雨连绵的晦暗日子
是无比美丽的，
她喜欢那些光秃干枯的树，
她走上黏湿的牧场小路。

她的快乐不会让我驻足，
我乐于记下她所说：
鸟飞走了她很开心，
她的毛衣沾上雾气
由灰变成了银，
她很开心。

那些可怜的被遗弃的树，
褪色的土地，沉重的天幕，
那些她如此真切看见的美，
我从没留意过，
这困挠着我，为什么。

我并不是刚刚才学会
爱这灰暗的十一月天，
在雪落下之前，
不告诉她这些无妨，
因他们胜于她的赞扬。

TO THE THAWING WIND

Come with rain, O loud Southwester!
Bring the singer, bring the nester;
Give the buried flower a dream;
Make the settled snow-bank stream;
Find the brown beneath the white;
But whate'er you do to-night,
Bathe my window, make it flow,
Melt it as the ice will go;
Melt the glass and leave the sticks
Like a hermit's crucifix;
Burst into my narrow stall;
Swing the picture on the wall;
Run the rattling pages o'er;
Scatter poems on the floor;
Turn the poet out of door.

致 冰 风 暴

一场声势浩大的风暴和着雨！
带来歌唱者，带来巢窠；

给入土的花朵一个梦；

使坚固的雪堤奔涌；

让白雪下的褐土裸露；

而你今晚要做什么，

洗涤我的窗，让它顺风而去，

让它像冰一样融化；

玻璃融化只留下条框，

像隐士的十字架；

冲进我逼仄的马厩；

摇撼墙上挂的画；

让书页沙沙作响；

将诗撒落一地；

诗人扔出门去。

AFIELD AT DUSK

What things for dream there are when spectre-like,

Moving among tall haycocks lightly piled,

I enter alone upon the stubble field,

From which the laborers' voices late have died,

And in the antiphony of afterglow

Andrising full moon, sit me down

Upon the full moon's side of the first haycock

And lose myself amid so many alike.

I dream upon the opposing lights of the hour,

Preventing shadowuntil the moon prevail;

I dream upon the might-hawkspeopling heaven,

Each circling each with vague unearthly cry,

Or plunging headlong with fierce twang afar;

And on the bat's mute antics; who would seem

Dimly to have made out my secret place,

Only to lose it when he pirouettes,

And seek it endlessly with purblind haste;

On the last swallow's sweep; and on rasp

In the abyss of odor and rustle at my back,

That, silenced by my advent, finds once more,

After an interval, his instrument,

And tries once-twice-and thrice if I be there;

And on the worn book of old-golden song

I brought not here to read, it seems, but hold

And freshen in this air of withering sweetness;

But on the memory of one absent most,

For whom theselines when they shall greet her eye.

黄 昏 出 离

入梦的是什么,当恐惧似的东西

在轻悄堆起的高耸干草垛之间游走,

我独自进入收割后的田野,

那里农人声音刚刚消失,

在余晖的交响中,

一轮满月升起,我不由坐

在第一个草垛上,满月侧旁

我在如此多相似的草垛间迷失。

我在时间的逆光之上做梦,

阻挡阴影直到月亮上升;

我梦到夜鹰充斥天堂,

一个围着另一个发出含混怪异的尖叫,

或和着远处猛烈的拨弦声俯冲；

而蝙蝠古怪的缄默，似乎

幽微地营造出我的秘密空间，

只为了在他快速盘旋时失去它，

再急促地用半瞎的眼没完没了的寻找；

在最后吞噬般的扫荡中，在刺耳的刮擦

在气味的混沌和背后的窸嗦中，

那随着我的出现安静下来，将被再次找到的，

片刻之后，他的乐器，

奏了一次、两次、甚至三次如果我在那儿；

我随身携带记载老歌的旧书，

不打算在这读而只是拿着

它使这空气，这枯萎了的甜蜜重新变得清新；

但在最容易忽视的记忆里，

他们将会遇到她的眼睛，那么这些诗行又给谁呢。

OCTOBER

O hushed October morning mild,

Thy leaves have ripened to the fall；

To morrow's wind, if it be wild,

Should waste them all.

The crows above theforest call；

Tomorrow they may form and go.

O hushed October morning mild,

Begin the hours of this day slow.

Make the day seem to us less brief；

Hearts not averse to being beguiled；

Beguile us in the way you know.

Release oneleaf at break of day；

At noon release another leaf;

One from our trees, one far away.

Retard the sunwith gentle mist;

Enchant the land with amethyst.

Slow, slow!

For the grapes' sake, if they were all,

Whose leaves already are burnt with frost,

Whose clustered fruit must else be lost—

For the grapes' sake along the wall.

十 月

呵让十月的早晨逐渐沉静，

你的叶子已为秋天成熟；

明天的风，如果很大

就不要它了吧。

森林里的鸡啼，

明天可以免去。

呵让十月的早晨逐渐沉静，

让今天的时间缓慢开启，

使日子对我们来说不再那么短暂。

心不会介意被欺骗，

用你熟悉的方式欺骗我们吧。

在早晨放走一片叶子；

在中午再放走一片；

一片从我们的树上，一片从远方，

用轻薄的雾减弱太阳的威力；

用紫水晶对大地施咒语。

慢下来，慢！

看在葡萄的份上，如果它们就是一切

谁的叶子已经被霜灼伤，
谁的果实还要尽皆失去——
看在满墙的葡萄份上吧。

FIRE AND ICE

Some say the world will end in fire,
Some sayin ice.
From what I've tasted of desire
I hold with those who favor fire.
But if it had to perish twice,
I think I know enough of hate
To say that for destruction ice
Is also great
And would suffice.

火　与　冰

一些人说世界将毁于火，
一些说毁于冰，
从我品尝到的欲望来看，
我同意火的说法。
但如果世界毁灭两回，
我所了解的憎恶告诉我，
毁于冰也不错
而且足够用的。

NOTHING GOLD CAN STAY

Nature's first green is gold,

Her hardest hue to hold.

Her early leaf's a flower;

But only so an hour.

Then leaf subsides to leaf.

So Eden sank to brief,

So dawngoes down to day.

Nothing gold can stay.

金 难 存

太初生物始为金，

然难以为继。

初始之叶为花

然须臾

叶归叶矣。

亚当遂悲之

黎明堕白昼

凡金皆难存。

STOPPING BY WOODS
ON A SNOWY EVENING

Whose woods these are I think I know

His house is in the village though;

He will not see me stopping here

To watch his woods fill up with snow.

My little horse must think it queer
To stop without a farmhouse near
Between the woods and frozen lake
The darkest evening of the year.

He gives his harness bells a shake
To ask if there is some mistake.
The only other sound 's the sweep
Of easy wind and downy flake.

The woods are lovely, dark and deep.
But I have promises to keep,
And miles to go before I sleep,
And miles to go beforeI sleep.

雪 夜 驻 林

我知道这些是谁家的树
而他就在村里居住；
他不知我在此停留，
看他的树林被雪渐覆。

我的小马一定疑惑，
为何停驻无人之所，
在树林与冰湖之间，
一年中最黑的夜晚。

它摇了一下脖上的铃，

问我有何不妥。
此外惟一的声音是轻风
与鹅毛雪花的扫撒。

棵棵秀木黑而深。
可我已承诺不停步，
睡前还要走很多路，
睡前还要走很多路。

C

B. Franklin's Autobiogrphy (Exerpt)

My brother had, in 1720 or 1721, begun to print anewspaper. It was the second that appeared in America. I remember his friends trying to persuade him not to attempt it, since it probably would not be successful. One newspaper was, in their judgment, enough for America. He went on, however, and I was employed to carry the papers through the streets to the people.

He had some clever men among his friends whose writings added to the success of the newspaper. These gentlemen often visited us. Hearing their conversation, and their accounts of the approval their articles had received, I became excited and decided to write a piece of my own. But still being a boy, and suspecting that my brother would object to printing anything of mine, I wrote an article and left it unsigned. At night, I put it under the door of the printing house. It was found in the morning, and shown to his writing friends when they came to visit. They read it and gave their opinions. I had the wonderful pleasure of finding it met with their approval, and that, in their different guesses as to the author, they named men of learning and imagination. I suppose now that I was lucky in my judges, and that perhaps my writings were not as good as I then thought.

Encouraged by this judgment, however, I wrote and delivered in the same way several more articles which were also approved; and I kept my secret till I just about ran out of ideas. When my brother finally found out, he was not exactly pleased. Perhaps this might be one cause for the arguments that we began to have about this time.

Though a brother, I was his apprentice and he considered himself my master. He expected the same services from me as he would from another; while I thought he asked too much of a brother. Our arguments were often brought before our father, and I guess I was either generally in the right, or else a better debater, because the judgment was usually in my favor. But I disliked my apprenticeship and wished for some opportunity to end it. I sold some of my books to get a little money and, with the help of a friend, made arrangements for my trip with a captain of a New York ship.

In three days I found myself in New York, nearly 300 miles from home. I was but a boy of 17, without the least recommendation to or knowledge of any person in the place, and with very little money in my pocket.

Having a trade, and supposing myself a good worker, I offered my services to the printer in the place, old Mr. William Bradford, who had been the first printer in Pennsylvania before he moved to New York. He could give me no employment, but he said, "My son at Philadelphia needs an assistant and if you go there, I believe he may hire you."

Philadelphia was 100 miles further. I started out, however, and leaving my trunk of clothes to follow me by a larger ship, I hired a small boat to carry me as far as Amboy. Just outside New York harbor, a storm drove the little boat upon the shore of Long Island. With night approaching, the boatman and I had no choice but to wait until the wind stopped. We tried to sleep but we were so crowded and uncomfortable with the water crashing over the boat and leaking through to us, we had very little rest that night. We managed to reach Amboy the next evening, having been thirty hours on the water, without food or any drink.

That night I became very feverish, and stayed in bed drinking plenty of cold, fresh water. The next morning I felt better, and I continued my journey on foot. I had been told I would find boats at Burlington—fifty miles away—that would carry me the rest of the way to Philadelphia. It rained very hard all day and when I stopped at a small hotel that first night, I was beginning to wish I had never left home. I proceeded, however, and on the third day reached Burlington. Walking in the evening by the side of the river, I found a boat with several people in it that was going toward Philadelphia. They took me in, and, as there was no wind, we rowed all the way.

We arrived at Philadelphia about eight or nine o'clock the following morning and landed at the Market Street pier. All the money I had was one Dutch dollar and some small coins. I gave the coins to the owner of the boat, who at first refused to take it because of my rowing; but I insisted. A man is sometimes more generous when he has but a little money than when he has plenty, perhaps through fear of being thought to have but little.

I was in my working clothes; my best clothes were supposed to arrive at a later time by sea. I was dirty from my journey, my pockets filled with shirts and stockings, and I knew no one nor where to look for a room. I was exhausted from traveling, rowing, and lack of sleep and I was very hungry. I walked up the street, looking at the many clean-dressed people till near the Markethouse I met a boy with bread. I had many a meat on bread, and asking where he got it, I went immediately to the shop on Second Street and bought three great puffy rolls. Having no room in my pockets I walked off with a roll under each arm, eating the third. Thus I went up Market Street, passing by the door of Mr. Reed, my future wife's father; when she, standing at the door, saw me and thought I made, as I certainly did, a most awkward, foolish appearance.

富兰克林《自传》（节选）

张平功　译

　　我哥哥在 1720 年也许是 1721 年开始办报，那是当时美国的第二家报纸。我记得他的朋友曾劝他不要办报，因为可能不会成功。他们认为，美国有一家报纸就足够了。可是，我哥哥还是办了，于是，我就成了在街上递送报纸的雇员。

　　哥哥有些朋友颇有才气，他们写的文章给报纸增色不少。这些人经常来访我们。听到他们谈话，说他们的文章受到好评，我激动了，自己便决定也写一篇。可自己还是个孩子，恐怕不管写什么哥哥也不愿登，于是我写了篇文章没有署名。夜晚，我把它放在印刷间的门底下。次日早晨有人捡起，并在哥哥的那些撰稿朋友来访时递给他们看。他们看了，评论了一番。我听到文章博得他们的赞赏，观他们对作者猜来猜去，提到一些博学多思的人，真是高兴不已。现在想来，我有他们来评判真算走运，我那些文章也许并不像我当初想象的那样妙。

　　不过，他们这一评鼓励了我，我又写了几篇并以同样的方式投送。文章也得到了肯定。我一直保守着这个秘密，后来简直想不出写什么好了。哥哥终于发觉了，他很不高兴。我们大概是这个时期开始争吵的，也许这要算个原因吧。

虽说是亲兄弟，我可是给他当学徒，他也以我的老板自居。他要我和别人一样干活，可我觉得他这样要求亲兄弟也太过分了。我们往往吵到父亲那儿去，我想若不是我总占理，那就是我嘴更硬，因为父亲评起理来通常是偏向我的。不过我讨厌学徒生活，想找机会辞掉不干。我卖了些书挣点钱，在一个朋友的帮助下，找到一个船长，安排好搭他的船去纽约。

三天后，我到了离家近三百英里的纽约。当时我年仅十七，既没人介绍我去见谁，自己也不认识谁，兜里也没几个子儿。

我会一门手艺，自信活儿干得不错，就向当地的印刷师威廉·布莱德福特老先生找活干，他本来是宾夕法尼亚的第一位印刷师，后来去了纽约。他没能雇我，可是说了："我儿子在费城，需要个帮手。你要是去那儿，我相信他会用你"。

到费城还有一百英里。不过我还是出发了。我把一口衣箱托给一艘大船随后运去，自己雇了一条小船直奔安姆波伊。刚出纽约港，一场风暴把小船刮到了长岛岸边。眼看夜色来临，船主和我只好等风住了再说。我俩想睡下，可是太挤了，再说海水不住地涌上船来，渗得到处都是，简直不得安身。那一夜，我们几乎没睡。第二天晚上，我们总算到达了安姆波伊，没吃没喝在海上度过了 30 个小时。

当晚我发起高烧，躺在床上喝了不少凉水。第二天早上觉得好点，继续徒步赶路。听人说，在五十英里外的波灵顿可以找到船一路坐到费城。一整天大雨下个不停，头一晚我在一家小客店投宿，这时才后悔真不该离家外出。不过我还是走了下去，第三天到了波灵顿。傍晚我沿着河边走，找到一条去费城的船，船上坐着几个人。他们让我上去了，因为没风，我们一路划去。抵达费城已是第二天早上八、九点钟了，我们就在闹市街码头上的岸。我身上只剩下荷币一块钱零几枚小硬币了。我把硬币付给船主，他先是不愿要，说我不能白划船。但我非要他收下不可。人有的时候钱少了反倒比钱多了大方，也许是怕人嫌贫吧。

　　我当时身穿工装，最好的衣服要等些时间随船运来。我风尘仆仆，衣袋里塞满了穿脏的衣袜。我不认识人，也不知上哪儿找个地方住下。赶路、划船，缺觉，搞得我疲惫不堪，还饿得要命。我沿街走去，一路注意到许多人穿着整洁。快到市场，遇见一个手拿面包的小男孩。我啃过好多顿干面包了，问明小孩在哪里买的，便连忙去了二道街的商店，买了三个又大又暄的面包圈。衣袋里装不下，只好在腋下各挟一个，边走边吃着第三个。我就这样，走上了闹市街，走过了我未来的岳父里德先生的家门口；他女儿正好站在门边，看见了我，心想瞧这人出的洋相——可不，我是真亮了相——好一付笨手笨脚、呆头呆脑的傻相。

　　（译文原刊于中国翻译工作者协会会刊《中国翻译》，1990 年第 6 期。）

D

Sayings of Dr. Samuel Johnson
(Translated from his
literary works and biography)
约翰生博士言谈
张平功　译

1. Children and Education　少年与教育

"I love the young dogs of this age; they have more wit and humour and knowledge of life than we had; but then the dogs are not so good scholars."

Boswell, *Life of Johnson*

"我喜爱现在的年轻人。他们比我们更机智、更幽默，比我们更懂得如何享受生活。但是，年轻人不见得都能做出扎实的学问来。"

鲍斯威尔《约翰生传》

Amongst other pleasing errors of young minds, is the opinion of their own importance.

Rambler

诸多后学确有不少美中不足之处，自峙高明当在其中。

《闲谈者》

"I would put a child into a library (where no unfit books are) and let him read at his choice. A child should not be discouraged from reading anything he takes a liking to, from a notion that it is above his reach."

Boswell, *Life of Johnson*

"我愿意把孩童引到图书馆去（当无不良藏书），任其阅读。儿童不论喜爱什么书都应该受到鼓励。不说'这本书对你来说太深奥了'"。

鲍斯威尔《约翰生传》

"I would rather have the rod to be the general terror to all, to make them learn, than tell a child, if you do this, or thus, you will be more esteemed than your brothers or sisters."

Boswell, *Life of Johnson*

"我时常使用棍头来威吓我的孩子，并告戒他们，学习不用功就要吃苦头。家长对子女的教育不能只是好言劝诱。"

鲍斯威尔《约翰生传》

"That lad looks like the son of a schoolmaster, which is one of the very worst conditions of childhood. "

Piozzi, *Anecdotes*

"说某个孩子长得像教书先生的儿子，将会成为这孩子的童年恶梦。"

皮亚兹《轶事》

Names which hoped to range over kingdoms and continents shrink at last into cloisters and colleges.

Rambler

那些曾传遍遐迩的名字最终溶于暮鼓晨钟。

《闲谈者》

"Babies do not want to hear about babies, they like to be told of giants and castles and of somewhat which can stretch and stimulate their little minds. "

Piozzi, *Anecdotes*

"儿童不喜爱听有关他们同类的故事，那些能开启想象力的关于巨人和城堡的传说才会使他们着迷。"

皮亚兹《轶事》

"Endeavouring to make children prematurely wise is useless labour. "

Boswell, *Life of Johnson*

"试图让儿童过早成熟和聪慧的种种努力和尝试都是徒劳的。"

鲍斯威尔《约翰生传》

2. Food and Cookery   食物和煮调

"A cucumber should be well sliced, and dressed with pepper and vinegar, and then thrown out, as good for nothing. "

Boswell, *Journal of a Tour to the Hebrides*

"如果黄瓜切片、佐以胡椒和醋那还不如不吃的好。"

鲍斯威尔《游赫比蒂斯岛》

"For my part, I mind my belly very studiously and very carefully; for I look upon it, that he who does not mind his belly will hardly mind anything else. "

Boswell, *Life of Johnson*

"我十分注重饮食，决不让胃口受到委屈。对餐饮不重视的人可能不会认真对待别的任何事情了。"

鲍斯威尔《约翰生传》

If an epicure could remove by a wish in quest of sensual gratification,

263

wherever he had supped, he would breakfast in Scotland.

A Journey to the Western Islands of Scotland

如一个老饕想得到满足，不管他选择了何地用餐，早饭是一定会在苏格兰吃的。

《游历苏格兰西部诸岛》

"Claret is the liquor for boys; port for men; but he who aspires to be a hero (smiling) must drink brandy."

Boswell, *Life of Johnson*

"小伙子要喝波尔多红酒，成熟男子喝波特紫葡萄酒，要想成为英雄豪杰（笑）非饮白蓝地不可。"

鲍斯威尔《约翰生传》

The death of great men is not always proportioned to the lustre of their lives. The death of Pope was imputed by some of his friends to a silver saucepan, in which it was his delight to heat potted lampreys.

Lives of the Poets

大人物的死因常常无法和其在世时成就辉煌大业时相比拟。蒲伯的友人认为他死于一个长柄银锅，其时他正在煎鳗鱼。

《诗人传》

"A tavern chair is the throne of human felicity."

Hawkins, *Life of Johnson*

"酒馆里的椅子是享受人伦之乐的王座。"

霍金斯《约翰生评传》

3. Love and Marriage　情爱与婚姻

Marriage has many pains, but celibacy has no pleasures.

Rasselas

结婚有许多痛苦，独身生活却毫无欢愉可言。

《拉塞雷斯》

He that thinks himself most secure of his wife should be fearful of persecuting her continually with his presence.

Idler

丈夫常常认为，与妻子形影不离一定会使其放心。可怕的是，这样做无疑等于让她时刻感到折磨。

《闲谈者》

"A man is in general better pleased when he has a good dinner upon his table than when his wife talks Greek. "

Hawkins, _Life of Johnson_

"对丈夫而言，妻子能做一桌好饭要比善于高谈阔论来得更加实惠些。"

霍金斯《约翰生评传》

Same ladies have taught themselves to believe that every man intends love who expresses civility.

Rambler

不少女士这样认为，男人在献殷勤之后就会示爱的。

《闲谈者》

Marriage is not commonly unhappy, otherwise than as life is unhappy.

Rambler

盖言之，婚姻生活并非不幸福。否则，人生也就索然无味了。

《闲谈者》

Wretched would be the pair above all names of wretchedness who should be doomed to adjust by reason, every morning, all the minute detail of a domestic day.

Rasselas

夫妻之间最大的烦恼和悲哀莫过于把每天平俗的生活细节都逐一理论清楚，辩明谁是谁非。

《拉塞雷斯》

"Why sir, being married to those sleepy-souled women is just like playing at cards for nothing; no passion is excited and the time is filled up."

Piozzi, *Anecdotes*

"不是吗，与笨女人结婚如同打牌而不计输赢：毫无激情可言而时间却悄然逝去。"

皮亚兹《轶事》

4. Politics and Society　政治与社会

"Patriotism is the last refuge of a scoundrel."

Boswell, *Life of Johnson*

"爱国主义是暴徒最后的避难所。"

鲍斯威尔《约翰生传》

The Europeans have scarcely visited any coast but to gratify avarice, and extend corruption; to arrogate dominion without right, and practise cruelty without incentive.

Introduction to *The World Displayed*

欧洲人造访别国的目的无外乎是为了满足自己的贪欲,或展延腐败,或推行强权统治,或让他国人民无端承受苦难。

《世界览胜》之"导言"

Kings see the world in a mist which magnifies everything near them, and bounds their view to a narrow compass, which few are able to extend by the mere force of curiosity.

Life of Frederick the Great

君王在雾中观察世界而又放大了他们之所见,于是就把视野局限在狭窄的范围内,仅凭好奇心是无法拓展视界的。

《弗里德力克大帝的一生》

How small of all that human hearts endure, that part which kings or laws can cause or cure.

Lines contributed to Goldsmith's "The Traveler"

人们心灵的苦难,庶几可在王权的威严和法律的判例之中显现。

《献给哥尔斯密"旅行家"的诗行》

I would wish Julius Caesar and Catiline, Xerxes and Alexander, Charles XII and Peter the Great, huddled together in obscurity and detestation.

The Adventurer

让凯撒大帝、谋反者加蒂蓝、波斯泽克西斯一世、亚历山大王、查尔斯七世和彼得大帝一并光耀不再，遗臭万年吧！

《历险者》

It has been observed that they who most loudly clamour for liberty do not most liberally grant it.

Lives of the Poets

有据为证，那些高调宣扬自由理念的人往往最不愿让人们充分享有自由的。

《诗人传》

No scheme of policy has in any country yet brought the rich and poor on equal terms into courts of judicature.

A Journey to the Western Islands of Scotland

从古到今，任何国家的政策法规从未让富人和穷人在法庭上享有同等的权利和义务。

《游苏格兰西岛》

There may be community of material possession, but there can never be community of love or of esteem.

Rosselas

虽然社会的物质生活富足，可人们之间不一定充满爱和尊严。

《拉塞雷斯》

The prosperity of a people is proportionate to the number of hands and minds usefully employed.

Idler

一个国家的繁荣有赖于脑力劳动者和体力劳动者的数量均衡与合理分工。

《闲谈者》

Such is the state of life, that none are happy but by the anticipation of change: the change itself is nothing, when we have made it, the next wish is to change again.

Rasselas

这就是生活的状态：人们期盼从变化中获得幸福。但变化本身是不足道的，因为变化一旦实现，新的愿望又会促使我们对此加以改变。

《拉塞雷斯》

5. Lichfield 家乡——里奇菲尔德镇

"I remember…when all the *decent* people in Lichfield got drunk every night, and were not the worse thought of."

Boswell, *Journal of a Tour to the Hebrides*

"不可想象的是，里奇菲尔德镇上的体面人士每天晚上都大肆酗酒，酩酊大醉之时却不为世人所耻笑。"

鲍斯威尔《游赫比蒂斯岛所想》

"Sir, we are a city of philosophers; we work with our heads, and make the boobies of Birmingham work for us with their hands."

Boswell, *Life of Johnson*

"请记住，我们的市镇多有贤达的智者，他们从事脑力劳动，并指使伯明翰的粗人为我们干活儿。"

鲍斯威尔《约翰生传》

I am not wholly unaffected by the revolutions of Sadler Street, nor can forbear to mourn a little when old names vanish away, and new come in to their place.

Letters

对于赛德勒大街所发生的暴动，我并非未受到震惊，"新桃换旧符"也叫我颇感伤情。

《书信》

"I lately took my friend Boswell and showed him genuine civilized life in an English provincial town. I turned him loose at Lichfield…that he might see for once real civility."

Boswell, *Life of Johnson*

"日前我领着友人鲍斯威尔去感受英国小镇生活的魅力。我让他自行在里奇菲尔德镇上走走，看一看什么是雅致的生活和品味。"

鲍斯威尔《约翰逊传》

They have cut down the tress in George Lane. John Evelyn tells of wicked men that cut down trees and never prospered afterwards, yet nothing has deterred these audacious aldermen from violating the hamadryads of George Lane.

Letters

约翰·伊夫林告诉我，缺少德行的市政官员指令胡乱砍伐树木，却不在原址上补种，甚至连乔治大街两旁的植树也不放过。这些无耻的官僚竟然对于老街的树神缺少敬畏之心，实在太可悲了。

《书信》

This place grows more and more barren of entertainment.

Letters

此地（里奇菲尔德镇）正在变得越来越缺少生气和趣味了。

《书信》

He expatiated in praise of Lichfield and its inhabitants, who were "the most sober, decent people in England, the genteelest in proportion to their wealth, and spoke the purest English".

Boswell, *Life of Johnson*

　　他（约翰生）不惜言辞颂扬家乡里奇菲尔德，夸赞镇上的人们，称他们是"最沉稳、最优雅的英国人；个个都注重仪表和身份，操纯正的国语。"

鲍斯威尔《约翰生传》